PRAISE FOR

HER DARK WINGS

"Salisbury's voice sings at the crossroads of classical and urgently modern. She perfectly captures the violence of teenage friendship between girls and the holy terror and hunger of seventeen. Her storytelling is tight and focused and moves at a breathless pace: as all good mythmaking should. This story is strange, elegant, and chilling: I devoured it."

—**SARAH MARIA GRIFFIN,**
author of *Other Words for Smoke*

"Melinda Salisbury is a lush, magical writer who isn't afraid of the dark. *Her Dark Wings* captures the glory of having a real best friend, and the mythic pain of being betrayed by one."

—**RAINBOW ROWELL,** *New York Times* bestselling author of *Eleanor & Park* and *Carry On*

"Infused with myth, *Her Dark Wings* is darkly enchanting, bold, and unexpected. I loved experiencing this richly imagined world through the eyes of such a well-drawn, nuanced heroine."

—**MARY WATSON,**
author of *The Wickerlight*

"A skilled contemporary reimagining full of friendship and fury."

—**DEIRDRE SULLIVAN,** author of
Perfectly Preventable Deaths

"All the hallmarks of Salisbury at her best: raw emotion, searing prose, and a darkly imagined world."

—**NON PRATT,** author of
Every Little Piece of My Heart

Also by Melinda Salisbury

The Sin Eater's Daughter
The Sleeping Prince
The Scarecrow Queen
The Heart Collector and Other Stories

State of Sorrow
Song of Sorrow

Hold Back the Tide

NONFICTION

The Way Back Almanac 2022: A Seasonal Guide to Connecting with Nature
The Way Back Almanac 2023: A Contemporary Seasonal Guide Back to Nature

HER

DARK

WINGS

MELINDA SALISBURY

DELACORTE PRESS

Text copyright © 2023 by Melinda Salisbury
Cover art copyright © 2023 by Leo Nickolls

All rights reserved. Published in the United States by Delacorte Press, an imprint of Random House Children's Books, a division of Penguin Random House LLC, New York. Originally published in the United Kingdom by David Fickling Books, Oxford, in 2022.

Delacorte Press is a registered trademark and the colophon is a trademark of Penguin Random House LLC.

Visit us on the Web! GetUnderlined.com

Educators and librarians, for a variety of teaching tools, visit us at RHTeachersLibrarians.com

Library of Congress Cataloging-in-Publication Data is available upon request.
ISBN 978-0-593-70558-2 (trade pbk.) | ISBN 978-0-593-70559-9 (ebook)

The text of this book is set in 11-point Adobe Caslon Pro.
Interior design by Megan Shortt

Printed in the United States of America
1st Printing
First Edition

For Franzi, Katja and Antje,
my Furies, my sisters

HER
DARK
WINGS

Tell me, of a world where the gods still rule
in Olympus, where they spread across the
world as sure as rosy-fingered Dawn and held
their own these many years; sing, Muse, of
the Titan spawn: Zeus, Poseidon, Demeter.
Sing of Hades, the Receiver of Many, alone
in his unchanging, unyielding realm.

Sing of the Boatman, of the Furies, of
the rivers that flow in and around the land
of the dead. Tell me where the triple goddess
Hecate now dwells. Tell me of silver-tongued
Hermes, who moves between the land of
the living and the world of the dead, foot in
either, belonging to neither.

Then tell me of the flower-touched girl
hidden at the ends of the earth; of betrayal
and vengeance, of blossoming and blame.
Tell me of heartbreak and healing, tell me
what it means to forgive, to plant a seed, to
watch it grow.

Tell me what happens next, Muse.
Sing.

SEEDING

THE MORNING AFTER THE FESTIVAL, MR. MCKINNON, who wrote and edited the *Island Argus* when he wasn't teaching us, published an emergency edition of the paper. He must have started working on it the second he got home, then cycled around the Island in the dark to make sure everyone had a copy before breakfast. He went to so much effort.

The headline he used was "Daly's Hero."

I knew he meant Hero from "Hero to Leander," because we'd just finished the double Heroides in his class. It must have been the first thing he thought of: how fucked up to teach a poem that ends in a double drowning to someone who'd actually drown before he handed our essays back. But everyone else read "Hero" and thought about film characters or stupid warrior men from epic poems. People who lived and died starting wars or fighting wars or ending wars; there was always a war involved

3

somewhere. They'd forgotten about the actual Hero, who was just a girl.

So the headline did not go down well.

Cally Martin, who runs the Spar in Daly, went door to door with a wheelbarrow collecting every copy she could get her hands on; I didn't let her have ours. She dumped them on Mr. McKinnon's front step, where, allegedly, Thom Crofter pissed on them, but only on the back page, out of respect. He was careful to avoid the photo of the girl found dead in the lake at the Thesmophoria festival.

Daly's Hero.

I'll tell you something about Bree Dovemuir—she was no Hero.

Bree Dovemuir was my best friend for almost my whole life, until she became the person I hated most in the world. Sometimes second most, depending on the day.

Three months ago, it was still Bree-and-Corey, Corey-and-Bree, said as one word, treated as a single, double-headed entity; a mini Hydra. The photo Mr. McKinnon used in the paper was actually of the two of us, taken from the school website, except he'd cut me out so it was just Bree. The irony was not lost on me.

Despite Mr. McKinnon's best cropping efforts, you could still see the seashell curl of my ear pressed against Bree's, the matching double-helix piercings that got us both grounded two summers ago, me for a week and Bree for the whole holiday. We'd held each other's hands as the needle went in once, then again, pulses syncing with the beat of the song the piercer tapped her foot to.

4

I hadn't wanted my ears pierced, but Bree begged me not to make her do it on her own. And when mine got infected—of course—it was Bree who insisted I keep the earrings in and made me swear I wouldn't take them out. And the sad thing is that when we walked into school the first day of autumn term, the rings hidden under our hair, it felt like it was worth it.

I should have known she was a snake then; she'd changed her hoops from the steel ones they were pierced with to tiny silver ones, so we didn't quite match.

As if the headline wasn't bad enough, Mr. McKinnon had changed the dimensions of the photo and he'd messed it up, stretching Bree's jaw wide, making her forehead huge. If it hadn't been her obituary, I would have been thrilled by her mutant Wanted-poster face. If it hadn't been her obituary, I would have graffitied it—blacked out her teeth, added a monobrow, some hairy warts. Stabbed out her eyes with the compass from my math set. Glued it to a doll made from grass and hair, spit and blood, and asked the Furies to curse her for her crimes. But it was her obituary, so there was no point; the worst had already happened.

The photo had been taken at the end of term, just before the summer that was supposed to be the best summer of our lives, because we were seventeen and Bree swore the summer you were seventeen was the best summer you'd ever have. And it wasn't quite the truth to say it was of the two of us, because Alistair Murray was in the original photo too.

I was in the middle, the bridge between them; Bree's best friend and Ali's girlfriend. Until Bree and Ali decided they didn't need a bridge after all. They'd cut me out of the picture too.

When someone dies, there are certain things you have to do. The body has to be cleansed and oiled, a coin left on the lips for the Boatman so he'll carry the soul away to the Underworld. There is the prothesis the night before the funeral, when the body lies in state and women sing the dirges over it. The next day is the ekphora procession to the graveside, where milk and honey and wine and water are poured into the grave as offerings to Hades. The chief mourners sometimes offer a lock of their hair too. Finally, the perideipnon feast to celebrate the dead.

Without the proper rituals the dead are left behind on the shores of Styx, unable to move on. It's kind of the same when someone breaks up with you. There are rituals you have to do then too—not official ones, they don't appear in any sacred text. But everyone knows them, the tried-and-true ways to get over heartbreak. And you have to do them, or you won't move on either.

First, you call all your friends and they come for a sleepover—they come to you so you don't have to get dressed, or risk bumping into your ex on the street. This is the relationship's prothesis, but instead of singing dirges you sing your favorite songs, starting with the sad ones and then getting to the real angry shit, the fuck-you-forever songs. Once your blood is boiling, you delete your ex's number, all the messages they ever sent and block them online. You do it to them before they do it to you—this is especially important if you're the dumped, not the dumper.

Then, everyone lies and says they actually hated your ex, that they were never good enough for you. They promise better, brighter things, offer up rumors of who's newly single, who always had a thing for you. These words and deeds become your bread. They feed and nourish you. They are your perideipnon. Really good friends will bring ice cream, too.

Slowly, you start to come back to life.

A week later, you ceremonially remove a lock, or several, of your own hair and get some new style, or you dye it rainbow colors, and a week after that, you kiss someone's brother or sister or cousin behind the old abbey ruins in Fraser's Field. After a month, when it's obvious it's really, truly over, you take everything they ever gave you and set it alight in your back garden, an offering to Aphrodite to send you a better lover next time. The fire makes your neighbors worry about sparks and wooden fences, and mutter darkly about the noise as you and your friends dance around a metal bin full of burning memories, but it has to be done.

These are the rites of the breakup, and if you do them properly, they fix you.

But when Ali and Bree left me for each other, there was no ritual, because Bree wasn't there to be the chief mourner. I was left marooned, somewhere in between.

Now Bree is actually dead. And if you're wondering if I'm sad about it because it means we'll never get to mend our broken friendship, no. I'm not.

I wished for it.

INVASIVE

JUST BEFORE BREE WAS FOUND, I WAS BEHIND the south barn with Astrid Crane, who'd adopted me after the Ali-and-Bree betrayal, and some of the others from our year at school, far enough from the fire that the parents could pretend not to see us.

Astrid had passed me the bottle of wine she'd stolen from somewhere. I never used to drink, but that was the old, happy Corey, who'd had a boyfriend and a best friend. The new Corey had neither, so I'd let the sour liquid spill over my tongue, and scanned the crowd again for Bree and Ali.

I kept doing it: in the village, at school, everywhere. They'd become my north, my internal compass swinging straight for them any time they were around. I couldn't decide if I was relieved or gutted when I realized they'd disappeared.

I also couldn't decide how I felt about the boy I'd just kissed.

The Thesmophoria was good for that kind of thing. It's an

old festival; older than greeting the hamadryads when you drive through Green Wood, even though almost nobody has seen one in centuries; older than throwing pine dollies off Amphitrite Cliff to ask Poseidon to keep the fishermen safe. The Thesmophoria used to be a three-day celebration before the winter wheat was sown, to honor Demeter, and only women were allowed to go, but these days it's a one-night-only bacchanal, where everyone on the Island gets absolutely blasted and behaves stupidly. Including me, this year. Kissing a random boy.

It's not that I'd believed I'd be with Ali forever, more that I hadn't really thought about life *After Ali,* until it happened. Kissing someone new wasn't unexpected, but it's not like I'd gone to the Thesmophoria planning to. On the one hand, I was satisfied I'd proved I'd moved on so everyone could stop pitying me. On the other, I worried I'd put a nail in a coffin I already knew was welded shut.

Most of all, I was afraid Ali and Bree would think I was doing fine without them, and that I didn't need them anymore. I didn't need Ali, but Bree . . .

I *hated* her. But I'd never, ever considered a life *After Bree.*

When the random boy had come to me, hand outstretched for mine, I was standing at the edge of the festival, trying to drum up the courage to either stay and find someone I could hang out with or just go home and listen to my playlist of sadness for the thousandth time.

And then he appeared, with wide shoulders, a smile full of promises and shadowed eyes, offering a place by his side. I slipped my fingers between his and followed him into the crowd, deliberately not looking for *them*, trying to act as though he was the only thing in the world on my mind as we started to dance.

I didn't know for sure they were there, but it was the Thesmophoria and I couldn't imagine them being anywhere else. And, honestly? In that moment I wanted them to be there. I wanted them to see someone else wanted me. I wanted the whole Island to see that I was fine, because some other boy with a beautiful mouth he'd painted gold, and a hammered copper mask that looked like scales in the red firelight, had picked me out of the crowd. Here was the proof that my world didn't begin and end with Alistair Murray and Bree Dovemuir.

I needed to believe that. And the boy had, for one moment, kissed me with gilded lips and made it real.

His mouth was cold, he tasted like ice, or salt, or diamonds— something clear and sharp and glittering, something that would quench or call a thirst, or buy an army, start a war. His hands were cold too, cooling my burning skin where they touched me, and my fingers gripped the lapels of his coat so tightly that they cramped. I wanted more; his kiss made me *hungry*. I wanted to swallow him down, like honey. I wanted to be like the legendary mellified men we'd learned about in history, I wanted to consume this boy until he was my sweat and my tears, until it killed me, and then I wanted to be buried in him for a hundred years.

I'd only ever kissed Ali, so I didn't know how different it could be. I'd thought it would just be a kiss, like a hundred kisses before. I thought I knew what to do, how it would go.

I didn't know anything at all.

And this was a kiss without love, or liking, or even knowing.

This was a kiss just for kissing's sake. Imagine if I had cared. Imagine if it had actually meant something.

I could hear the sound of drums, my own heart thundering. I knew with certainty that the ground beneath us had opened and we were going down, down, down, until the earth would cover us and bury us alive, and I was fine with that. I *wanted* that. I wanted him.

I pressed my whole body against his, and shivered when his hands moved from my face to my waist, holding me to him, keeping me there. Somewhere close by I heard a wolf whistle, long and loud, piercing through everything. I remembered where we were and pulled back, embarrassed. But my fingers were still curled into his coat so he couldn't get away because I wasn't done—we weren't done. And he was still holding me just as tightly. When I looked up into his eyes, they were dark and shining, like he knew exactly what I was thinking and he agreed, and I turned away because suddenly it was too much.

That's when I saw Ali and Bree. It took me a second to realize it was them, partly because of their masks, but mostly because Bree didn't look like Bree anymore. At school the day before her hair had been in the usual topknot, chestnut waves bound up and out of the way. Now it was short, cut to her chin, the curls bouncing without the length to hold them down.

We'd always had long hair. She'd wanted to cut hers for years, but her mom wouldn't let her. Whenever they fought, Bree would threaten to chop it off, though she never did; even she wouldn't go that far. Until now. I felt a starburst of hurt that she'd do something so huge without telling me first, without us doing it together, even though it was stupid and we hadn't spoken for months. I felt like she should have told me, or warned me. Asked me if I thought it would suit her. It did suit her, and that hurt too.

And it never stopped hurting to see her in his arms. To see them without me.

Bree was in a long tartan coat, cinched tightly at her tiny waist, that flared as she spun, her wind-tanned skin glowing warm in the light from the bonfire. Next to her I'd always looked like a child: short, soft and round, milky skin, wheat-colored hair. And Ali, holding her, tall and broad-shouldered, like a warrior prince. They looked like equals. They looked like they *belonged*.

It killed the kiss. It soured the honey.

The boy followed my gaze and said something, but I didn't hear his words over the roar of blood in my ears like a thousand birds taking flight at once.

I wished her dead.

I wished for it with my whole heart. Because for a moment I'd forgotten about her and Ali and I'd been happy. But the second I saw them, all of the hurt and humiliation and anger came rushing back and I remembered everything.

How they must have spent weeks laughing together at what a gullible little idiot I was. How, when Ali took longer and longer to reply to my messages, I told Bree I thought something was wrong, and she said I was being paranoid. How when *she* started taking longer and longer to reply, she told me it was because I kept going on about Ali being weird and she was bored of it. How they were probably together when I sent most of the messages, how they probably showed them to each other.

How I'd tried calling her all the way home after Ali broke up with me and she never answered, never replied, never once said sorry. How she sent her little brothers to my house to bring back the stuff I'd left at hers and collect the things she'd left at mine. She'd made a list: books, a cardigan she didn't even like, a set of pajamas, three nail polishes, an almost-empty tube of hand cream and, worst of all, Ali's big blue sweater that I'd had longer than he ever did. How she'd excised me from her life so neatly and I was here, months later, still clawing at myself to tear all the little bits of her out of me.

I hated her so much in that moment.

So I sent a cursed dart out from my mind, straight into her chest, and wished she'd drop fucking dead. That she'd be dragged to the Underworld and left there to rot.

The boy spoke again.

"What?" I'd said, barely looking at him, too busy with my hate.

He didn't repeat himself, just drew me back into the dance, away from Bree and Ali, around the fire so it blocked them from view. But the magic was gone, and I'd smelled the fat and onions from the burger stand overpowering everything, could hear the guitar in the band was out of tune, see how stupid we all looked, most of us wearing jeans and bundled up against the weather, faces covered by cheap masks with feathers and sequins that fell off and were crushed into the mud. As if they might be enough to fool any gods who walked among us that we were like them. As if we could be anything other than human.

There was no more kissing. The boy left me the moment the music ended, giving me a funny little bow, like a character in a play, before he disappeared into the crowd. I didn't blame him, because why would he have stayed? No one stayed with me. For me.

For a second, I was lost and alone, terrified Bree and Ali would notice. Then I saw someone waving from the barn, and the relief when I realized it was Astrid almost knocked me down.

I dropped into the space Astrid made for me, my thigh pressed against hers, and took the bottle she offered. When I raised it to my mouth I could feel her lipstick, greasy on the rim. The boy's lips had been cool and velvety. I ran my tongue over my own and tasted salt and honey.

Realizing no one else was wearing a mask, I pushed mine back and Astrid leaned forward and took it, putting it on and grinning. Stained dark by the alcohol, her smile was a chasm. I shivered.

"Who was that?" Astrid leaned into me, sloppy and wine-friendly.

"Dunno."

Astrid gave me a look, and I realized how stupid my answer was. There were just twelve hundred people on the Island and the only tourists here right now were a middle-aged couple staying at the B&B. I took a deep gulp of wine and tried to place the boy—he wasn't from school, I was sure of that. He could be from one of the other islands, gate-crashing our party, I supposed, instead of staying at his own. I wondered how I could find out.

Then I realized, with a sharp, almost-electric shock, that I wanted to know who he was because I wanted it to happen again. That at some point soon I was going to kiss someone—him— not just to prove something, but for real. And I didn't know what to think about that, because it sounded like healing and moving on and I wasn't ready yet. There had been no breakup rites and I wasn't done tending my garden of grudges.

"*They* were watching," Astrid said, distracting me. "Ali looked *furious* when you kissed him," she continued.

"Ali can kiss my ass," I replied, pleased at how calm I sounded. I didn't feel calm; I felt shipwrecked. "What do you think of Bree's hair?" I asked, still cool, still casual. *As if I care.*

"It looks like a helmet. She looks like she's about to ask for the manager."

"Right," I said, laughing, even though we both knew it wasn't true.

Astrid prized the bottle from my fingers and brought it to her mouth, tilting her head back as she drank, exposing her throat to the night like a sacrifice. I looked up. It was cloudy; no stars glittered above us, no chance of catching the Orionids. No wishing on a star for me.

I wondered what Bree had thought when I kissed the boy. If she'd been shocked or relieved. Maybe even a little proud. If she had even cared at all.

Hunter Kelley lurched to his feet, his eyes glazed and fixed on the distance as he staggered away, obviously willing himself not to puke until he was alone. He did this at every party—he couldn't take drink at all. I pulled out my phone and checked the time. Five to midnight. I wanted Bree and Ali to break up horribly and publicly. I wanted to go home. I wanted to find the boy. I wanted.

Lars and Manu started kissing noisily, and I remembered last year when Ali and I had snuck away from the festival, running down the lane hand in hand to his house to make the most of it being empty. I looked around for him and Bree but couldn't see them. *They've gone,* my traitor-brain whispered. *Probably at Ali's house, in Ali's bed, while you stay here, with your long, boring hair, drinking shit wine.*

That's when Hunter screamed.

Astrid pulled me to my feet and we joined the crowd running toward the lake. People were yanking their masks off, frantically looking at everyone around them, searching for their people. You could see the relief as they realized the ones they loved were safe.

Everyone safe but her.

The crowd parted for me, though no one remembered it like that afterward. Thom Crofter told my dad he physically tried to stop me from approaching the shoreline, and Mr. McKinnon said to Merry he ordered me to stay back. But a lot of people misremembered things on the Island. You couldn't really trust anything that happened here.

Bree was facedown in the lake, her brand-new hair like a halo around her head, flirting with the weeds at the edge. The tartan coat was gone; she was wearing a white dress, the kind of thing her mom was always buying her and she pretended she hated, but she never wore anything else. It was bunched up around the tops of her thighs, and even though I hated her I wanted to get in the water and cover her up.

"Is he the one you love?"

"What?" I turned toward the voice.

"I said, look away, love," Cally Martin said, trying to force me back. "For gods' sake, child, don't look." But I was made of stone, and even her strong hands couldn't make me stop staring at the girl in the water. *Bree.*

After Bree and I learned to swim, we used to play a game called Dead Man's Float. To win, all you had to do was keep your face in the water the longest. She always won. Always. And just when you started to panic that maybe this time something had actually gone wrong, she'd roll over and shout in triumph.

But she wasn't rolling over this time. People were crying and she wasn't rolling over. The water made her skin look green and mottled. She looked like a naiad. She'd like that. I'd tell her, if she rolled over.

I'd wished her dead. But I hadn't really meant it. It was just the heat of the moment. I'd just meant a little bit dead.

Not dead like this.

She wasn't rolling over.

Someone called for Bree's father. "Where's Mick Dovemuir?"

"Where's young Alistair Murray?" someone else said.

"Bree?"

Ali appeared, walking unsteadily over to us, a bottle of something dark and sticky-looking in his hand. His brown hair was tufted, his cheeks reddened.

"Who screamed? What's going on?" he asked.

He dropped the bottle when he saw Bree floating in the lake. It didn't break, just hit the wet ground with a dull thud. He stared at Bree, frowning, and then he started to walk past me, into the water.

Mr. McKinnon grabbed him then, and Ali lashed out, clocking him in the face, but Mr. McKinnon didn't let go, clinging to Ali as he screamed Bree's name over and over.

Or did she break your heart?

I whipped around again, and saw Manu being comforted by Lars. They were the only people nearby, and neither of them were close enough to have said it. Lars gave me a bleak smile as he stroked Manu's neck. His face was buried in Lars' faded lavender hair, and I paused, torn between pressing back into the mass for comfort of my own or running far, far away.

The foghorn boom of the Island police sergeant's voice cut across the night as he moved through the crowd, issuing instructions for everyone to keep back, and Merry appeared by my side, gripping my arm. Then the sergeant was in the lake, pulling Bree's dress down, his back to us. I thought I saw his shoulders hitch once, but when he turned his expression was grimly professional.

"Go home. All of you," he ordered. "There's nothing more to be done here."

His eyes fell on me, his expression full of pity, before he looked away, as the Island's sole other police officer appeared.

"Should I make a list of people here?" Declan Moretide—only

18

three years older than me but somehow a policeman—asked the sergeant.

"I know who's here."

Which was true. It was the Thesmophoria. It was the Island. Everyone was there.

"Meredith, you should get Corey home," Cally Martin told Merry, who nodded and tucked my arm into hers.

"Let's go home, pet. Come on now."

I'd let her guide me away, leaving my ex–best friend dead in the lake.

RESIDUE

DAYS PASS—FOUR OF THEM, TO BE EXACT. THE following Wednesday, I'm on my bed, messing with a Dione flytrap, when Merry knocks on my door. I consider pretending to be asleep, but I like Merry. And she isn't stupid.

"Corey?" she calls through the wood. "Can we chat, or are you pretending to be asleep?"

I almost smile. "We can chat."

Merry opens the door and peers around it. "Hey. How're you going?"

I shrug. "Fine."

She looks around the dim room and I do the same, then wince. There's a collection of cups on the bedside table, all full of cold, abandoned coffee. We're out of bottled water and I hate the taste of the Island's tap water, so I don't drink more than a sip, even when I'm desperate. The curtains are cracked just enough to give my plants some light; my bedclothes are rumpled about me in a kind of nest; the muddy jeans I wore to the Thesmophoria lie on the floor where I shucked them off Saturday night. I know the room has a smell, because I noticed it when I came in from the garden yesterday. It isn't necessarily a *bad* smell, just what I smell like when I stop using apple shampoo and lemon body wash. A bit sweet-sour. Organic. Animal.

Another kind of stepmother would take all this as a sign I was not, in fact, fine, and would tell me to take a shower or at least open the window. But Merry isn't like that.

"Your dad's doing tacos for tea," she says. "He made seitan for you. He says if there's anything you want to add from the garden, you'll need to fetch it for him."

I shake my head. "It's just your cabbages and a few parsnips left."

"No bother." Merry hesitates, clearly building up to something, and I brace myself for it. "He's just gone down to the Dovemuirs'."

My heart falters. "Right." I gently tickle the fringe on one of the flytrap's leaves and watch it slowly close. Ali gave it to me for our six-month anniversary but I can't get rid of it. I look up to find Merry watching me.

She sighs, then sits beside me on the bed, her weight tipping the old mattress so I fall against her; I put the plant on the bedside table so I don't squash it. Merry wraps an arm around me and I lean into her, inhaling rose water, the black castor oil she rubs into her scalp, the almond cream that softens her hair. At the moment it's in long twists, tied up with a white silk scarf; she had them done fresh for the Thesmophoria.

"It's the prothesis tonight at the temple. For Bree," she says. "The ekphora is tomorrow."

"Tomorrow?" I turn to face her, fighting a wave of dizziness. "But it's Thursday tomorrow. She only . . . It only . . ." My words bottleneck in my throat.

"The Dovemuirs don't want to wait to . . ." Merry pauses, and I know she's considering how to phrase it. "To lay her to rest," she finally chooses. "You know what they're like. They want it done properly."

I swallow. I do know what Bree's parents are like.

"Right. But isn't it a bit fast? Is there not going to be an investigation?"

Merry frowns. "Why would there be?"

"Because no one knows what happened. How she got in the water."

The answering silence is suspicious.

"Do they?" I ask. "Merry?" It comes out sharper than I mean it to. "Sorry," I apologize.

She squeezes my arm. "We just weren't sure if you'd want to know."

"I do."

"All right." Merry releases me, shifting so we're face to face, and I reach for the flytrap again, cradling it in my hands, running my fingers along the leaves and letting the few that are still open close over them, holding me. "Well . . . Alistair says the last time he saw her, she told him she was going to the bathroom and he went to get them something to drink. Cally Martin confirmed that Bree was behind her in the line and they chatted for a bit, until Bree said she couldn't wait anymore and left. Cally was the last person to see her."

I blink. "Is that it?" I ask. "She just ditched the line and fell in the lake?"

Merry nods. "Pretty much. Declan—Constable Moretide—thinks she tried to get behind the reeds for privacy and slipped. They found her coat folded nearby."

I remember how it flared when she spun, like a cape.

"No," I say. Because that can't be it. I shake my head and repeat, "No. Bree's a good swimmer. And the lake isn't even that deep where she was."

Merry's voice is so gentle when she replies. "Alistair said she'd had some vodka; they both had. And it was pitch-black, and the water would've been ice cold. Paralyzing. It only takes a few seconds."

"But it doesn't make any sense." My voice cracks, and I clamp my mouth shut to stop anything else escaping me. My lips are chapped; I press them together and feel the skin come away.

Merry's eyes glisten and she swipes at them with her sleeve. "I know. I know, pet. It's awful. No matter what happened between you . . . it's awful."

She pulls me close for another quick, hard hug, before standing up and clearing her throat at the same time. "Anyway, I just wanted to let you know what the plans are so you can decide if you want to go. No pressure, either way." She looks around the room. "Mind if I take a few of the mugs? Oh, and there's bottled water now, your dad picked some up. I could bring you a fresh coffee?"

"No, thank you," I manage. "Sorry. I should've brought them down."

"It's no bother." Merry offers a sad smile and gathers up the cups, hooking the handles with her fingers, careful not to spill anything. As soon as she's gone, I wriggle out from the blankets and close the door behind her. I lean against it, stomach full of eels.

She wouldn't die like that. Not Bree.

If she thought the line was too long, she absolutely would leave it and find somewhere that suited her better, because that *was* Bree—she always did what she wanted, when she wanted, and she hated to wait for anything. But she wouldn't die because of it.

Except she did, I think. Barely two hundred meters from where we'd all been dancing and laughing, she drowned.

In early summer, before everything went wrong, me, Bree and Ali had been down at the south of the Island, at Thetis Point. There is a bit of cliff the older kids jump off into the sea, but we'd never done it. Usually, we followed the worn path down the cliffside to the small, black-sand cove, and waded into the water from there. But this summer we realized we *were* the older kids and Bree wanted to jump. So she had; no hesitation, flinging herself off the top the moment we got there, so impatient that she'd peeled her dress off on the walk, leaving me to pick it up.

I didn't believe she'd actually do it until she did, caught in the air for one shining moment, her arms outstretched like wings before she dropped out of sight. I'd gripped Ali's hand as we edged forward, looking at her in the glittering sea below. Far, far below. My insides lurched and I pulled back.

"Come on!" Bree had shouted up to us. "It's amazing!"

I'm not scared of heights, but I am scared of falling. Of spaces with edges and not being connected by hand or foot to the ground. There was no way I'd be able to do it, and I knew it.

"I suppose we should start the walk down," Ali had said when I'd stepped back from the edge.

I could hear in his voice that he wanted to jump. And I wanted him to have what he wanted, because we were in love.

"I don't mind walking alone," I'd said.

I'd meant it too. I was worried about Bree being in the open water by herself for the fifteen or so minutes the walk down would take. I'd be safe on the path, but if she got a cramp, or if something else happened . . . it felt like it was tempting the Fates to leave a young woman alone in the sea. We know people from the mainland call us backward and think we're all superstitious weirdos, but they don't have to live here. It's easy for them, in their concrete towns with their subways and skyscrapers, to forget what it's like to live where there are things in the woods, watching and waiting. There are winter days when the wind blows the wrong way and we hear the singing far out at sea; I've *seen* people with my own eyes being held back from the icy water, swearing they're being called. And people out here still die with Poseidon's name on their lips every now and then.

It doesn't hurt to keep one eye on the gods. Just in case.

"You jump," I'd insisted to Ali. "We can't leave her by herself in the ocean. Go on. I'll meet you down there."

He didn't even pretend to mull it over. "All right." He was undressed in seconds. "See you down there," he'd said, kissing me fast on the mouth, tasting like the chocolate we'd all shared on the way up. Then he was gone.

I waited until he surfaced with a cry of joy, and then I'd gathered up his and Bree's forgotten clothes and shoes and started toward the path, scrambling down as fast as I could, cutting a full five minutes off the usual time. I took my shorts and T-shirt off, left all our stuff in a tangled heap, then swam out to them.

They were treading water close together as I approached, and when they turned to me, Bree's eyes were shining.

"Holy shit, Cor, there was a seal!" Ali shouted.

I turned, looking for it. "Where?"

"Right here! Just after Ali jumped in it popped up, right next to us," Bree added, her voice high and excited. "It was so beautiful."

"It was unreal," Ali said. "It just started swimming with us. Like, just swimming around us."

"Are you sure it was a seal?" I asked, still spinning in the water, scanning for dark shapes.

"Yes," Bree said, her voice sharp. "What else would it be?"

I ignored that and turned to her. "Were you scared?" I asked.

"No." Bree's mouth twisted as if the idea was ridiculous. "It was really sweet. Like a water dog."

"Yeah," Ali agreed. "It was like it wanted to be our friend."

"Wow," I said, my voice flattened by jealousy, but they didn't notice, or they didn't care. They started racing each other and I leaned back and floated, staring up at the sky.

The seal didn't reappear, and I wondered if maybe they were making it up to tease me; it sounded too good to be true, too convenient that it happened at the exact time I wasn't there, but they insisted it was real and talked about it for the rest of the day. Not just the rest of the day, but for weeks after: *Remember when we swam with the seal?*

I think that's the day it started with them. When they saw the seal together.

I wonder if Bree knew what was happening to her, in the lake. Whether she fought it, or gave herself over to it. They say you see your whole life flash before you when you drown.

A tiny part of me wonders if she thought of me.

Because I'd been thinking about her. I'm almost always thinking about her.

CATCH CROP

IT'S NOT THAT I ACTUALLY THINK I KILLED HER. You can't wish people dead, any more than you can wish them in love with you, or wish yourself a million dollars. I know it's just a horrible coincidence that she died after I'd thought it, but I feel weird now that I've remembered it; I can't help feeling a little guilty.

Which is good, I tell myself, because if I didn't feel bad, I'd be a monster and I'm not. I'm the victim.

Are you still the victim if your enemy is dead? a voice whispers in the back of my mind. *Doesn't that make you the victor?*

Screw this. I need my garden.

Merry is pacing in the living room, on a call with her PhD supervisor judging by her expression, and she gives me a stressed wave as I pass her, heading for the kitchen. I pick a sweater out of the clean laundry pile and pull it over my pajama top, shove my feet in the boots waiting by the back door and then go outside.

The air is a cold, sharp shock after the closeness of my bed-room, pinching my skin through the sweater. I pause to breathe it in, all the mingling smells: woodsmoke from fireplaces across the Island, the salt of the sea and seaweed rotting on the strand-line. And under it all, the rich, soft earth of my garden.

Pretty much everything I grew ripened early this year, so I've already covered the beds, except one that still has a few strag-gling parsnips I hope might get a little chunkier, and a trio of red cabbages I'm growing for Merry. I want them ready for the Haloa feast next month—Merry does this thing where she spices and caramelizes them and it's my favorite—but when I check them over, they look small and fragile, struggling against the circumstances.

"Me too," I whisper, then feel like an idiot.

I give them a little pat and leave them to it.

Then, I dig. It's messy, boring and painful work—I've never started digging a bed without regretting it halfway through—but the thing is, you can't just leave a hole. You either keep going or fill it back in, and with those as your choices you might as well carry on. Plus, it's good to slam a hoe into the mud when you're pissed off.

My mother was a gardener too, according to Dad. Maybe she still is—we last spoke for approximately four minutes on my sixteenth birthday. She phoned and wished me many happy returns and asked if I planned to stay on the Island. I thought she was hinting that I should visit her, but she sounded scared when I suggested it. Maybe whoever she's with now doesn't know she has a kid. For all I know, I have brothers and sisters.

When my mom moved here, she started an organic fruit and vegetable business, which was ambitious considering there are so few people and mostly everyone grows their own stuff. But not like her—Dad says she had greenhouses full of pineapples and peaches, figs and olives, things that would never normally grow here. It's how she met him; he was cycling down to the lighthouse and she stopped him by the road and offered him a basket of June strawberries. Nine months later, I was born.

And three years after that, she left us and didn't look back.

Too warm once I'm working, I pull the sweater off and toss it behind me. The cold air feels good against my hot skin and I pause to let it wash over me. Then I look down into the shallow hole and realize it's the same shape as a grave.

Bree never liked the garden at this time of year. She said it was depressing, that it looked dead. I tried to explain that even the bare parts weren't really dead, just sleeping, but she didn't understand. She liked it when it was full of flowers.

I lean on my digging hoe and close my eyes.

"I thought you were leaving that bit for my barbecue pit?"

My father, still dressed in the boilersuit he wears to work in the lighthouse, lopes toward me, carrying two steaming mugs. He's the kind of tall that means he always stoops a little, as if his whole body is apologizing for making you look up that far. I guess I inherited my height, or lack thereof, from my mother too.

"I was. But it's not like you're going to build it in winter, and the land's a-wasting, Mr. Allaway."

He doesn't laugh. "For the love of Zeus, Corey, are those

your pajamas?" He nods at my T-shirt and shorts. "It's forty-five degrees out. Are you trying to catch pneumonia?"

I fetch my sweater and haul it over my head, knocking my bun askew. I leave it lopsided, the grease of the last five days holding it mostly in place, and take the mug he holds out to me, sniffing it.

"I made it with bottled water," Dad says with a sigh.

When I was eight and refused to drink the tap water, wouldn't even brush my teeth with it anymore because it tasted like sucking pennies, he took me to the doctor, who said I had something called pine mouth, even though I'd never eaten a pine nut in my life. She said it would go away in a couple of weeks, but it didn't. A few weeks later my dad replaced all the pipes with new plastic ones, but I still wouldn't drink the tap water. The Island's water comes from a spring, deep underground—the kind of water, he reminds me, that rich people pay through the nose for. They're welcome to it. Whatever it is, I hate it.

"Talk to me, Cor." He sits on the edge of the bed with the cabbages, balancing delicately. I perch beside him, press my free hand into the soil and rub it. It feels nice between my fingers. Soft and warm. I press into it further, planting my whole hand up to the wrist.

"About?"

He gives me a look. "I've just seen the Dovemuirs."

"Merry said."

"Mick was asking after you. Wee Aengus too."

I lower the cup and look at him. "How are they?"

"Mick's holding up. Trying to be strong for Ella and the boys. Ella's a wreck, of course. You know how she was about Bree. I think things will get easier for them after tonight, and tomorrow. They'll be able to start healing. He wanted you to know you're welcome there any time."

I always did like Bree's dad.

"Little Mick doesn't seem to understand Bree's gone," my dad continues, gray eyes soft and sad. "Mick said they might send him and Wee Aengus to stay with one of their mainland cousins for a bit, after the funeral." He pauses. "I think you should go. Maybe not to the prothesis. But to the ekphora, tomorrow."

"I don't know." I shrug. What's the etiquette for going to your former best friend's funeral? "Everything was so bad between us."

"I think you'll regret it if you don't. And it would mean a lot to Mick and Ella, you were practically their kid too, before . . ." He backpedals when I glare at him. "I don't condone what Bree did. Or *him*. They both betrayed you and you're right to be angry and hurt. But . . . she's dead, Cor. It changes things."

Annoyance flares. "It doesn't change anything for me. She's still a b—"

"Don't speak ill of the dead," my father snaps.

In that moment, I wish Bree dead all over again; outrage lightning in my veins, because it will always, *always*, be like this now.

I know, as clearly as if Cassandra herself had delivered the prophecy, that what Bree and Ali did to me won't matter to anyone anymore. I won't be allowed to hate her. Or even him. She'll always be young and beautiful and dead too soon, and that will eclipse everything. Every shitty thing she did and said, wiped away. It's so unfair, and I can never, ever say that aloud, because at least I'm alive, right?

I bite my tongue to keep from screaming. I *hate* her. I will always, always *hate* her.

"Hey," my father says when I keep my mutinous gaze down, too scared to look up in case I say something to him that I can't take back. "I know things have been hard for you. I'm on your side, you know that, right?"

Then be on my fucking side, I think. Understand why I can't go and cry over her, or watch Ali cutting a lock of his hair off over her. Understand why this doesn't change anything for me, why it makes it worse.

I make a fist in the earth and hold on for dear life.

He reaches out and rubs my shoulder, then stands, knees clicking as he does. "OK, kid, I'd best get on. What's it going to be?"

It takes me a few seconds to understand he means the new bed.

"Flowers," I murmur, then change my mind. "No. I don't know yet."

"All right. Think about tomorrow," he says before he returns to the house.

As my anger fades, I pull my hand out of the earth and shake it clean. A little dirt flies onto the cabbages and I lean over to brush it off, realizing as I do that they're bigger than I thought. If they carry on like this, they will be ready in time for Haloa.

I turn back to the hole I've made and wonder what it would feel like to climb into it.

ENTROPY

I EXPECT I WON'T BE ABLE TO SLEEP THAT NIGHT, so much so that I steal one of the sleeping pills Merry brought back from the US last time she visited, and try to pass out before they get back from the prothesis.

It doesn't work.

The walls in our house are thin, so I hear every word they say to each other in the bathroom as they brush their teeth. Dad insists I should go to the funeral, because I *clearly need the closure.* Merry disagrees, says that what I need is time.

"She needs more than time," my dad replies.

I sit up, straining to hear.

"Like what?"

"I don't know. Some proper help, maybe. She's so angry lately. You should have seen her earlier. It was coming off her in waves. I could practically feel it."

"Her boyfriend cheated on her with her best friend. Damn right she's angry," Merry says.

I feel a burst of gratitude, which my dad obliterates when he replies: "It's not Corey, though. She's always been so placid. And now she's shouting at people on the phone and slamming doors."

"She shouted once on the phone and, to be fair, she's been waiting for that netting for ages. They're stringing her along. If they don't have it, they should refund her."

"She never used to talk to people like that. And last week, when she told Cally Martin to piss off just for asking how she was doing. I'm still getting grief for it."

"Frankly, Cally Martin does need to piss off. She's a nosy cow, Craig."

I laugh in the dark and miss my dad's response.

"Corey's a teenager," Merry says, and even though I love her, I roll my eyes when she adds, "Mood swings are part of the process."

"I'm just . . ." My dad pauses and my heart gives a weird little lurch. I have to press closer to the wall to hear the next part, his voice is so soft. "I'm worried if she doesn't get a handle on it, she'll end up in real trouble. Go to some dark place she can't come back from."

"You're overthinking it. She's still Corey; it's not like she's had a personality transplant and given up gardening, or started taking drugs. She's just grieving, working through her stuff. And Bree's death isn't going to help her heal."

"I know that. But I don't want to see it escalate to a point where she needs help we can't easily get on the Island. You read about kids and mental health. . . ."

"I honestly don't think Corey's having some kind of breakdown. But we'll keep an eye on her. All right? She'll be fine. She's a great kid."

"Let's hope so."

They're still bickering softly when they close their bedroom door.

I lie back down, curling on my side, my stomach in knots. I didn't think I was having a breakdown, either. This is just what it's like living with the aftermath of having your heart ripped out and stomped on by the one person who was never, ever supposed to do that. This is what happens when you have your entire world turned upside down.

I roll onto my back, place my hands on my belly and close my eyes, taking deep, meditative breaths, trying to picture a forest. Something soothing and peaceful. The sea, or a lake—

No.

Because then I can't help but think of Bree, who must be lying in the same position across town in a coffin.

I wonder how she looks. People always say the dead look peaceful, like they're sleeping, but I'd gone with Bree to her granny's prothesis a few years ago and Mrs. Dovemuir hadn't looked asleep, or especially peaceful. She'd looked dead; whatever had made her herself was gone. She wasn't Bree's granny anymore, just an empty vessel.

I panic as I realize I can't fully remember what Bree looked like alive. All my mental pictures of her are superimposed over by her face down in the lake.

I get out of bed and open my underwear drawer, searching for my phone. I tossed it in there Saturday night after Merry brought me home, not wanting to talk to anyone, or see anything online. The battery's run down, so I bring it back to bed and plug it in to charge, turning it on.

There are a bunch of notifications, from Astrid, from Lars, from the group chat Astrid added me to. I ignore them all and open my photos, scrolling until I come to the ones of her, of us, the history of Corey-and-Bree in full color: in my garden, in my bedroom, on the beach, at school. Further back, and further back, until I find one from last year. I stop scrolling. In the picture Bree is kneeling by a stream in the woods, a piece of ragged old net curtain over her head, her expression fake solemn, on the knife edge of laughter.

It was another game we used to play, when we were about eight or nine. We called it the Brides of Artemis. It started because we had to pick one of the gods to do a special project on at school. We chose Artemis because she had a bow and arrows, could talk to animals and didn't like boys; all things we could get on board with.

We found out that right up until the 1980s, girls our age would be sent to one of her temples to serve her for a year, and we loved the idea, imagining a grotto full of girls like us, running and hunting and howling at the moon. I remember asking my dad, in the pre-Merry days, if I could go and serve Artemis on the mainland—I knew there were temples to her in the south, and our teacher said some girls still went, though you didn't have to anymore—and he'd said no, almost got angry about it, which was weird because he never usually told me no.

Bree's mom also said no, but that wasn't a surprise because Bree's mom always said no.

And it never stopped us.

I stole a pair of net curtains for veils, and Bree contributed two of the endless smocked, pastel cotton dresses her mom bought for her, and we dedicated ourselves to Artemis in secret.

Our worships were ridiculous: gathering rainwater in jam jars and adding petals to make "perfume" for Artemis, dancing, chanting, making bows and arrows out of sticks and stolen yarn, trying to talk to squirrels. Kids' stuff. We hid our props in a plastic box we wedged between the roots of a tree. We didn't tell anyone what we were doing; we weren't allowed to play in the woods.

Once, Bree said she saw a hamadryad smiling at us before she vanished into the oak tree we hid our supplies in, and I refused to go back for a week, terrified a tree woman would appear and do whatever tree women did to girls who were playing in the woods unsupervised. But when I told Bree why I wouldn't go back, she said she never saw a hamadryad and I must have dreamt she did. Of course, she was lying to get me to go back. And it worked.

We'd stopped eventually—I can't remember why, just one day we didn't go to the woods and dress up and then we never did it again. Except once, last year.

We were in my room while I was supposed to be cleaning. Bree was painting her nails red and I was shoving things in my wardrobe when I found our Artemis project book in the back.

"Remember this?" I threw it at her.

"Nails!" she shouted. Then, "Oh my gods," she'd said, flicking through it. "Do you remember the Brides of Artemis?"

It was a match to a wick. We'd raced to the woods to find the box, still in the tree, the net curtains and our bows still inside. They were a bit damp and smelly, but that hadn't stopped Bree ruining her nails and swinging her old veil over her head. I'd taken a photo of her on my phone and she'd taken one of me on hers. We'd brought the box back with us and shoved it all in the bin outside the post office. Game over.

I've deleted every photo of Ali, even the ones I looked good in, but not a single one of her.

Before I can think about what I'm doing, I'm out of bed, grabbing a pair of socks from the drawer and then feeling on the floor for my jeans. They're stiff, showering splinters of dried mud on the wooden floor when I pull them on over my pajama shorts, but they'll do for now, it's not like she'll be able to see them.

Besides, Bree told me once that you shouldn't wash jeans, only sponge them down and freeze them, and even though we later discovered that absolutely isn't true, I never stopped feeling guilty for putting mine in the wash, unless they were totally wrecked. Bree didn't even own a pair of jeans, so I don't know where she would have heard that.

Silent as the grave, I leave my room and move cautiously down the stairs, avoiding the steps that would betray me. I grab the first jacket I touch from the cupboard—Merry's, from the scent of rose water I get as I slip my arms into the sleeves and zip it up over my pajama top—and rummage for a pair of boots. Then I creep out of the cottage, into the night.

I nearly turn back three times, but force myself to go on, walking through silvery, silent streets. It's a bitterly cold night, the air like tiny knives.

Twenty minutes later, I find myself outside the Island's temple, reaching for the spare key I know the priestess hides in the eaves of the porch, because Bree, Ali and I have used it more than once to break in when it's raining or we don't want to be at any of our homes. It's so quiet I can hear the sea whispering and shushing against the rocks on the other side of Lynceus Hill, and the wind in the cypress trees in the graveyard.

I don't really know what I'm doing here, or why I've come. Maybe it's what my dad said—I need closure. Just without the entire Island watching me. Then I can go back to hating her in peace.

The sound of the lock releasing snaps like a gunshot and I step inside.

I wash my hands in the bowl by the doorway and then look around. The temple is lit by candles that flicker in an oddly rhythmic way. They surround the coffin—*there is the coffin*—and I'm shocked: What if they fall, what if there's a gust of wind or a spark falls into one of the jars of oil circling the coffin and the whole place goes up?

"Hello?" I call, my voice echoing off the pillars. Surely someone's here to make sure there isn't an accident. No one replies.

I have to blow the candles out. I can't leave them going. Not near the coffin—*that's her actual coffin*. If she's going to burn, I want it to be in the Underworld, not here.

Her coffin is on a raised platform in front of the altar. To the left, someone's put a copy of Bree's last school photo on a stand, cypress and celery flowers woven around it. My heart lurches as my eyes meet hers in the picture, and I begin to walk toward the coffin— *Bree's coffin, Bree's really dead, that's really her coffin, oh gods, oh fuck.*

As I get closer, I realize the reason the candles are flickering so strangely, and the reason no one is here to stop a potential inferno, is because they're battery operated, and I feel both stupid and relieved. Then I forget about the candles because I see her.

Bree.

There are more celery flowers in her hair and she's in a pale-blue dress, with three-quarter-length sleeves. It's rustic looking, balloon sleeves and smocked cotton, very Bree, very butter-wouldn't-melt. Her hands are clasped low on her belly, fingernails painted palest ballerina pink. Bree liked red or black—the trio of nail polishes she'd been so desperate to get back from me were all shades of red that she'd put on and then take off before she went home.

She's lying on a patchwork quilt, the kind of cottage-chic thing that's very much Mrs. Dovemuir's style. I look closer at it and then my stomach bottoms out as I recognize some of the fabric. A square of white cotton with embroidered yellow flowers, exactly like the outfit Bree had worn to Astrid's tenth birthday; I remember her complaining she was the only one in a dress while everyone else wore jeans. A gray square that suspiciously matches our school uniform color. A soft, worn pink square that I'm pretty sure came from a blanket she'd had as a baby. I try to remember what it's called, and then it comes to me: an heirloom quilt. You make it as your kid grows up, out of all their old clothes, and give it to them on their wedding day or when their first child is born. Neither of which will happen for Bree.

The back of my throat burns, and I swallow.

The mortician's makeup is pretty good, but Bree's cheeks are too poreless—probably the primer they've used—and the foundation or concealer or whatever has caked over the pimples on her chin, making them more obvious. She gets them every month, just before her period, and realizing she'd had them when she died shakes me, because it means we're still in sync and that feels like it shouldn't be allowed anymore.

There is a coin on her lips for the Boatman.

I didn't get, until then, that part of me believed this was all fake. The ultimate Dead Man's Float, the joke to end all jokes, a way to distract everyone from what she'd done to me. That I hadn't all-the-way believed she was dead, and was waiting for the next part of the story. But the coin is the proof. The coin and the quilt. She really is gone.

Oh, Bree.

And because no one will ever know, I take a tiny break from hating her, for old time's sake, and reach out and rest my hand on hers.

It's cold, and waxy, and I flinch away, but then I pull myself together and try again. I do it for those two girls who called themselves the Brides of Artemis and whose periods happened at the same time. Before she was the worst fucking person I have ever met, back when loving her was as easy as breathing.

I stand there for a long time, and when I don't want to stand anymore, I sit, leaning back against the stand the coffin rests on. I'll go home in a minute. One more minute.

Tolerance

MY EYES SNAP OPEN WHEN SOMEONE TOUCHES my shoulder.

Priestess Logan crouches beside me, still dressed in her street clothes, her shock at seeing me plain on her face.

Which is not lit by the light of a hundred electric candles, I realize, but weak winter sunlight.

It's dawn.

"Corey?" she asks. "What are you doing here? Who let you in?"

I leap up and run.

I make it to the top of the hill behind the temple before I collapse to the ground, panting, my legs shaking from the climb. I wrap my arms around my knees and stare out across the sea.

The sound of bells drifts up the hillside and I count them. Six. My dad and Merry will be getting up soon. I need to get home before then.

I haul myself to my feet and look for our cottage, checking for lights. I find it easily, nestled on the outskirts of Daly, not far from the fields where the Thesmophoria is held. My gaze moves to the lake, and I turn sharply away.

I haven't been up here for a while. We used to come up on feast days and holidays and dare each other to look over our left shoulders, toward the west. Legend has it, if you do, you might catch a glimpse of one of the entrances to the Underworld. It was another thing we'd been told by our parents not to try, not to even think about it, but that just meant we had to. Bree was always the first to dare, but also the first to look. She isn't here anymore, so I dare. I look.

Over my left shoulder, out to the west. I don't actually expect it to be there.

But it is.

Every inch of skin on my body tingles at the sight of the small island where there was just ocean a second ago.

I don't move, as if I might scare it off, but the island that has appeared from nowhere doesn't fade or sink back into the sea. It stays solid and true, like it's always been there, like it's *supposed* to be there. I turn to face it slowly, afraid to even blink.

It's real. It's really real.

It can't be.

I close my eyes, count to three and open them again, expecting it to be gone—hoping it's gone.

But it's still there. If anything, I can see it even more clearly now, like I'm looking through binoculars.

I watch milky bubbles of seafoam pop as the waves break on

the shore, see fronds of seaweed dance as salt water washes over them. The beach beyond is pebbled and leads to a dense forest. I can even see the individual trees, all evergreens, in so much detail it could be a few feet in front of me, not miles away.

I feel in my pocket for my phone—I have to take photos or film it, I have to get proof—and then remember it's still plugged in at home. Swearing quietly, I stare at the island instead, trying to commit every detail to memory. The thing I want to do most of all is run down the hill to the temple and tell Bree that I've seen it, finally, and she hasn't—

Then she's there.

She walks out of the woods on the island, wearing the same outfit she'd had on at the Thesmophoria: the tartan coat, the heeled boots. Her new hair, in its shining chestnut waves. I watch, my mouth bone dry, as she walks down to the waterline and sinks into the shingle, gripping fistfuls of wet pebbles, the waves lapping her knees.

At first, I don't understand how can she be lying down in the temple and over there too. How can she be in two places at once? But then it clicks: it's the Underworld. I'm not seeing Bree, but her shade. I'm looking at what comes next.

I wait, my heart pounding, for her to look over, to look up and see me. I want to shout, to get her attention. I'm desperate to do it, but I can't move. I can't speak. I'm a statue on top of the hill; like Niobe, locked in with all my sorrows.

There's movement in the shadows of the forest behind Bree and my heart stops as a figure emerges from the trees.

It's a man, and he hesitates, watching her, his arms crossed.

He's dressed in black, a long-sleeved T-shirt or sweater and trousers—mortal clothes—his dark hair ruffling in the breeze from the sea. He isn't as old as I first thought either, I realize, just a couple of years older than me. More of a boy than a man.

When the boy walks toward her, moving as smoothly as a snake over the rocky beach, shadows leak from him like oil and cover the stones.

And then I know who he is, what impossible, awful thing he is.

Hades.

I'm looking at an actual god. The worst of the gods.

I watch him approach Bree, his shadows curling around her, and I want to warn her that he's there, and she should run. For that instant it doesn't matter what she's done to me; I'd save anyone from him if I could.

Then Bree rises to her feet, facing him. As they look at each other, his expression is tender, sorrowful. Something twists inside my chest. Why isn't she screaming? Why is he looking at her like that?

He holds out a hand to her, and she turns and gives the Island a last, lingering look, but she still doesn't see me. The moment their hands touch, whatever has been keeping me prisoner releases me, my heart starts battering frantically against my ribs and I scream.

"Bree!"

My voice breaks over the water, but it doesn't reach Bree.

He hears, though.

He guides Bree in front of him, even as he turns, trying to find the source of the scream.

I throw myself to the ground, making myself as flat as I can, some feeling in my gut telling me he mustn't see me, can't know I've seen him, or that I'm here. With my heart thumping against the cold, damp grass, I lie there, counting the seconds, waiting to see if I got away with it, if I cheated death.

"What are you doing?"

For a minute I really do think it's him. Then I realize it's just Ali.

I sit up, turning to the water.

The Underworld is gone.

I peer over my shoulder, twisting to check from every direction, but it isn't there anymore. It's vanished.

"Corey? Are you all right?" Ali looks me up and down, staring at my jeans, my muddy boots, as I haul myself to my feet.

"How come you're here?" I say, bewildered by his sudden appearance.

"I'm going to the temple to fill up the lekythos for Mrs. Dovemuir, but I saw you doing . . . whatever you're doing."

I spin around and around, but the island doesn't appear again, leaving me with the unpleasant realization that it's likely I hallucinated the Underworld, Hades and my dead ex–best friend. Maybe it's sleep deprivation, or the sleeping pill I took. Possibly I am having a breakdown and my dad was right.

"Are you coming to the ekphora?" Ali says. "Because, no offense, you might want to get changed. And maybe shower."

I ignore him and pivot quickly, as if I might catch the island by surprise, like we're playing peekaboo. When it doesn't work, I try again, whirling the other way and then jerking my head to look over my left shoulder. Nothing. Definitely a hallucination, then. I laugh when I realize I don't know if that's a good thing or not. Which is better, losing your mind or seeing the land of the dead?

"Corey?" Ali grabs my arms and makes me face him. "What is going on with you?"

I pull myself from his grip, holding up my hands to keep him back. "Don't touch me."

For a second, he looks shocked, like I've bit him. Then he scowls. "Oh, for Zeus's sake. Seriously? Bree's down there in a coffin and you're still in a mood with me?"

"In a mood?" I repeat, stunned.

"About what happened," he says, like he thinks I might have forgotten. "We broke up, like, in summer. I thought you were over it. You seemed over it at the Thesmophoria," he adds sullenly.

Bitter triumph that Astrid was right and he is annoyed I kissed someone else is instantly eclipsed by my own anger.

I forget about Bree, the Underworld, everything, as my blood roars. "Are you serious? You think I should be over it because, what—some arbitrary amount of time has passed? Are you forgetting what you did, Ali? What I did?" He swallows and I lean in, thrilled when his skin pales. "You came to my house and said, 'Let's go for a walk.' And you didn't say a word—not one single word—about breaking up with me when we went down to

48

the cove. You chatted about school and some stupid film you'd watched and then you let me . . ."

I stall as I get to what happened next, losing momentum when I think about what he'd let me do just before he told me it was over. How I'd believed everything was fine, because I'd thought he still wanted me, still fancied me. My voice breaks when I say, "You waited until I was done before you dumped me. Remember, Ali? Because I do."

He looks at the ground. "I didn't ask you to do anything."

"But you didn't stop me. You let me think everything was normal between us. Did you tell her? When you got to her house, did you tell her about it?"

"Will you shut up?" He peers behind him, as if checking that no one can hear us, and then I know he didn't tell her. Just took one last freebie before chucking me, and my temper flares higher and brighter.

"Why, Ali? Why her?" The words are out of my mouth before I can stop them. "Of everyone on the Island, in the world, why did it have to be her?"

He can't look me in the eye. "I dunno. She was just different."

"Different how?" I grind the words out. "How was she different?"

"I dunno," he repeats.

"You don't know?" I snap, and he flinches, eyebrows rising like he's surprised.

I remember my dad in the bathroom, saying how I used to be so placid and almost smile. *Not anymore, folks.*

"Well?" I say.

The shock must have worn off, because Ali's eyes narrow and his face turns mean. "She was more fun. More up for stuff. You never wanted to do anything, or try anything. You were always messing around in your garden. It was boring."

It lands like a kick, knocking the rage out of me hard enough that I curl in on myself, crossing my arms and turning away. I hear him leave, and keep my head bent. I don't want to watch him walking away. Not again.

I stay hunched over, his words ringing in my ears. *You never wanted to do anything. You were always messing around in your garden.* I think again about my dad saying how placid I am. Placid. Stolid. Bovine. Boring.

I crouch down, kneeling in the grass, and press my hands to the earth, pushing my fingers into the wet soil. Immediately I feel better. *Gardening isn't boring,* a fierce voice says inside me.

Then my skin tingles again.

I stand and straighten, and when I look over my left shoulder, I'm not surprised to see the Underworld is back.

And so is Hades.

Even with the distance, I can feel the fury in his gaze, a heat that makes my skin burn. He *hates* that I can see him, that I saw Bree. His rage rolls toward me, carried on the waves, and I'm desperately grateful for the sea between us, praying that small barrier will keep him from getting to me.

Then I remember he's a *god*.

I didn't really believe in the gods. I didn't *not* believe in them—I live on the Island; only a fool wouldn't believe. But I believed in them like I believed in Antarctica and the Mariana Trench; I knew they were out there, but it wasn't like I was ever going to see them. They had nothing to do with me.

So I thought.

We watch each other, playing chicken; one of us has to look away, or run away, first. We both know it will be—must be—me and yet I don't move. Don't blink. I can't take my eyes from him.

Overhead the sky flashes and I flinch, for a second convinced that Hades has taken my photo. But the light is chased by a roll of thunder that crashes through me so hard my bones shake, and I realize a storm has broken. I glance back at Hades, who's looking up at the sky with a faint frown on his face.

A bolt of lightning forks between us, striking the ocean with a neon pink blast, the light radiating over the surface, and we lock eyes again, the dark heat of his boring into mine.

"Go home," he says. I hear him as clearly as if he's standing beside me and realize I recognize his voice, that I've heard it before.

As rain begins to hurl itself down, I catch sight of another figure, hooded, standing back in the tree line and I pause. Is it Bree? Waiting for him?

"Corey, go home. Now." He doesn't sound angry. He sounds worried.

Lighting flashes again, with thunder rolling immediately after. The storm is on top of me.

I turn and run.

I slip and slide my way down the hill, toward the high street, running like the hounds are chasing me to drag me to the Underworld.

The Underworld. Hades.

I stop running, a stitch in my side, hands on my knees as I bend double and try to catch my breath. Rain lashes my back like a cat-o'-nine-tails. I am not built for this kind of exercise.

A low boom ricochets through the sky, startling me, and I look up, catching sight of my reflection in the darkened window of the Spar, hair plastered to my face, rain dripping from my nose.

Behind me, a figure towers. Icy skin, inky hair, shadows spreading out behind him like dark wings.

He's here.

I whirl around, but the street is empty. No Hades. No shadows. Nothing. I walk forward with my arms outstretched, groping the air where he'd been. It feels warm, sticky. Charged.

I smell ozone, sharper than chlorine.

The hairs on the back of my neck rise, followed by the ones across the rest of my body, and I remember too late that I'm standing outside in a storm.

There is a flash, and then nothing.

ELECTROTROPISM

WHEN NOTHING FINALLY RESOLVES ITSELF TO something, I'm here.

Here is identical to the high street in Daly. I'm standing exactly where I had been, outside the Spar, just before the flash. Except it's wrong. I don't know why, but it is.

The rain has stopped. The streets are deserted; no signs of life, no lights in any of the windows. Which could be because it's still pretty early, but that doesn't explain why there are no cats slinking along the lane—Lars's feral ginger tom is almost always around—and there are no birds flying about. The village feels abandoned, a *Mary Celeste* town, like everyone has downed tools and fled while I was on the hill.

I walk forward slowly, waiting to see what, if anything, will happen. Only to stop dead as I realize why it's so strange, my mouth opening in wonder.

It's as if someone's built a replica of the high street, but only the fronts of the buildings. Everything is made of plywood and plastic—the whole street is fake: the doctor's surgery, the tea-room, the post office, the secondhand shop—all pretend, like a film set. I step into the alley between the butcher's and the chemist, peering at the struts holding the facades up. Back here, there's no paint or effort to disguise it; the chipboard and nails are clear for all to see.

I turn back to the street and trip over the hem of . . . my gown? What?

I look down at myself. Gone are my jeans and boots, and Merry's coat. Instead, I'm wearing a long white dress or robe, sleeveless and pinned at the shoulders. No shoes, just my bare feet on the tarmac, which is neither cold nor warm. The air is ambient too, not the stormy November I've been in. In fact, the ground is dry. No puddles. No sign of the storm. . . .

The storm.

The flash.

I freeze. "Oh, shit," I whisper. "I'm dead."

"You're not."

I spin around and trip over the gown again, knocking into the front of the fake tea shop and making it wobble. For a second, I think it will fall, taking me with it, but it stays upright and I use it to find my balance before I turn to the boy leaning against a lamppost on the opposite side of the street.

"Elegant," he says, his smile thin and pointed like a crescent moon. "Relax. You're fine. This is a dream."

I scan him for shadows. I should be relieved when I see none, but I'm not, because though he's not Hades, he is still one of *them*—his silver skin makes that obvious, shining dully in the dim morning light. *Shit.*

As well as the knife-edge smile and argent skin, this boy-god has light brown hair, falling in loose curls to his shoulders, amused hazel eyes watching me from beneath arched brows. He's tall and slim, stretched like taffy: long limbs, a long, thin nose, a long neck. I must outweigh him by a good twenty pounds, though he's at least a foot taller than I am. Like me, he wears a white robe, though his ends at the knee. And when I look down at his feet, I see he's wearing sandals. Winged ones. My heart sinks. *Shit, shit, shit.*

"Who are you?" I ask, though I already know. The sandals are a dead giveaway.

Hermes confirms it with his reply: "I have a message for you."

I force myself to stay calm. "Who from?"

His smile widens. "I think you know that, too."

My palms turn clammy.

"Where am I?" I ask, my heart beating hummingbird fast against my rib cage. "Where is this?" I gesture at the buildings.

He inclines his head, still grinning. "As I said, it's a dream. Your mind has put you in the last place it remembers you being— well, a dream version of it. You're actually at home, on your bed, asleep and well. Look."

No sooner has he said it than we're standing side by side in the doorway to my bedroom.

I melt against the frame, disoriented by the sudden change of scene and the sight of myself lying on top of the covers, curled on my side, my eyes closed. That is *weird*.

"That's me? Right now?" I look up at Hermes.

He nods. "Sleeping like a baby."

"But how . . . ? This isn't real," I murmur.

He lifts an eyebrow as he looks at me. "No, it's a dream. Do pay attention, Corey."

I take a deep breath. "I mean, things like this don't happen. Not to me." I hadn't seen the seal. I hadn't seen the hamadryad waving. Dreaming about gods bringing messages was Bree's kind of thing.

I walk to the bed and stare down at myself, fighting off chills as I look at my own sleeping face. My clothes are wet from the rain, soaking the blankets beneath me, my hair sticking to my face. I wait for the rise and fall of my chest, relieved when I see it. I look all right, except the soles of my boots are missing. I can see my socks, framed by ragged strands of rubber. They look melted. . . .

"I was struck by lightning." I remember how charged the air felt, how my skin crawled when I saw Hades reflected behind me. The sudden sharp stink of ozone. The flash of light. Then I remember how Hades looked up at the sky and something else occurs to me. "Was it on purpose?"

Hermes understands what I'm asking. "A little bit." He grins again. "But it wasn't intended to kill you."

"Is that supposed to reassure me?"

When he doesn't reply, I turn around to find him peering into my open underwear drawer, his expression one of delight.

The absurdity of a god staring at my bras roots me to the spot, and even after all this time the first thing I think is that I can't wait to tell Bree, because she'd love this. It's remembering that I can't, and that *I saw her in the Underworld,* that snaps me back to attention.

I cross the room and nudge the drawer shut with a hip, folding my arms. "Do you mind?"

Deep dimples appear in his cheeks as he gives a lazy, one-shouldered shrug. "Apologies. I just find mortal things fascinating."

"Hmm," I hum. "So, this message?"

"Ah, yes." His eyes flash. "I'm here because you saw something you weren't supposed to. You got a glimpse of what happens next—a spoiler, in your modern parlance," he says, leaning toward me like he's telling me some great secret. I have to crane my neck to look up at him.

"All right. But how did I see the *something I wasn't supposed to* in the first place?"

"That I can't answer. All I have is the message."

"And then what?"

For the first time, the smile slips from his face; he sounds almost bitter when he says, "Your guess is as good as mine. Like I said, I'm just the messenger."

Here's what I know about the gods: they are capricious; they never take back their gifts and can't undo their own curses; they protect what's sacred to them fiercely; they are easily offended.

They love a destiny.

They like to interfere with mortals.

So I know there will be a catch, because with them, there's always a catch. They don't give out messages or warnings. They turn you into trees, or animals. They curse you to always tell the truth but never be believed, or to only be able to speak in rhyme until you piss someone off so much that they kill you. Gods don't know the meaning of subtlety. Or clemency.

I pull a skeptical face.

"I swear." He holds up his silver hands. "On my honor, as a god. On my name, as Hermes, son of Zeus. All I'm here for is to give a warning, nothing more."

"So, after your warning I'll wake up fine, and I can go back to my life and everything will be exactly as it was?" I ask.

"You'll live your life, as the Fates have measured it."

"That's not an answer."

"It's the only one I can give." Another wide grin. He has far too many teeth.

I weigh it up. If Hades really wanted to hurt me, he could. He could have sent Thanatos instead of Hermes and had me dragged down to the Underworld to be at his mercy for all time. And Zeus—if it was him with the lightning—wouldn't have hesitated to kill me if he'd really wanted me dead. So maybe, *maybe*, Hermes is telling the truth and somehow I'm going to get off with just a warning. Only an idiot would argue with it. Only an idiot would argue with *them*.

"All right," I say, as if I have a choice. "What's the warning?"

Immediately his expression changes, the dimples vanishing as his face becomes severe and remote, like the face of a statue. His hazel eyes pale to amber, then burn crimson. I want to look away but I can't. Whatever playfulness he had is gone, burned away by the fire of an immortal, and I turn icy with dread.

"I am here with a warning from the Receiver of Many, the king of the Underworld. Your friend is not your concern anymore. From this moment, you saw nothing. You know nothing. You will speak of it to no one and you will strike it from your thoughts."

It should be stupid; a bad actor reading from a worse script, a metal-skinned boy in a white gown saying doom-laden words in my filthy, stale mortal bedroom. It should be a joke. It shouldn't be happening.

If I thought for even a second earlier that Hermes was almost human, I realize my mistake now. He wasn't, never had been, never could be. If he wants to, he can squash me like an ant, grind me into a smear of greasy powder like a moth under a thumb. I'm a blink of an eye to him. A fleeting, fragile, silly little thing.

His voice is an iron fist around my heart, squeezing tighter with every word.

"Well?" he asks, the ring of command faded from his voice. He sounds like a boy again.

I can't move. Can't speak.

His smile is sheepish. "Was it a bit much? I haven't had to give a warning in a long time."

I manage to shake my head.

"All right. Why don't we go and get you some water?" He reaches gently for my arm to guide me from the room, and I allow it, too numb to stop him.

We go downstairs single file, me first, and I'm aware of him behind me the whole way, heat radiating from him even though he isn't particularly close, the air scented with oranges and cloves. I wonder what will happen if Merry or my dad comes out of their room now and sees us, what it would look like to them, me sneaking a boy out at dawn, but then I remember he's not a boy and this is a dream.

Nightmare, I amend. *This is a nightmare.*

"How're you feeling?" Hermes asks, leaning against the dresser while I go to the cupboard to find a clean glass.

"Fine." I find my voice.

"Glad to hear it. Sorry if I came on a little strong."

"Not at all," I say, still stunned. "I suppose I should be flattered you thought I was worth the whole shock-and-awe thing."

He laughs, and I open the fridge.

"Water would be best, I think," Hermes says.

I pull a bottle from the door and show it to him. "It is water."

"No. Running water." He nods toward the sink.

"I don't drink that. I don't like the taste."

He narrows his eyes at me.

An alarm, soft but insistent, begins ringing in the back of my mind. He's not smiling anymore.

"Is that a problem?" I ask.

"I didn't know. I apologize."

Before I can ask what for, he launches himself at me. The glass falls to the floor, shattering, as one of his arms locks around me, holding me fast, while his free hand moves toward my face. As I open my mouth to scream, he shoves something inside it, something bitter and foul. He clamps his hand over my mouth and jaw, forcing them closed.

"Swallow," he commands.

I shake my head as violently as I can.

"I can't let you go until you do."

I try again to struggle free, but he's immovable. I might as well try to fight a tree, or a mountain.

Why aren't I waking up?

"Just swallow," he says. It sounds like a plea.

I swallow, my throat bobbing against his thumb.

He releases me and I stumble back, glaring at him with pointlessly raised fists.

"Good girl. Now sleep." He blows air into my face and the world disappears.

Etiolated

I SIT UP WITH A SHARP GASP AND IMMEDIATELY begin choking when something wet and vegetal hits the back of my throat.

I lean over, coughing violently, trying to force it out of my windpipe, thumping my own back, stars in my eyes. Just as I think I'm in real trouble I manage to dislodge it and it shoots across the room, leaving the coppery taste of blood in my mouth and tears streaming down my face as sweet air floods my lungs.

I collapse onto the bed, panting. My limbs feel heavy and aching, my left arm and shoulder are tender against my sleeve like they're sunburned.

Oh . . .

Forcing myself to sit up, I perch on the edge of the bed and pull the zip of Merry's coat down, wincing as the lining rubs my left arm. Then I gasp.

It looks as though someone has traced tree roots onto my

skin with red pen. The marks feather along my shoulder, like veins, like seaweed, trailing down my arm. When I carefully press a fingertip to them, the pain is sharp, making me swear.

I leave Merry's coat on my bed and open the wardrobe door, peering at the mirror inside, my mouth open in shock. The same marks run down my back, disappearing under my pajama top. I lift it, following the marks to where they taper off just an inch above my hips.

The lightning.

Hermes . . . I bend and pick up the lump he tried to make me swallow.

In the dream, I pinned it to the roof of my mouth with my tongue, only pretending to swallow it. I did it out of reflex, not wanting to be poisoned.

I didn't think it would still be in my mouth when I woke up. That isn't how dreams work—you don't bring things from them back with you. Dreams aren't real.

The lump, solid in my palm, disagrees.

I lean against the chest of drawers and lower myself to the floor. What the *fuck*?

My brain feels too big for my head, beating against my skull like it wants to escape, done with my body and all the dangers that come with it. Suddenly, I'm furnace hot, sweat prickling along my back and under my arms. It stings against the lightning scars, which tingle as if electricity is still running through them. I feel sick, and dizzy, and breathless. *It's a panic attack,* I tell myself, though naming it doesn't actually help. What are you supposed to do in a panic attack? Which god do you pray to?

Forget that. Knowing my luck, they'd show up.

It wasn't a dream. It can't have been. Hermes, *the actual Hermes*, god of trickery and thieves, had stood here, in my bedroom. He had looked at my bras. He had had silver skin and dimples and he had made me promise to forget I'd ever seen him—ever seen anything.

And then he tried to poison me.

I look at the glob of green leaves, then give it a tentative sniff, recoiling from the metallic bitterness. What is it? *How* is it?

I lower my head to my knees, my whole body shaking. *Get it together*, I command. I'm safe at home. I'm still alive. I'm awake—I pinch my shin to check, assuming that actually works. And Hermes must believe I'd swallowed the poison, or whatever it is, or he wouldn't have left. So in theory, I'm OK, for now at least. I count my pulse until my heart begins to slow, until the haze in my mind clears. I feel empty and hollow, as though my insides have been scooped out. I need coffee.

I stand, my legs shaky, planning to go to the kitchen, get caffeine, and find a bag or some Tupperware to put the leaves in, only to gasp as I open the bedroom door and find Merry is there, a cup of coffee in one hand, the other raised to knock. She's wearing her good black dress, her hair in a matching black scarf.

The ekphora, I remember, a flash of Bree on the beach darting across my mind. I shift to hide my injured arm behind the door.

"What the . . ." Her jaw drops when she sees me, my jeans stuck to my legs, hair drying into straw. "Corey? Have you been in the garden? You're drenched." She looks over my shoulder to my bed. "Is that my coat?" She sniffs the air. "Have you been straightening your hair? Or lit a candle? I can smell burning."

"I had to— I went— I saw— Yes." None of my sentences have ends, so I shut up, hoping the *yes* answers all of her questions.

"Did you drop a glass too? The kitchen was covered."

My breath catches, but I manage a nod. "Sorry. I'll clean it."

"I've done it. I couldn't exactly leave it."

"Sorry. I'm sorry."

Merry looks me up and down, her expression shrewd.

"You'd better go and have a shower, get warm and dry, and leave those clothes in the wash basket," she says finally. "Bedding too, I suppose. Put the duvet over the radiator. And hang my coat up."

I nod, but stay where I am.

She raises her eyebrows, then holds out the coffee, and I reach for it with my right hand. I can see she's fighting not to ask what's going on. I know I'm getting a lot of free passes because of Bree, but Merry's patience is wearing thin, and I don't blame her.

"Thank you," I say softly. "I'm really sorry, Merry."

"All right." She gives me a this-isn't-over-yet smile and heads back downstairs.

I take the coffee with me to the bathroom, only to throw it away after one sip when I start shaking again, deciding that maybe caffeine isn't a good idea right now. I try to keep the panic at bay by focusing on each task: shampoo, now rinse; *Hermes was in your bedroom;* conditioner; *you saw Bree;* wash, now rinse; *you saw Hades;* now rinse, now rinse, now rinse. The water stings the lightning scars, sending waves of heat through me.

I'm still shivering when I get out of the shower.

In my bedroom, Merry has changed my sheets and taken the duvet away, and I feel guilty as I climb onto the bed, still in my towel, rolling into a ball on my right side. She's left my phone plugged in at the pillow end and I reach for it but change my mind. I hear my dad come back from the lighthouse, and listen to his tread on the bottom step, stalling when Merry asks him where he's going.

"To get Corey up."

"Leave her, Craig."

"She'll regret it for the rest of her life if she doesn't say a proper goodbye."

"Craig." Merry's Glaswegian accent thickens in warning, and the next step doesn't creak under his weight. Instead their voices move away, into the kitchen. Talking about me. I could get down and press my ear to the floor to listen, but I honestly don't want to know.

An hour later, just as my trembling has settled into occasional spasms and most of the horror has faded into a kind of manageable dread, Merry comes upstairs and knocks on the door.

"Corey, we're off. I don't know when we'll be back, but I've got my phone and I'll leave it on vibrate in my pocket. If you need anything, call." She pauses. "OK, pet. See you later."

I hear her go back down, and then the front door opens and shuts. I'm alone.

Maybe I can let it be a dream. Maybe if I go to sleep right now, I could wake up new. No leaves in my mouth, no glass on the floor, no gods in my bedroom. The lightning scars might be a problem, but it's winter; long sleeves will hide them and they'll surely fade, right? Everything fades with time. That's what everyone has told me. It's a great healer. So I'll wait.

And yet . . .

I sit up.

I can feel *His* eyes on me, despite the distance and the walls between us. Like Hermes said, I've seen something I shouldn't have, and it has seen me.

I need to talk to the Oracle.

Exposure

She isn't really an oracle, not like the celebrity ones in Athens and London and New York who claim the gods speak through them—and who knows, after what I've seen today, maybe they actually do—but that's what Bree had called her when we were little and the name stuck. What she actually is, is a witch.

A genuine spell-casting, card-reading, dancing-sky-clad-under-the-full-moon witch. I used to be *obsessed* with her. Not because she was a witch, but because she lives on an islet all of her very own, about three miles from the Island, growing her own food and doing whatever she pleases. I'd wanted to be her when I grew up. Then I met her.

The first time I went to the Oracle was with Bree, the same year we got our ears pierced, a few days before the Thesmophoria. We "borrowed" (stole) Bree's cousin's boat and made our way across the choppy sea, because Bree had got it into her head that she needed to know what her future held, and she was convinced the Oracle would be able to tell her.

"Cor, I have to know there's more to life than the Island. I have to."

I went along with it, because I needed to know my fortune too.

At some point during the summer break, which he'd spent on the mainland, Ali Murray had gone from being an annoying little pip-squeak to almost six feet tall, broad-shouldered, home haircut grown out and curling at the nape of his neck. He'd dashed into our classroom seconds before the bell went, slid into his seat, winked at me, and I'd blushed, realizing in the same moment that he was *hot*. I spent the next two months praying to Aphrodite to make him notice me, fancy me.

It was the first secret I'd ever kept from Bree.

The second time I went to the Oracle was almost two years later, when I stole Bree's cousin's boat at night and headed out to the islet alone, because my boyfriend was barely answering my messages and kept disappearing, and my best friend had vanished into thin air too, right when I needed her most.

The Oracle hadn't even bothered getting her cards out that time. She'd simply looked me up and down, shaken her head, and told me to repeat what I'd just said. Still not getting it, I'd done so, and she'd nodded along with my words, slowly, like I was stupid. Then I'd understood that I *was* stupid.

I'd called her a word that rhymed with *witch* and left. Three days later, I finally managed to get a reply from Ali, who'd suggested we go for a walk down to the cove and . . .

I doubt the Oracle will be thrilled to see me again, but I don't see what choice I have. If anyone can tell me what the leaves are, it's her. And once I know what they are, maybe I'll know how much trouble I'm in. Hermes said to forget everything, but he'd also said there would be no punishment and then tried to poison me. I need any help I can get.

Draping the towel over the radiator, I wrap the leaves in a tissue. Then I dress in fresh jeans and a sweater, drag a brush through my hair and knot it on top of my head.

In the kitchen, I shove my gardening boots on and take a bottle of red wine from the pantry to apologize for last time. I scribble a note for Dad and Merry—*Had to get out, don't worry, I'm fine*—just in case they come back before I do, and then grab my rain mac from the cupboard. The pockets rustle and I dig my hands in, pulling out a mix of loose seeds. I peer at them, trying to see what they are, before I decide it can wait and push them back into the depths of the coat. I squeeze the bottle in on top of them. The tissue-wrapped leaves go carefully in the other pocket.

The storm has passed and the streets of Daly are quiet; all of the shops have black signs in the doors saying they're closed for mourning. If it wasn't for those, the puddles, and the faint sounds of sheep bleating, I'd worry I was back in the dream, beginning the morning over again like I was trapped in some horrible, Sisyphean nightmare. I'd feel more reassured if there was at least one other person around, but it seems like everyone has gone to the funeral.

All the better to steal a boat without being seen, I think as I jog

70

through the wet lanes. And sure enough, the harbor is deserted, the office dark and empty.

Connor's boat is a small cuddy cabin, docked at the far end of the tiny harbor, opposite my father's lighthouse. In summer, Connor takes the few visiting day-trippers we get out around the Island in it to see seals and basking sharks that hunt in our waters, vaguely hinting they might see mermaids or sirens if they're very lucky—it's a lie, the water here is way too cold for them—but in winter, like most of the small boats, it bobs forlornly in the harbor. Ripe for the taking.

I hop into the boat and check the petrol level, then feel under the tank for the key Connor has thoughtfully left taped there. Scrambling back out, I unmoor it, winding the wet dock line with me before I jump in and haul the anchor up. Checking there's no one around, I grip the wheel, put the key in the ignition and start her up, slowly guiding the boat away from the dock, out of the harbor and onto the open sea.

The Oracle's islet is on the opposite side of the Island from where I saw the Underworld, which is a relief. I keep an eye out for other boats, and animals too, watching as cormorants and gulls fly above and around me. A long, dark shape under the water a few meters away catches my eye and I put the boat into cruise, reaching into my pocket for my phone.

It's then I remember it's still in my room, still plugged in on my bed. Swearing, I wait for the animal, probably a seal or maybe a porpoise, to surface, but it never does, which at least takes the sting out of my absent phone. I really need to start carrying it again; this would all be so much easier if I'd been able to take pictures of the Underworld earlier. I put the boat back in gear and continue on, toward the islet that's just visible on the horizon.

As I round the islet to get to the small dock, I see another boat, out on the open water, rowing in the direction of the Island. It's the rowing that catches my attention, the sea spilling from the oars as they breach the surface before plunging back under the waves and propelling the boat forward. The rower must be incredibly powerful to row in the ocean, but also more than a little stupid, especially at this time of year. I slow my boat so the wake doesn't make their job harder, and peer out as we draw level.

I falter when I see the pale, grayish passenger sitting in the bow, head down, hands clasped in their lap. And again, when I notice that manning the oars is a hooded figure with powerful arms.

No. No way.

It's the Boatman. *The* Boatman.

As though he senses my gaze, the Boatman looks up and I meet red eyes in a long, gaunt face. He pauses, then raises a hand to hail me, and I raise one back automatically, my fingers shaking. We pass each other like that, hands raised, before he takes up his oars again, cutting expertly through the choppy sea. When I look around, he is gone.

Hermes said the lightning didn't kill me. And I've spoken to Merry, drunk coffee, showered.

But you're not supposed to see the Boatman unless you're dead.

I lean against the steering wheel and press two fingers against my wrist, feeling for my pulse. I find it, jumping, spiking, but unmistakably there. I check my throat; there it is, my own internal clock ticking away. I exhale, hard, holding my hand before my face to feel my breath. Good.

Still, I don't like it. Don't like that I've now seen a third immortal and had some kind of contact with a fourth if you count the lightning, and I do. Don't like that they're trespassing into my world.

I gun the engine, continuing to the Oracle's islet. She'll help me. She'll have answers. She has to.

When I reach the tiny jetty that serves as the dock, I guide the boat alongside and drop anchor. My legs feel strange and I wobble as I tie the boat off to a rusting post, tugging on the rope to make sure the knot, and the ancient mooring, holds. Then, carefully, I climb the narrow staircase carved into the cliffside that leads to the top, where the Oracle's cottage is.

I'm tired when I reach the summit, thighs aching from the effort, lightning-struck arm tingling under my sleeve. A quarter of a mile away I see the Oracle's cottage, as gray as the sky, squat and rounded, its windows glowing gold from the light inside. I start to walk down the trail rehearsing what to say to her. An apology, to begin. Then I'll give her the wine. And after that . . . I guess I'll find out.

One of the things I'd liked—still like—most about her is that she's a gardener, too. Like my mother. Like me. I wonder if they ever met when my mother was here; I should ask.

The first time I came to the islet it was summer, and her

garden was alive with flowers and plants, fat bees bobbing drunkenly between blooms, butterflies sunning their open wings. I don't remember much from the second time; it was dark and Ali was the only thing I could think of. Now, in winter, the garden is barer, but still productive; as I walk toward the Oracle's door, I see leeks thicker than my forearm in the beds, not in rows like I grow them, but dotted here and there around cabbages and some other plant with deep-purple leaves. I don't recognize it and step off the path to get a closer look.

"Thief." A strong voice speaks, and I turn to see the Oracle standing in the doorway of a small shed, watching me, her black dog beside her wagging its tail.

Last time I was here, when I'd sworn at her, she'd been an old woman, bent over a cane that looked as if it was made of bone. The first time Bree and I came to have our fortunes read, she'd barely looked older than us, though her hair was gray. I'd thought she looked cool, like the kind of girls on the internet we imagined being late at night during sleepovers. I'd assumed the Oracle was her own granddaughter, until she'd corrected me with a crow-caw laugh when I asked where her gran was.

"I'm who you're seeking. I'm always she. No matter the face I wear."

I'd been stunned, but not frightened. It made sense to me, somehow, that she could change her face, age backward if she wanted. She's the kind of person you expect it from.

She knew who I was too, inviting me into her house by name. Bree hadn't liked it, until I reminded her that Merry probably told her who I was; Merry comes out here twice a year to survey puffins, so she and the Oracle are friendly.

Today the Oracle is somewhere around Merry's age, her hair in a thick braid over her shoulder. She wears a dress similar to the one I'd worn in the dream, floor length and sleeveless, exposing brown, well-toned arms, only her dress is black and there's no belt at her waist. And, as mine were in the dream, her feet are bare. I shiver. It's just a coincidence.

"I wasn't going to touch anything," I say. "I just wanted to see what you were growing."

"I wasn't talking about the plants. That's the second time you've stolen Connor Dovemuir's boat. Once more and it's yours."

"I don't think that's the law."

"And what would you know about the law?" she replies. "Little enough, it seems, arriving once again in a stolen vessel. What do you want? Come to hurl more abuse at a poor lonely woman?"

I blush. "I'm sorry, for what I said last time. I shouldn't have spoken to you like that."

"You were angry," she says, not looking at me but beyond me. "You're still angry. In fact, you're all anger, it leaks from you like wine from a cracked glass."

Her words fluster me. They're too close to my dad's, but they also remind me of the peace offering I've brought. I pull it from my pocket and hold it out. "Speaking of wine, this is for you. To apologize. You were right. I should have listened."

"I'm always right. Is it stolen too?" She nods at the bottle.

"It's from my house," I hedge.

"Yes, then." She moves forward and takes the bottle from me, turning it to read the label. "A good bottle. You must be sorry. Or else you didn't know its value when you took it." She looks at me and frowns. "What have you been up to?" she murmurs, raising a hand toward my mouth.

I lean away, and she gives me a shrewd, searching look. "You'd better come inside."

With that, she walks past me, dog at her heels, and I follow her into the cottage, straight through to the kitchen.

In the corner, an ancient stove heats the room and the dog takes itself over and flops before it. Atop it, something sweet and sleepy-smelling bubbles away in a chipped cast-iron pan. The floor is tiled in black and white, a giant chessboard. I follow the Oracle, pawn after queen, though my eyes are on the countertops, dirt scored deep into the wood and covered in bottles and jars that are all filled with powders, herbs, leaves, liquids. The only window is obscured by more plants, jam jars acting as makeshift greenhouses protecting whatever grows in them. In storybooks, witches' houses are awful things, but I'd be happy in a place like this. Just add a couple of cats. Maybe a handsome woodsman who pops by. From nowhere I think of the boy at the Thesmophoria and butterflies thrash in my stomach.

The Oracle places the wine on top of the scarred oak table that dominates the middle of the room, and goes to the sink, washing her hands. I watch as earth and dirt fall away and look at my own hands, the semipermanent dirt moons under my nails. *Gardening is boring,* Ali said. Idiot.

She turns back to me, dries her hands on her skirt and gives

76

me a sly smile. "Tell me, then, Corey Allaway, what brings you here again? If it's about the Murray boy, don't waste my time. He's not for you, I've told you that twice before."

My cheeks burn. "It's not."

"Finally." Her smile turns wicked, like we're conspiring. "Tell me, then."

I take a deep breath, and pull the tissue from my pocket. As the Oracle watches, I carefully unwrap it, then hold it out to her, the leaves a dark mound in the center. She takes it from me, stares at it, sniffs it, then looks at me. Her grin has vanished, a piercing gaze replacing it. Suddenly we're not conspirators anymore.

"Where did you get this?" Her voice is sharp.

"What is it?" I ask.

"Tell me where you got it."

I hesitate. "I had a dream," I begin. "Except I don't think it was a dream. Not completely." It sounds ridiculous saying it aloud, but the Oracle nods at me to continue, her expression stern.

"It started when I was heading home from . . . somewhere," I amend. "And I was struck by lightning."

Her eyes widen.

"Show me," she demands. "Show me where."

"It wasn't supposed to kill me, apparently," I mumble, unzipping my coat and shrugging the left sleeve off. I lift my sweater and turn, showing her my back.

She runs cold fingers along the wounds, tracing some of them. "You're fine," she says. "You'll be sore for a few days, and your chest might feel a little tight, but you were lucky. I can give you something to help it along. Who told you it wasn't supposed to kill you?"

I pull my sweater down and put my coat back on as I speak.

"The person—the one who gave me the leaves," I say, too scared to name him in case he somehow hears me; I'm in enough trouble as it is. "I think he must have taken me home after the lightning, while I was passed out, and then broke into my dream. In it, he asked me to do something. Then he tried to make me swallow those leaves. But I didn't; I just pretended to. And when I woke up, they were still in my mouth," I finish. "So, I don't think it was a dream. But I don't understand how it was real."

I realize I could apply that sentence to everything that has happened so far.

The Oracle is looking at me, her expression shrewd. "I ask you again, what have you been up to?"

"I haven't been up to anything. Do you know what it is?" I nod at the bundle in her hand. "Is it poison?"

She tips the leaves into her palm. "It's nepenthe."

"What's nepenthe?" I ask. I've never heard of it.

She chews her lower lip for a long moment, as though choosing her words carefully, before she replies. "It's a kind of water lily. It grows on the River Lethe. *Only* on the Lethe. You know what that is? Where that is?"

I give a shallow nod, my heart sinking. I should have guessed. "The Underworld."

The leaves come from Hades, then. He must have given

them to Hermes in case I refused to forget or tried to fight. Or to be sure I kept my word.

"You're not surprised," the Oracle says. "The one who gave you these—what did he look like? Dark-eyed? Dark-haired? Pale as the grave?"

"It wasn't him. It wasn't"—I mouth his name—"*Hades.*" I continue, my voice barely a whisper, "It was Hermes who gave them to me. But he came with a message from . . . the other one. So . . ." I trail off.

The Oracle puts the nepenthe down on the table and crosses to the bureau, opening a drawer, rummaging violently through it. I look at the bunch of soggy green leaves. They don't look like something that comes from the Underworld. They look like the time I tried to brew nettle tea. But then, plants are tricky like that. It's easy to eat or touch something deadly without knowing what you've done, and by the time you realize, it's—

Then something occurs to me.

The Lethe is the river of forgetting. You drink from it if you want to forget being alive, because living makes you too sad, or hurts you. So Hermes wasn't exactly poisoning me. He was trying to make me forget. I'd asked what if I couldn't forget, and it's this—nepenthe. A plant that makes all your cares fade away.

"How much would that make me forget?" I ask the Oracle's back, my voice casual. "How far back?"

"I'm not sure," she says, slamming the drawer and opening another.

It would at least cover this morning. Hades would want to

make sure there was enough to make me forget the Underworld, and Bree. And *Him*.

But what if it could do more? What if it could make me forget the last six months? The last nineteen? What if it could take me back to before Bree and Ali, before Ali and me, even?

I could forget what they'd done. I wouldn't hurt anymore.

I reach for the leaves, and the Oracle spins around, moving faster than she—than anyone—should be able to, snatching them up and stepping out of my grasp.

Stunned, I stare at her. "I need that."

"What is it you're supposed to forget?" the Oracle asks.

"I can't," I say through clenched teeth as my temper lashes. "I promised I wouldn't. So please give it back to me."

She shakes her head. "Not until you tell me."

I look her up and down. She's the same height as me, a little thinner. I could overpower her and take the leaves, swallow them before she could stop me.

Then I'm horrified—how can I even think that? She's a little old lady. Sometimes.

"Tell me." Her eyebrows are raised, and I have the eerie feeling she knew what I was thinking.

I growl in frustration. "I saw the Underworld, OK? They want me to forget it. And I want to forget it. So please, *please*, will you give it back?"

"You're sure? He wants you to forget something you saw? Not something you've done?"

The Oracle steps forward, reaching for my face with her free hand.

"What are you doing?"

"Look," she says. "Your mouth."

I raise my hand, touching my lips.

And when I draw them away, my fingertips are golden.

What?

I move to wipe my fingers on my jeans, but the gold is already vanishing. I rub my mouth on my sleeve, shocked at the smear of gold that glistens along the navy oilcloth, before it fades to nothing. Above me, copper pans hang in a rack, garlic and onions strung between them, and I reach up and grab one, holding it to my face.

In the reflection, my skin takes on the rose-gold cast of the pan, making me look every bit as metallic as Hermes was. But my mouth . . .

As if I'd painted it, my mouth is bright gold.

BOLTING

"WHAT IS IT?" I ASK. "WHAT'S ON ME?"

I touch my lips again, horrified when my fingers come away covered in a dusting like pollen, before it vanishes. When I look back at my reflection, the gold is still there, and I measure the contrast between the warm copper glow the pan gives my skin and the bright slash of gold beneath my nose.

Wait—

I've seen this combination before. I *kissed* someone wearing a copper mask above a golden mouth, five days ago.

The night Bree died.

Is he the one you love?

The words come back to me, the ones the strange boy spoke as I stared at Bree and Ali dancing and pretended I hadn't heard, fury buzzing like bees in my ears, making wax and wishes from hate. Wishes for death.

Is he the one you love?

Or did she break your heart?

His hands on my waist and my face, in my hair. The funny little bow as he'd left me. And then he'd vanished, and Bree had died.

Every hair on my body stands on end.

"No," I say aloud, shaking my head. "No. There's no way."

The mysterious boy, my wish, her death. Hermes coming to me, the Boatman hailing me. The Underworld, Bree. And *him*.

No no no no no no no no no no no.

He was the boy. That's why I recognized his voice when he told me to run.

I'd kissed Hades. I'd *enjoyed* kissing Hades. Then I'd seen Bree and wished her dead.

And she'd died.

My stomach bottoms out and I collapse into the sideboard behind me as the full force of what happened—*what I've done*—slams into me like a tsunami.

Bree is dead because of me. I did that.

A strange, weighty feeling fills my chest, my lungs feel full of honey, or oil, or something warm and thick, rich and viscous. It sticks to my ribs, coating my insides, and I gasp, afraid for a second that I'm drowning, like Bree did, but here, on land.

Then it settles, I can breathe, and I realize what the feeling is. Satisfaction.

Because she betrayed me and look what happened to her.

I did that.

Good. I hope she is fucking miserable. I hope she cries herself to sleep every night, until there aren't any tears left inside her. Let her be alone, let her be as lonely and empty as I've been since she and Ali left me. Let her know what it's like to be snatched from the world you know and love, and to live in the cold and dark. Let her pine and cry for the life she had. Let her only have memories of what it was like to be in the sun, to love and be loved. To trust.

"You kissed the Receiver of Many," the Oracle says, pulling me back from my thoughts. "At the Thesmophoria, I take it?"

I'd forgotten she was here. I turn to her and touch my mouth again, only this time my fingers come away clean; the gold is gone.

"The same night the girl died." Her eyes bore into mine, steady and unblinking.

I shrug, unease prickling a path over my shoulders.

"She was your friend once, that girl. You came here with her. Hand in glove the two of you were."

My stomach cramps. "Yeah. Until she slept with my boyfriend behind my back," I snap.

"And now she's dead."

"It was an accident. The police said so."

The Oracle simply stares at me.

People wish for things all the time and they don't come true. People pray to the gods to ask for favors and blessings and miracles and most of the time nothing happens. I didn't ask him to do anything, I didn't know he was a god; I didn't even say it aloud. I only wished it.

And it's not like I meant it literally. I meant dead like humiliated, abandoned, shunned by everyone. I meant dead like forced to go and live on the other side of the world, or grounded forever.

I meant socially dead. I didn't mean actually dead. I didn't mean coin-on-your-lips dead.

Except that isn't quite true. In that moment, I had meant really, truly dead. And I could lie to everyone else about it, but I know what was in my heart in that moment and it was vengeance.

I just never imagined I'd get it.

She stole Ali from you, I remind myself fiercely. But even I can see they aren't the same thing. And it doesn't matter that I didn't know it would actually happen. The result is the same. Bree drowned. Because of me.

I look up at the Oracle, whose face has changed while I've been reckoning with myself, aging decades in moments to make her look at least a hundred years old, as if what I've done has taken its toll on her.

"I think I made a mistake."

"No shit," she says, then starts to laugh, a loud magpie-gunshot sound that rattles the window and pans.

I watch her, horrified, while she wheezes and huffs, tears springing from her eyes and traveling the wrinkles of her face like ancient rivers, like it's the funniest thing she's ever heard.

"Why are you laughing? She's dead because I wished for it. How is that funny?"

It only makes her laugh harder. "A moment ago, you were thrilled with yourself, it was all over your face. You felt vindicated," she manages between chuckles, and I close my eyes, mortified, because it's true.

Even now, I'm not as ashamed as I should be. I should be

wretched about this. But I'm not. There is a dark spot on my heart that's insisting this is justice.

It isn't, I think fiercely.

Isn't it?

I look at the Oracle. "I didn't think. . . ."

Her expression is suddenly solemn, as if she'd never laughed, and my words fall away.

"No, you didn't think. What a pretty mess you've made. Look at you, Bringer of Death."

"What can I do?" I must be able to do something. There has to be a way to fix this. "Can I ask him to undo it?"

"He's not a genie, Corey Allaway. You don't have two more wishes you can use to solve your troubles."

"So what happens now?"

She makes a huffing sound. "You go home. You learn a valuable lesson—be careful what you wish for, especially when the gods are involved—and you get on with your life."

"That's it?" Go home. Eat dinner with Merry and Dad, ask how the ekphora was. Go to school tomorrow, or next week, and sit with Astrid and the others and bitch about homework, look at Bree's empty seat and pretend it's not my fault. "Won't I be in trouble?" I ask.

"Is that what worries you? Getting in trouble?"

"No, I just . . ." This can't be the end of it. There are always consequences.

"You wanted a boon, and it was granted. Sounds to me like you've got the gods' blessing. Or at least one god's blessing." The Oracle smirks, and I turn hot.

"I didn't ask for it." For some reason it's important she knows that. I never said it out loud. I never prayed to anyone—least of all *him*—for it. "I didn't kiss him to get a favor."

Do I regret wishing it? I think. Yes, obviously. Obviously I do.

Really?

"Are you sure? Are you sure there's nothing I can do?" I ask, silencing the voice in my head.

The Oracle gives me a look that makes me worry she knows what I'm thinking, and approaches the table, moving the wine and a pile of papers aside, making space before her. "Come on. Let's see what your choices are."

She pulls a deck of tarot cards from her pocket.

The first, and only, time I saw the tarot was when I came here with Bree, to find out if Ali Murray would ever like me back. Bree went first, and I waited in the garden, cataloging everything the Oracle grew, planning to replicate it at home. Bree came back out in under five minutes, two red spots high on her cheeks.

"She's a fake," was all Bree would say. She never did tell me what her fortune was.

Then it was my turn, and it was like this, the same table, same battered cream-colored cards with their blue meandrous border.

The Oracle shuffles them with an ease her crooked old fingers shouldn't have, then, with a croupier's flair, spreads them in an arc.

That first time, she'd asked me to keep my question in my head as I chose a single card, but this time she simply says, "Pick three. Pick the three that want to be chosen."

"Should I think of something?"

"As long as you don't wish me dead, you can think of whatever you want."

She cackles and I turn beetroot, reaching out and holding my left hand over the cards, moving it slowly along the splayed deck. I think about Bree, and *Him*. I think about how he reached for her on the beach, the sadness in his gaze, and something uncurls in my stomach. He kissed me, but took her. My fingers twitch, and the Oracle knocks my hand aside and pulls out the card that was beneath it.

"Continue."

I exhale slowly, trying to clear my thoughts. He must have gone straight to her at the lake, after leaving me. He must have still been able to taste me on his lips when he found her. I picture him holding out his hand to her like he did to me, that smile on his face.

My hand jerks so violently I hit a card and the Oracle's long fingers dart out to snatch it. I close my eyes one last time.

This isn't the same as with Ali. She's dead. It's not like he chose her over me and they ran away together or eloped. She *died*. He took her to the Underworld and I'm still alive.

I'm still alone.

"Stop!" the Oracle cries.

I open my eyes.

My index finger is extended, pointing at a card. I didn't feel it move.

Feeling sick, I snatch my hand back as the Oracle reaches for the card I chose. Am I *jealous* of Bree?

One by one, the Oracle turns the three cards over.

The Three of Swords. The Three of Cups. Justice.

I don't know what they mean, but it's a relief not to see Death or the Tower, or any of the ones that are obviously bad. "What is that? Past, present and future?"

She shakes her head. "No. We're trying to determine what lies ahead for you. They represent you, your path and your potential."

"Is it good?" I look pleadingly at her.

"The cards don't deal in bad or good."

I look at them. The Three of Swords is a sad woman holding a broken bird, three swords piercing a shattered heart she wears as a hat. And that's me. Of course it is.

I turn to the Three of Cups; three women in jewel-bright gowns toasting each other. My path. For a second I think it's supposed to be Bree and me, some kind of unlikely reconciliation, but there are three women. So, new friends, maybe? The card looks a lot happier than sword-hat woman, so I'll take it.

Then my potential. Justice holding her sword and scales, her expression peaceful. Justice done now that Bree is dead? Or justice to come?

"What does it mean? All of it?" I gesture at the cards.

The Oracle, who's been studying the cards with the same intensity as me, looks up, and I startle when I see she's young again; my age, face guileless, eyes clear as crystal. And she's smiling. A huge, beaming grin, like she's just been given the best present in the world.

"All growth begins in the dark," she replies. "From the smallest daisy to the mightiest oak. It all begins in darkness."

"OK." I wait. "And what does *that* mean?"

The Oracle gives an elaborate shrug. "I can't tell you any more than that."

I'm stunned. "But—this was your idea; I didn't come here for a reading."

"So what did you come here for?"

"Advice. Answers," I say. "Help!"

"And you shall have it all. When you've paid your dues."

I shake my head. "I brought you wine."

"To atone for last time. This isn't just another teenage heartbreak, Corey Allaway. This is much, much more."

"Are you serious?" I say. When she doesn't reply, my blood begins to boil. "I don't have anything else with me. I don't have anything at all!" I snap, reaching into the pockets of my oilskin and pulling the contents out. When I slap them onto the wooden surface, seeds scattering, my palm stings with the impact. "See? Nothing. I have *nothing*. Everything I had is gone. Gods, I'm such an idiot. I came here because you were the only person I could think of and all you talk is riddles and shit."

"That temper could be the death of you too, you know," she says, grinning, teeth white and straight.

"Why won't you help me?" I shout, leaning across the table until my face is inches from hers.

"Why won't you help yourself?" she replies, deadly calm.

I stare at her for a moment. Then I sweep her cards from the table and leave while they swirl around me like a storm.

THRESHED

THE ORACLE CALLS AFTER ME AS I RUN FROM her kitchen, her dog barking loudly, but I don't want to hear anything else she has to say. I should have learned my lesson after the last two times. She's a mad, attention-seeking hag, changing her face and peddling mysteries to build a legend around herself like some stupid—

Fuck.

I go too fast down the steps and slip, my legs flying out from under me. There is a horrible moment when no part of me is touching the ground and I'm suspended in the air, high above the water. Then my fingers find the rope handrail and I manage to keep myself from tumbling into the water below. I scramble back to standing and pause, forcing down shock as I stare at the dark sea beating against the cliffside.

If I fell, I'd die. From the cold, being battered against the rocks, or drowning. It would just be a case of what killed me first. Then I'd end up in the Underworld too. I shiver.

When I continue, I'm careful, one foot at a time, both hands gripping the makeshift railing until I'm safely on the dock.

As soon as I am, my patience vanishes and I burn my fingers on the rope as I tear open the knots and free the boat from its mooring. I throw myself in, winding the anchor up with such force that the winch creaks ominously. As soon as it's clear of the water I stab the key into the ignition, firing the cuddy up and pulling away from the jetty. I turn to see the Oracle on the hillside, watching me, a shawl pulled over her shoulders, wisps of hair like clouds around her face. She looks ancient again, as though decades passed once I bolted from her. She doesn't wave, and I certainly don't, but I sense her gaze on me until I round the islet and am gone from her sight.

On the open water I speed up, bouncing over the waves, while I think about what to do next. It's clear that the Oracle can't, or won't, help me. Which leaves me with exactly no one else to turn to.

And then I realize I've left the nepenthe behind, so I can't even forget it all.

"Fuck!" I scream at the empty sky. And then again. And again, slamming my fists against the steering wheel of the boat, sending shockwaves of pain along my lightning-burned arm, which only makes me angrier. I want to kick. I want to tear. To bury. To kill—

I stop, clapping my hands over my mouth in horror. What is *wrong* with me?

Idling the boat, I lean against the side of the cabin, wrapping my arms around myself like I can keep my fury caged inside. Maybe my dad is right. Maybe I actually *do* need help.

What kind of help is available to someone like me? Therapy? Prison? I imagine myself walking up to Declan Moretide with my hands held out before me and telling him solemnly that Bree is dead because I wished for it. I snort.

Then the horror returns.

I should be in bits, shattered under the weight of *getting my ex–best friend killed*. But alone at sea, with no one to hold me responsible, no one to pretend to or put on a show for, there's no point in lying. Bree is dead because of me. While I sat with Astrid and drank wine I didn't even want, she drowned.

And I don't feel bad about it.

The fact I don't feel bad about it makes me want to be sick, because the feeling should be there and it isn't. I feel like I've lost not just Ali and Bree but part of myself too. The good, best part . . . Leaving me a monster.

All because of a kiss.

That's another thing: I can't align the boy I kissed with the being who walked in shadows, who's surrounded by them, wears them like a cloak. Can't fit his cold, salt mouth and gentle fingers with the image of an actual god—especially *that* god.

He was supposed to be a rebound. Part of the ritual. Kiss a stranger, prove you've survived, carry on. This is all so messed up.

There wasn't supposed to be any more to it than that.

Why did he take her and not me?

No, I don't mean that.

I really do need help.

The boat bobs on the sea, the same view in every direction, and I'm exhausted. Suddenly, the only thing in the world I want is to curl up on the bottom until all this is over. Until whatever's wrong with me is fixed, or starved, or dead. I thump the steering wheel again and in response waves slap against the boat, making it rock, and I stumble, grabbing the wheel to steady myself. I can't just stay at sea forever. Slowly, I put the boat in gear and turn west, heading back to the Island.

When I pull into the harbor, it's still deserted, so I leave Connor's boat in his dock, the key taped back under the wheel, and trudge through town along the back lanes, at the last minute veering away from the cottage and toward Lynceus Hill. I take the long way around, approaching it from the cliffside so I don't accidentally crash the funeral or bump into anyone.

Climbing the cliff path is harder than from the road, and I'm sweaty and hot when I get to the top of the hill, where I collapse to the ground. I look down at the temple, then beyond, to the Island cemetery, the rows of weather-beaten graves and old mausoleums. It's empty of people, but there is a single mound of fresh earth on the far left, old graves to one side, empty space to the other, and my heart squeezes because it means it's over. I missed it all, and everyone will be at the perideipnon now, toasting Bree.

Who is dead. Because of me.

I stand and look over my left shoulder, out to sea, half expecting to see the Underworld with Hades on the shore, staring back at me. But it isn't there, and he isn't there, only gray, churning ocean and heavy sky as far as the eye can see.

There are, or were, ways you can call Hades to ask for his favor, but they're all grim. Fast for a week and then eat six asphodel seeds, dig a pit in the ground, lie facedown in it and knock the earth three times. Take a pure black ram and sacrifice it in a grove of cypress trees at midnight, on a full moon, and while its blood spills you call His name. I guess you can also wait for him to come to a local festival in disguise, kiss him, and think your wishes too. That wasn't in any of the textbooks at school. Things might be different if it had been.

I don't think I could actually fast for a week, and I don't know where to get asphodel seeds. I'm pretty sure there aren't any black rams on the Island, and even if there were, I don't think I could kill one.

You killed your best friend.

Stop.

Anyway, what would I say to him even if I did see him. Ask him to undo it? Ask him why he took her? Ask him if it was ever going to be me and the kiss changed his mind?

One last look over my shoulder. Nothing.

I turn for home, and stop.

In the earth before me is a single narcissus. It's the white-and-yellow kind—*fried egg flowers,* me and Bree used to call them every spring when they finally came around again.

But it's November. And I'm pretty sure it wasn't there a second ago.

I crouch down and look at it.

Narcissi were Bree's favorites. I grew them for her so she could fill old glasses and milk bottles with them for her bedroom, even though Mrs. Dovemuir worried about pollen or attracting insects or the smell of stale water.

Maybe it's a sign.

I reach out and take the flower.

And the ground beneath my feet opens, swallowing me whole.

I surface in water, warm and green, and I panic, flailing for a second before the lifesaving lessons from school kick in. I lean back, letting myself float, grateful for the air trapped under my coat because without it I would be drowning right now. *Like Bree.* My boots are dragging me down, so I slowly move my legs until I can reach the laces. I tug at them until my boots fall away, then take a break while I figure out what the fuck is going on.

As the water buffets me about I catch a glimpse of evergreen trees in the distance and my stomach sinks as I realize where I am. Where I've come. The narcissus is still clutched in my hand and I let it go, hoping that I'll be sucked down and spat back out on Lynceus Hill, but all that happens is the waves push the flower against my cheek, so I grab it again.

I twist my head to look at the shore. I think I can make it.

I have to fight the tide to swim inland far enough for my feet to find the bottom, then keep fighting as I wade up the steep incline to the shore. By the time I get there I'm exhausted, my clothes heavy, soaked and clinging to my skin. I collapse onto the shingle, the pebbles digging into my palms, knees and shins.

Then I hear footsteps, loud on the stones. They stop behind me and I brace for his voice. For his fury.

"Well, well, well. I should have checked you'd swallowed it. Though I would never have guessed you'd come here, even if you hadn't. You've managed to surprise me again."

I look up into the sly, smiling face of Hermes.

HYBRID

HE WEARS THE SAME WHITE ROBE HE WORE IN my dream, or whatever it was, but now his skin is molten, no longer dully metallic but gleaming, moving like liquid over his muscles when he crosses his arms in what I assume from his grin is mock disapproval. Even in the dull, weak light of the Underworld, he's star bright, forcing me to squint and blink rapidly so I can look at him.

"Whatever are you doing here?"

Despite his words, I don't get the impression he is surprised to see me. There's something pleased and knowing about his expression. *Don't trust him.* I remind myself of what happened last time I saw him. He's the god of thieves and liars.

"I don't know," I manage, hauling myself to my feet, water cascading from my clothes.

His smile widens. "Did you swim here?"

"I picked a flower." I hold up the bedraggled narcissus. "And the ground opened under me and then I was in the sea."

"Not the sea, sweet Corey. The Styx."

I gag. Thank the gods I didn't swallow any of it.

"Is this another dream?" I ask hopefully.

Hermes shakes his head, and panic starts to creep through me. I hold out my wrist, feeling for a pulse, relieved when I find one.

Hermes laughs. "You're still not dead, Corey. I . . ." He stops, his smile faltering as he looks over his shoulder at the woods behind him.

I look too, but there's nothing there. "Listen, can you help me? I know—"

Hermes holds up a silver hand to silence me.

For a long moment there is no sound except my breathing.

Then something deep in the forest screams.

It's followed immediately by the sound of twigs snapping, as if something huge is barreling through the trees at great speed, coming this way. My flesh crawls, fear like a vise compressing my chest.

I turn and race down the shore, skidding in the stones, and throw myself back into the Styx, arms flailing as I try to swim against the tide. I hear Hermes call out; I don't know if it's to me and I don't turn around, or stop.

Waves slap against my face and I throw my head back to keep water from getting in my nose, then take a deep breath and dive. I don't know where I'm going, there is no plan, all I know is I have to get away from the beach, from whatever is in the trees.

Something scrapes my back and then my coat tightens, binding me, as I'm plucked out of the Styx.

Wet hair sticks to my face, covering my eyes, but I can't move my arms to push it away. Then the pressure at my back releases and I'm falling. I just have time to cover my face before I crash, belly-first, onto the pebbles.

I roll over, body stinging from the impact, and then I forget everything as I stare at the three creatures stalking around me.

"She's here," the one closest to me says, and I jerk away, unable to tear my eyes from her.

She has the beautiful, serene face of the Mona Lisa—they all do—but no human woman has snakes for hair, or skin the color of dried sage. Her scalp is covered in writhing emerald-green serpents that coil and hiss and fight and caress each other while she watches me with jet eyes.

Her voice is low and musical, head tilted as she observes me.

"Finally." The second one speaks softly, slowly, as though every syllable has a flavor and they are all her favorites. This one is scaled, bronze overlaid with interlocking black diamonds, a cobra hood framing her lovely face like a medieval halo.

"You can feel it," the third says in an eager whisper. Her skin is dark, and she has feathers instead of hair; soft down covers the part of her chest I can see, and a thick plume cascades down her back, deepest indigo shot through with iridescent emeralds and blues.

At her words, they all move closer, three pairs of black,

iris-less eyes, fixed on me. When they blink, a second eyelid, white and filmy, lingers before retracting. Talons curl at the ends of fingers, whispering of violence and pain, and their feet are rough and scaled, with three long claws instead of toes.

And behind them, wings are folded.

My mind turns white with terror.

"She is ours," the first creature says, decisive, and her kin nod.

"Now, now, ladies." Hermes finally steps forward and all three turn in unison to him, movements as coordinated as a murmuration. I take advantage of their distraction to edge backward, trying and failing to move silently over the shifting stones, desperate to get away from them. "Are you responsible for Corey being here? Because you know you're not allowed near the mortal realm."

"You cannot command us," the bronze-scaled creature says. "Nor trick us."

"Tisiphone, I would never," Hermes flirts.

My stomach plummets, and I falter as I recognize the name. No. No . . .

Tisiphone; vengeance and destruction.

"You would, liar," the snake-haired one speaks. "You rely too much on your pretty face."

"I have little else, Megaera. Just a pretty face. Though not as pretty as yours," Hermes replies smoothly.

Megaera; O green and venomous jealousy.

My mouth turns dry, and gooseflesh stipples my skin.

"Mercury-tongued boy," the bird woman says, as though he

isn't an immortal god but a frisky teenager. "Your quicksilver flattery falls on deaf ears."

"Alecto . . . ," Hermes says, giving her a winning smile. "Come now. Let's talk about this."

And Alecto; implacable, impassable, immolating anger.

I stop breathing.

The Furies.

They turn to me in a single, synchronized motion and my heart leaps into my throat.

"No more talking," Megaera says. "We have come for her, and we shall have her."

Divine retribution. I killed Bree and now I'll pay for it.

I look at Hermes, silently begging for his help. For once he's not smiling. He gives a single shake of his head, and tears spill from my eyes.

"Please," I whisper, wiping my face uselessly. "Please. Please let me go. I'm sorry. Please. I just want to go home."

Alecto turns to me, unblinking, her eyes boring into mine, and I know *she knows* I'm not sorry, knows I'm only saying it to try to save myself.

She spreads her wings, and a rush of air disturbs the stillness as the others do the same. Alecto's wings are feathered, but Tisiphone's are leathery and veined, like those of a bat, and Megaera's thin and membranous, insectoid and fragile-looking. I can see Hermes through them, the pity on his distorted face clear.

"Help me!" I beg him.

"I'm sorry." He shakes his head. "I truly am. But I can't interfere in this."

"Good boy," Megaera says.

I close my eyes, curl in on myself, as if that might protect me from them. I cry out as I'm scooped up in arms that are bird-boned and thin, and nestled against a cold, feathered chest. No heart drums inside it; my own is a wild thing, trying to smash its way clean out of my body. The rest of me is paralyzed, petrified. I can't move. Can't fight.

"Please," I say again, eyes still squeezed shut. "I didn't know it would happen. I never even said it aloud! I was just sad and heartbroken, and it went too far. I'm sorry. Please. Listen! I'll fix it, just tell me how!"

My pleas make no difference, she doesn't give any sign she's even heard me.

When I feel the Fury lift off the ground, I cling to her, winding my fists into the thin black shroud she wears. I don't want to fall. I don't want to die. I don't want any of this.

We move at a dizzying speed, the air whipping past us, and I force myself to open my eyes so I can see where we're going in case I have to find the way back. Soon we've passed over the forest and are above a large, featureless plain that stretches for miles in every direction.

I look at the Underworld. And I am repulsed by it.

It's flat and colorless, like sun-bleached concrete, like a car park, like three a.m., like Tuesday, like January.

There's nothing. No buildings, no structures or features of

any kind, save a mountain range on the far horizon. The sky is clear, pale, cloudless and sunless, the soil a muted gray, and the two blur where they meet. Miles and miles of earth, utterly barren. To someone like me, it should be a dream—endless ground to plant in. Yet nothing grows. There's not a tree, nor a bush. Not a blade of grass, not even a lone weed. It looks like the surface of Mars, or some planet that can't hold life. It's terrifying in its emptiness; like it isn't quite finished, or hasn't really been started.

The only thing that draws the eye is a wide river, cutting the landscape in half. The Acheron. And when I spot a streak of crimson, I know I'm looking at the Phlegethon, the river of fire that leads to Tartarus, where the worst of the worst are kept. I wonder if that's where they're taking me, and shudder. Alecto makes a strange, cooing noise and holds me tighter, and I tremble again at the hollowness inside her chest.

I'm relieved, but only slightly, when we veer away from the Phlegethon, following the Acheron, flying lower to the ground. And I realize it isn't quite as flat as I'd thought; small mounds and valleys dot the landscape.

I'm still staring at the ground, something niggling in the back of my head, when Tisiphone swoops and one of the mounds throws itself down. With nauseating horror, I understand it's not the ground. It's people. It's the dead, falling and pressing themselves as close to the earth as I had on the hill when Hades looked at me.

Because they don't want to be seen. Like I didn't. They're trying to hide, as best they can in the empty, wide-open land that offers no friendly trees or shelter; no salvation at all.

They all wear the same kind of long, hooded shrouds, in the same muted beige blankness as the earth, so when they lie on their fronts, with their arms beneath them, they're camouflaged against the ground. They're like those photo challenges online, where at first it looks like nothing, just some woods or a plain, and then suddenly your eyes find the lion, or the snake, or whatever is cleverly hiding, and your heart catches, even though it's just a photo, because you didn't know something was there until you did. And if you were really there, it would be too late.

I scan them as they fall like dominoes, looking for Bree among them, trying to catch her face in the slivers I see before they hide. When Megaera follows her sister into a dive with a piercing shriek, I see people flinch and reach to grip their neighbors. As we fly over them, their fear is electric in the air, and I understand. The dead saw the Furies coming and they'd tried to hide.

A powerful dread courses through me.

The mountains are closer now and Megaera and Tisiphone begin to rise, higher and higher above the peaks, and Alecto pushes upward too, her wings working harder than before. They climb in a loose spiral, and I close my eyes as my stomach threatens to rebel, clenching my jaw, begging myself not to throw up.

Without warning, we plunge downward and my eyes fly open as Alecto's wings fold back and she dives behind her sisters, heading straight for the solid walls of the mountain.

My scream lodges in my throat and I grab Alecto, holding her tightly. I bury my face in her chest, braced for impact.

I hardly feel it when she lands. It's only when she tries to put me down and I won't let go, forcing her to pry my fingers from the thin shroud she wears, that I realize we're on solid ground. She's landed high up the range on a thin ledge of rock barely two feet wide and not much longer. In the side of the mountain is a small opening. Tisiphone and Megaera have disappeared.

I make the mistake of looking down and reel at the sight of the ground impossibly far below, bile rising in my throat.

Alecto steadies me before I fall, then places her hands on my shoulders, turning me toward the opening in the rock and urging me forward. I take tiny steps, terrified, until I can reach out and grip the sides of the fissure.

"What is this place?" I ask, staring up at the rock face.

"Erebus," the bird woman replies behind me. "Home."

LODGING

ONCE INSIDE, I STAY BY THE ENTRANCE, CLING-
ing to the wall. Alecto passes me, then leaps into the air, flying
upward. My eyes follow her and I look at where I am.

It's a large cavern, roughly circular, carved from the rock
as though a giant has scooped out the insides to form a long,
deep hole inside the mountain. It's darker than outside; there's
no roof, but there is a kind of ceiling made from a honeycombed
mesh that seems knotted together out of scraps of net and fabric.
The gray walls have recesses gouged out of them, some only big
enough to put a hand inside, others large enough for multiple
people to sit comfortably in, stand in, even.

In three of the largest ones are the Furies. Megaera sits on
the edge of the one opposite me, legs dangling over the side,
her hands in her serpent hair. I watch her carefully untangle
the snakes, pausing to let them to rub against her, occasionally
picking something out and tossing it to the ground, which is

littered with small stones and, I realize when I bend to look, the shiny carapaces of insects. I grimace and turn away. Tisiphone is in lotus position to her right, gnawing on something I'm not sure I want to identify, her wings half open above her, as though shielding her. In a third, on the left, Alecto squats, watching me watching them, her head cocked.

Erebus smells familiar to me, sweet-sour and musty, and as I try to puzzle out why that is, Alecto leaps from her perch, dropping silently in front of me. Without speaking, she reaches out and takes me by the waist, then launches upward, vast wings beating only twice before she deposits me in one of the large alcoves in the wall.

I scramble backward until I feel reassuring rock behind me. Alecto remains at the edge and we examine each other.

She's so *strange*. I have to break her up into separate parts to be able to look at her. If I just look at her face, her human face, it's all right. Or even her wings, or her hair. But only separately. The second my mind tries to put them together and see her as a whole, my vision blurs and there's a high-pitched buzz in my ears, like my brain is trying to reset itself. I close my eyes, giving myself a break. She's still there when I open them.

"You don't like heights," she says.

I almost laugh, like being this high is the worst of my problems right now. Then I shake my head. "Not heights. I don't like falling."

"You're not falling."

"No . . ." She peers at me, waiting for me to explain what's wrong with being so high. "I don't have wings."

"No," Alecto agrees, then falls silent. Her eyes rake over me, assessing, and my stomach cramps with fear.

"What's going to happen to me now?" I ask, trying to keep my voice steady. I get the feeling that tears, or any sign of weakness, won't do me any favors with the Furies.

"I saw you," she says.

"Where? When?" I ask.

"In the mortal world. You stood atop a hill, and you stared at the Receiver with your head high. You did not falter, nor cower. You met his gaze as an equal."

I remember the cloaked figure in the trees, behind Hades. Not cloaked. *Feathered.* "That was you?"

"Yes."

"Did you bring me here?" I ask.

Alecto looks at me with shining eyes and shakes her head. "No. But we wanted you here. We hoped you'd come. We watched and waited. We have waited for so long."

I become aware that Megaera and Tisiphone are listening to us. Megaera has stopped preening and Tisiphone has closed her wings and is sitting like her sister, her legs dangling over the edge of her own alcove. Both are watching us with onyx eyes.

"She does not know," Megaera says.

"What don't I know?" I ask.

They don't answer, looking at each other.

There's a chill, like cold fingers playing scales along my spine, and I shiver again, then realize it isn't just fear that is making me shake but also the fact I've been in the Styx, and the sky, and my clothes are soaked through. My jeans are heavy, clinging to my legs; my sweater beneath the oilskin is dripping. As soon as I notice it, my teeth begin to chatter and I wrap my arms around myself.

"She's cold," Tisiphone says. "And wet."

With that, she launches herself from her perch and lands beside Alecto. A moment later Megaera joins them, a bundle of black rags in her hand.

"Let us help you," Alecto says.

The three of them advance on me and I try to get away, but there's nowhere to go, solid mountain behind me and a sheer drop in front. I only realize I'm still clutching the limp narcissus when Alecto takes it from me, staring at it with wide eyes as she lays it down gently. Then six hands begin to tug at my clothes, gentle but firm, struggling with the zip on my coat.

At first I stay motionless, terror of Megaera's snakes enough to hold me still, but when they manage to unzip my coat, pulling it off me and tossing it to the ground, the sudden exposure kick-starts my survival instincts and I struggle away, batting their hands aside.

I might as well hit the air. The Furies ignore me, and Tisiphone drags a talon down the front of my sweater, rending it in two as her sisters pull it from my arms, leaving me half-naked.

"Stop it!" I cry, trying both to push them away and cover myself.

Megaera's snakes hiss violently at the sudden loud sound and I cower against the stone, eyes squeezed shut.

"What's this?" Megaera says.

I open my eyes to see them all staring at the lightning scars with looks of shock.

Megaera bares her teeth. "Who did this to you? Did Ze—"

Tisiphone slaps a palm over her sister's outraged mouth. "Don't say that name here. You'll only make the other one angry and then he'll come."

Megaera shoves Tisiphone away and her snakes rise up, their mouths open in threat. "Don't silence me."

"Then don't be foolish," Tisiphone snaps.

"Peace," Alecto says to her sisters, holding her hands out to them. Then she looks back at me. "We only want to warm you. We mean no harm. Not to you. Who did this?" she asks, nodding at the scars.

Lying seems like the best option. "No one. It was just the weather. It happens sometimes."

They exchange another of those inscrutable looks.

"This is dry," Megaera says, holding out the black rags to me. "For you. Does your arm hurt?"

"I . . . No. It's all right. Thank you. I can dress myself. Please," I say.

They stand back and watch impassively as my shaking fingers pop the button on my jeans and pull the zip down, pushing them to my knees. I don't think I've ever been quite so aware of my soft, curved, human body before, not even with Ali. My skin is mottled, purple and red, which makes me think of corpses. I start to cry.

Immediately, all three of them crowd in, stroking my skin

111

and hair, all of them making cooing, purring sounds. Alecto pulls my head against her shoulder, extending one wing to cover my injured arm, while the other two press against my spine and side, their arms wrapping around my waist. I can feel Tisiphone's cool, dry scales, hear Megaera's snakes hissing softly somewhere above the crown of my head. Talons rake gently against my scalp, rhythmic and massaging, petting me the way I might a frightened animal.

When I breathe in, I can smell Alecto, a dustiness in her plumage, that same sweet-sour scent I know underneath it, and then it comes to me—it's how I smelled when I stopped showering after the Thesmophoria. The same mix of wild and girl. They smell like me, or I smelled like them, and that makes me feel better. It's less frightening, to know that something in us is the same.

And then they shove me away.

I cower on the floor of the alcove, terrified once more, unable to understand what I've done wrong, why they've suddenly turned on me.

"We did not give you leave to come here," Alecto hisses, and I look up, bewildered, to see that the three Furies have turned away, forming a wall between me and the cavern. They're not talking to me.

"I don't need your leave, Alecto," a calm voice drifts up to the ledge. "It's my kingdom."

My blood runs cold.

Is he the one you love? Or did she break your heart?

It's him. Hades. He's here.

"Erebus is our domain," Tisiphone says. "You agreed to that. You signed the treaty. You would stay in your places and we in ours. This is ours."

"I want to see the girl you took from the bank of the Styx."

"We found her first."

"Megaera," Hades warns. "Bring her down. Or I'll come up."

"If you do, you'll violate the treaty. And you know what that means."

"You have already violated it by bringing her here. *You* know what *that* means."

I grab the bundle of rags Megaera held and shake it out, finding a neck hole, arm holes, and yank it over my head. It falls to my feet; a black version of the white robe I'd worn in the dream, like the Oracle's. I shove my jeans down, fling them into a corner and find the tattered remains of my sweater, pulling it on like a cardigan to cover my lightning-struck arm. I smooth my hair and set my face.

"Let's see if she wants to talk to you," Alecto replies, looking over her shoulder. "Do you want to speak to the one who calls this realm his own?" she asks me.

I shake my head. Not if I can help it.

"She doesn't," the Fury informs the king of the Underworld.

"So be it," he says.

I gasp as he appears between me and the Furies, his back to me. He's taller than I remember, his shoulders somehow broader, shadows undulating from him like coils of smoke.

The Furies whirl around, hissing in annoyance, snakes and scales and plumage rising, but they don't attack him, or even try to get between us again. Instead, they watch, angry that he's defied them, but unwilling, or unable, to actually do anything about it.

He turns to face me.

"Hello," he says, cool and impersonal, like I'm just *a girl taken from the bank of the Styx,* like we've never met before. Meanwhile, my tongue is glued to the roof of my mouth and my heart is thundering between my lungs.

Behind him, the Furies wait, their black eyes watchful. Compared to them, the king of the Underworld seems so ordinary.

This close, and without a mask obscuring part of his face, I see Hades isn't handsome. His skin is white to the point of translucence; the almost-sickly complexion of someone who avoids the sun, which I suppose isn't surprising, given who and what he is. He looks far more human than Hermes, but he has none of the quicksilver god's beauty; his brows are thick and heavy, his eyes cold without the bonfire to lend them warmth. His nose tilts slightly to the left, as if it's been broken and set badly at least once. His angular face is surround by a tangle of dark hair, as wild and unkempt as the shadows that flank him, spiraling out from his clothes as though part of his outfit. The shadows are the only thing about him that is remarkable.

Almost the only thing. My gaze falls on his lips, unadorned this time, and I look away. His mouth is beautiful. It has no right to be.

"How did you come to be here?" he asks, his attention settling somewhere just above my head.

I fight to keep my voice steady as I reply. "I picked a flower and I ended up in the Styx." When he frowns at me, I search for the bedraggled narcissus and hold it out to him. "I didn't want to come here," I add for good measure.

Some expression flickers over his face, his half-raised hand falling back to his side. "Well, you need not be inconvenienced by my realm any longer." He holds out his hand, turning away from me. "Come."

I bristle at his tone. Every word drips with the power of a god used to everything around him reordering itself because he wills it to. It gives me the perverse urge to tell him I'll figure out my own way back, thanks, and see what he makes of that, but I master myself at the last second.

As I reach for him, he shakes his head.

"No," he sighs.

I freeze. "No?"

He turns to face me. "The answer to the question you were just considering. No."

I blink, confused. "I don't know what you're talking about. I don't have a question."

"Please." He fixes his dark gaze on me, his upper lip curling. "You want to ask if you can have your friend back."

"No I don't."

"That's all anyone wants when they come here." He gives a knowing, bitter smile. "You don't have to pretend."

Tangling with immortals never ends well for humans. We just don't have the stamina. I am literally shaking because the truth of who and what he is *terrifies* me.

115

But now I'm angry too.

It burns me up; the arrogance of him, of all of them. Don't bother answering any of my other prayers, don't bother helping me when I actually need you to, when my heart is fucking breaking and I can't eat or sleep or stop crying. When I feel so alone that I want to die. Don't come to me then. Show up when you feel like it, just when I'm starting to come out the other side, and make me the villain of the piece.

Does he really think I'm so desperate for everything to go back to how it was; going to school on Monday and watching Bree and Ali hold hands under the table, his thumb rubbing hers the way it used to rub mine? Does he think I want to stay back after the bell, pretending I need to talk to Mr. McKinnon, so I don't have to walk home behind them in the lane, stalling every time they stop to kiss so I don't have to walk past them? Does he think I want to live in a place so small I can never, ever get away from them? The least—the absolute *least*—he could do is wait to see what I say aloud before he calls me a liar. The least he could do is *let me speak*.

My hands curl into fists as I boggle at the *audacity* of him.

"Stop that," I snap.

The shadows surrounding him had been stealthily drifting toward me, but now they freeze, hovering in place like they're unsure. Hades's eyes widen with the briefest glint of surprise as they meet mine, enough for me to know he hadn't expected me to argue. So his telepathy skills aren't all that, then.

"Stop reading my mind and deciding you know what I want," I continue.

He raises one eyebrow and that annoys me even more because I can't. Bree could do it, but I never could, no matter how hard I tried.

"I didn't read your mind," he says. "I heard you call for her, from your island. I saw you watching her. And, like I said, there is only ever one question people ask of me when they come here. You want to know if I'll give Bree her life back. And my answer is no."

My stomach hurts when he says her name.

"I told you, I didn't choose to come here." I snap. His lips thin, but I carry on before he can interrupt. "But you know what? If I had come for her, it would be your fault."

Behind him, the Furies look at each other, and, for the first time, Hades looks nonplussed, blinking at me.

"How would it be my fault, exactly?" He bites off each word.

"At the Thesmophoria. After we—" I halt abruptly as his expression turns to one of absolute horror. He uses my hesitation to shake his head, just once, which is enough for me to understand he doesn't want to me to continue, doesn't want me to say aloud exactly what happened. Mortified, heat surges along my chest and back, my ribs squeezing against my lungs.

His eyes bore into mine as he says, "I assure you, what happened to Bree had nothing to do with you." He gives me another polite, closed-mouth smile.

The back of my throat is scorched with humiliation; my eyes smart. He's ashamed of kissing me. He regrets it and he doesn't want the Furies to know. He's embarrassed by it. By me.

I will not fucking cry in front of him.

A traitorous tear spills from my left eye.

"Leave us." He turns to the Furies, whose mouths are matching Os of curiosity as they look back and forth between us. "Now."

I expect them to refuse to leave their own home at his command, but they glance at each other and then Megaera and Tisiphone give synchronized, slightly mocking salutes and step backward off the ledge, opening their wings and flying out of sight. Alecto throws me a wink before following, and it strikes me how wild it is that the wink of a Fury can somehow make me feel better. A few moments ago, she was the scariest thing in the world and now she's the closest thing I have to a friend. I wipe my face with my ragged sleeve.

Hades looks back at me, the shadows collecting beside him.

"You must understand, there are rules," he says, his voice dangerously soft. "I can't undo what's been done. Not for anyone."

"I haven't asked you to undo anything," I say through clenched teeth.

His eyes lock on mine. "So you don't want her back?"

Yes. No. I don't know.

He raises his eyebrows, for once waiting for me to speak, his beautiful lips pursed, and my gaze moves to them.

"Why did you kiss me?" I say it before I can stop myself.

"I didn't . . ." I think he's going to deny it, until he continues. "It was a mistake, for which I apologize."

I knew he was embarrassed about the kiss by the way he

didn't want the Furies to know, but hearing him say it aloud, seeing how sorry he is for it, absolutely guts me.

"Wow. You're supposed to be one of the better ones in that regard, you know," I say, shame thickening my voice. Another tear falls before I can blink it away and I'm livid he's earned a second one from me. I shouldn't even care; it was just a stupid kiss. I didn't know who he was until this morning. "But you're not. You're just as bad as the others. Kissing mortals and killing their friends. Classic Olympian behavior."

Color flushes the tops of his cheeks, but his voice remains even as he says, "I have apologized for my actions and I do so again: I am sorry. If it helps, I didn't think we'd meet again for a long time, if at all."

Ouch. My skin burns.

"And I didn't *kill* your friend," he continues. "Although, if I remember correctly, you did wish her dead."

"Even if that's true—"

"It *is* true." He fixes me with furious eyes. "You didn't need to say it aloud, Corey Allaway, your entire being was screaming for it. I could hear nothing else." The words fall from him in a rush and he looks away, like the admission is something I've stolen from him.

I never told him my name. He never asked. *She* must have. I picture the two of them sitting close together, talking softly, and fire kindles behind my ribs.

"Are you even allowed to just kill—sorry, *take*—mortals whenever you like?" I ask. "Or was she special?" *Different*, like Ali said. Exciting.

His expression is inscrutable as he says, "What did you call it? 'Classic Olympian behavior.' Tell me, did you really think I was better than the others?"

I look him up and down, slowly, pleased when his jaw tenses. "No. But if I'm honest, I didn't think about you at all."

He blinks, then pushes his hands through his hair. "Enough." He reaches for me and I jerk away.

"Don't touch me."

He flinches like I have slapped him. My breath comes in harsh pants and I can feel the heat rolling off me, can almost see the haze of it in the air.

Then he leans forward, so close that so our noses almost touch.

"Fine," he says. "You want to stay so badly, then stay. Enjoy it."

Then he vanishes.

Cultivation

I STARE AT THE SPOT WHERE HE'D STOOD, RIGID with shock. He's gone. He left me here. He actually left me here.

My legs feel hollow, and I lower myself to the alcove floor, dropping the narcissus and crouching with my fists against the stone while my heart rampages. I want my home, my garden, my soil—any soil—want to plunge my hands in up to my elbows and let the cool earth ground me. The longing is a real and bright pain behind my rib cage.

As the adrenaline wears off, I realize it's a miracle I'm still alive—I'm *lucky* he just left me here. I shudder at what an idiot I was, how badly it could have gone. He could have ended me with a snap of his fingers. I cover my face with my hands, shaking so hard my teeth rattle. The way I spoke to him, the things I said to him.

The things he said to me.

I lurch to my feet and jump backward as a dark shape drops onto the ledge in front of me. Shining feathers. Alecto.

She folds her wings and I stare, adjusting to her appearance once more. Even in the few moments she's been away my mind has sanded down the edges of her, letting me forget how different she is compared to me, with her black quartz eyes, her talons and her feathers. That's the problem with Hades, I realize. He doesn't look like what he is, his stupid face looks human enough. At least the Furies don't let you forget they're something else.

"I listened," Alecto says. "He said to go, but I didn't want to leave you alone with him. Girls shouldn't leave girls alone with strange gods."

I snort. I don't have much faith in the sisterhood anymore.

"The girl you spoke of. The not-friend. She hurt you. And now she is here."

I pause, then nod. "I wished for her to die, and she did."

"She hurt you first." Alecto says. It isn't a question.

"Yes."

"So it was justice." Alecto looks pleased, her feathers puffing up. "You were wronged, and you had justice."

A flash of the tarot. The Three of Cups. The sad, lonely girl with the sword-pierced hat. Justice. The path that lies ahead of me. Justice at the end of it.

"Not really. I don't think stealing someone's boyfriend means you get to kill them."

Alecto looks unconvinced. "She betrayed you. It was your right to be revenged and you took it. An eye for an eye. Who is she?" the Fury asks before I can get into the ethics of manslaughter. "This girl. A lover? A sister?"

I shake my head. "Neither. Well, not by blood. But we were as close as sisters, once. She was my best friend."

"And yet she took something that you loved," Alecto says. "That was yours. She stole from you."

My sigh comes from deep inside. "He wasn't *mine*," I begin. "People don't belong to people. But I was with him, and I thought we were all friends, the three of us. I actually liked that they were friends too, it made everything easier. Until they liked each other more than me. So they left me. Both of them."

Each word is a little paper cut, sharply stinging. I haven't had to explain it to anyone before. Everyone on the Island knew what was going on straight after it happened, the gossip network more efficient than any other news source, even the *Argus*. And not a lot happens on the Island, so everything is news.

I just saw Corey Allaway running toward her house, crying.

She was out with Alistair Murray earlier. I wonder if they had a fight.

More than a fight, I just passed Alistair Murray and Bree Dovemuir holding hands outside the Spar.

Corey's Bree? With her Alistair?

Oh dear.

I taste something bitter and swallow it down.

"She was the last person I thought would do something like that," I say. "And I wanted to hurt her back. But I didn't think she'd actually die."

"What's done is done." Alecto shrugs as if that settles it and sits down, patting the ledge beside her. "Come, sit."

I shake my head. "I can't. It's too high."

"I won't let you fall."

She might, though. She might look away, or not react in time. I could slip and that would be it. Or she could say she wouldn't let me fall, but not mean it. Words aren't worth shit, I learned that the hard way. What you do is what matters.

I shake my head again.

Alecto gives me a long, inscrutable look. Then she dives from the ledge, and I panic that I've offended her by refusing to sit with her and now she'll leave me here too. But I've barely taken a step forward when she returns, laden with masses of rags. She drops them to the ground and flies off again without a word, returning a few moments later with another pile of fabric, which she deposits onto the first. The Fury takes one final trip and then lands, folding her wings back.

She sits down before the pile and sorts through it, pulling out long pieces of cloth, and I watch as she deftly weaves them together, knitting them to create a thick cord. I look up at the ceiling and wonder if she made that too.

Growing up on the Island, I learned to sail, and I learned to make knots, but I've never seen ones like those Alecto is making, intricate, confusing things. I watch as she tests each one, pulling to make sure it holds, amazed as I understand what she's doing.

I move closer and Alecto looks up, making a trilling sound, like she's pleased by my attention, and then returns to her work.

Soon she knots the last piece and stands, carrying the end of the cord to the back of the alcove.

In stunned silence I stare as she tears into the stone wall, chiseling out a deep groove with her bare hands. The mountainside might be clay to her, soft as play dough, and I know then that the Furies, not some Titan or giant, created Erebus, carved it out of the rock themselves. That's how strong they are. Strong enough to rend holes in a mountain with their bare hands. No wonder Hermes didn't want to help me get away from them.

I breathe in sharply, causing Alecto to turn to me.

"What is it?"

I am speechless, no words to say how impossible it is that I'm here at all, let alone here and seeing this. No words to express how messed up it is that this time yesterday I'd been in my bedroom, clicking *yes* when the streaming service asked if I was still watching, because of course I was, what else would I be doing, and now what I'm watching is a creature I've only seen as a word in a textbook, hacking at a mountain, wings on her back, feathers for hair. No words for the tangled mess of things I feel, this horror-terror—let me wake up—I want to go home—please don't hurt me—I want to be this powerful—I want—I want—

I shake my head.

After a moment, Alecto turns back to the wall and continues clawing.

Soon, she's gouged a deep recess, leaving a thick rim of rock, creating a ring. Through that ring she threads the rope she's made and ties it back on itself, knotting it over and over.

Alecto winds the rope, loops it over her shoulder and gives me a wicked grin. Then she rockets past me, soaring into the air, the rope unraveling behind her. She jerks to a stop as it reaches its limit, and then she turns, wings beating forcefully as she pulls it.

I know what she is showing me. What she's done for me.

Alecto flies back to me and holds out the rope. My hand is steady as I take it.

"Now you can feel safe. This is yours. A way to come and go, a way to secure yourself. It should reach the ground, I think, or near enough. You can hold on to it, or I can tie it around you."

I look down at the gift she's given me.

"I'll hold it," I say.

When she walks back to the ledge and sits, I follow.

I'm not brave enough to dangle my legs over the side, but I do sit, keeping a couple of feet from the edge and curling my legs to one side. I hold the rope tightly, winding it around my arm, and then grip it in a fist, my knuckles white.

"I would like to ask something," Alecto says.

Wary, I nod.

"How did you come to kiss him?"

The question takes me by surprise. I didn't think she'd care about kissing.

I shrug. "I didn't know who he was. And if I'd known he was such a dick, I wouldn't have."

Alecto gives a sly smile. "But you did. And you're not afraid of him."

I blush. "I am, actually. I just . . . He made me so angry I forgot, I guess?"

Alecto shakes her head. "No. We can smell fear. You were afraid of us, when first we met. But not him. There is no fear of him in you. Because you kissed him?"

"Maybe," I say. I still think I'm afraid of him.

"Tell me," Alecto says.

I hesitate. I'm embarrassed now that I know he regrets it. It changes the kiss, retcons it into just another mistake on a night that was probably full of them. One more bad decision to be swept under the carpet and forgotten.

"I gave that to you." Alecto nods at the rope in my hand. "I made it for you."

I know what she's saying. Friendship is built on stories—secret for secret, confession for confession, and each one weaves invisible threads between you, binding you to each other. The more threads, the stronger the friendship.

Two girls, sitting side by side in a woodland where they weren't supposed to go but always did.

I kissed Ali Murray last night.

No way. I wondered if you would. What was it like?

Weird. But good? I think. He wants to see me again tonight.

Oh. Will you go?

Yes.

A pause: *I don't think I'll kiss anyone until I leave the Island.*

Surprise: *Do you want to leave the Island?*

Yes. But only if you come with me.

Of course I will.

And so it goes. Weaving a tapestry that makes a whole picture only if you both do the work. It doesn't have to be at the same time; sometimes you hold the shuttle more, sometimes they do. But it comes together in the end.

Me whispering in the dark to Bree that I didn't think anyone would ever love me because if my own mother couldn't, if she could just leave me behind, then who would ever stay.

Bree telling me she wished she had a brother or sister because her parents loved her too much and she hated how she didn't have the freedom I did.

Me thrilled that my dad married Merry, who was cool and knew about birds, and she liked me, and she loved him, and he needed that. We needed that.

Bree ecstatic that her mother was pregnant, once, then again, little brothers as a distraction so that Bree could steal independence.

Us. Planning to visit the Oracle, the Brides of Artemis.

Me sleeping with Ali for the first time, then a second and third, and being disappointed by it. Bree confiding that she fancied Manu and was going to make a move, only to find out he was gay and in love with Lars.

Me crying on Bree's shoulder because Ali was distant and cold, his eyes were far away and he wouldn't kiss me or hold me after we'd had sex, insisting he had urgent things to do.

Bree telling me I was being ridiculous and demanding, and maybe the best thing I could do was give him space to figure out what he wanted.

I'd thought she was working for me. She was working for herself.

"So?" Alecto says. "Tell me what it was, to kiss a god."

I can't tell her now how the kiss had made feel hope for the first time in months, like a cut-rate Sleeping Beauty being woken from her misery. I can't explain how much it hurts that he's ashamed of it. Of me. But I have to tell her something, because she's right. Those are the rules. An eye for eye.

"All right," I say to Alecto, looking at the rope around my arm.

I give her the physical stuff, where his hands had been, the press of his hips against mine, because those were things I could afford to share—they were nothing more than anyone at the Thesmophoria saw.

I don't tell her the private things that no one saw, or knows. That I'd got lost in the kiss, for a little bit, at least. I don't tell her how I'd wanted to see him again. I don't say what I'd hoped. I don't tell her that I'm scared his embarrassment and regret will break me wide open again.

Alecto doesn't know me well enough to know I'm holding back. Only Bree would have.

"Would you kiss him again?" Alecto asks.

I shake my head, as if it's my choice.

She reaches out and pats me, roughly, on the arm. It's unexpected and sweet. It makes me brave.

"Can you help me get home?" I ask.

"We don't have that power. We can't go into the mortal world."

I reach for the narcissus, drooping and pathetic now. "What about with this? Or a fresh one? Would that work?"

Alecto shakes her head. "Flowers don't grow here. Nothing grows here."

"Is there no other way?" I say, biting back frustration. "What about Hermes, would he take me?"

Alecto shakes her head again. "He cannot interfere. He is sworn."

"So that's it? I'm stuck in the Underworld?" I put my head in my hands and rub my face. This cannot be happening.

"You can stay here with us," Alecto says softly. "We want you to."

"I can't," I say, lowering my hands. "It's not that I don't appreciate the offer, but I don't belong here. My dad and my stepmum will worry if I don't come home—I don't want to hurt them or scare them. And I have things to do. A garden to tend. School." By now Dad and Merry must be back from the perideipnon. They'll have read my note. They'll be expecting me back any moment. "You really can't get me home?"

She shakes her head yet again.

I'll have to swallow my pride. I'll have to ask Hades if he'll take me back. Apologize, or beg, or whatever his stupid ego demands.

"All right. Can you take me to Hades?" I say, lead in my stomach.

She looks thoughtful. "I could go to him. I could petition on your behalf. He is more likely to listen to me—we have a treaty."

Right. The treaty. I nod. "Are you sure? I don't want to cause a fight. It's not really your problem." It's my problem. My stupid temper. Just like my dad said.

"I'm happy to. And it will be all right. Trust me. I will not be long." She pats my arm again and then takes to the air.

Leaving me alone, in Erebus.

I move away from the edge, back to the middle where it feels safe and solid and I can't see the ground.

It's so quiet. I've always thought of the Island as a quiet place, but it isn't, not really. There is always the sound of the sea, the wind, birdsong, snatches of TV from houses, the rumbling of tractors. Here, there is nothing. The silence is absolute.

I think of Bree, out there somewhere in all this silence. Forever.

She doesn't like the quiet. She's always singing, or humming, always has music on. Is she allowed to sing here? Is there music?

What have I done?

She deserved it.

Two shapes fly through the entrance. Tisiphone and Megaera have returned, and I stand as they land on either side of me. I'd gotten used to Alecto, but seeing Tisiphone's scales and Megaera's snakes again sends new waves of shock through me; all those small, serpentine heads turned to me, tongues flickering, interlocking copper that looks like it's moving, even when Tisiphone is still.

"You're still here," Tisiphone says, smiling at me and exposing long fangs.

"But where is our sister?" Megaera frowns as she looks around.

I swallow. "She went to see Hades. To ask him to take me home."

"What happened?" Megaera says, looking at Tisiphone. "We thought he came to take you away."

I swallow. "We fought and he left me here," I say. "Alecto went to plead my case."

They look at each other again and smile.

"Then we shall wait and see what the Receiver of Many decides," Megaera says.

She and Tisiphone lower themselves to the ground on either side of me, tucking their wings neatly behind them, and I sit too, trying to act like this is all normal, all fine. I don't know what to say to them; I can't think of anything that isn't stupid or pointless. I can't ask what they do—I know what they do, and I don't want to know if they enjoy it. Do they have hobbies? Spare time? Hopes? Dreams? Lovers?

My stomach gives a low rumble, and I cross my arms over it as the Furies frown.

"What was that?" Megaera asks, looking at me as if I'm a bomb that might go off.

"Oh, it's nothing. It just means I'm hungry."

She stands. "We will get food for you."

"No, it's OK. Thank you. I'll eat when I get home. Alecto will probably be back soon, right?"

Megaera looks at me with fathomless black eyes and nods, lowering herself once more to the ground.

We lapse back into silence, which they seem fine with, so I try to be, but I'm relieved when Alecto returns in a rush of feathers, landing in front of me with her hands clasped before her.

"I'm sorry," Alecto says, before I can speak. "He will not change his mind."

There is a high-pitched sound in my ears. "So I'm stuck here?"

Alecto reaches out a taloned hand and strokes my hair. "He's punishing you," she says.

"He is cruel like that," Megaera adds. "Cruel, vindictive, volatile. They all are, those godlings."

"What am I going to do?" I say, panic rising.

"You will stay with us," Megaera says. "We will keep you safe."

The Furies smile at me.

HARDEN OFF

It's funny how fast you can get used to things and yet not actually accept them. I always thought getting used to something automatically meant you'd accepted it, but that isn't true. Acceptance is a choice; you have to do the work to achieve it and make peace with the outcome, even if—especially if—it's not what you want. But getting used to things doesn't require any work, all you need to do is stop fighting. The last few months have taught me the difference. For example, I *got used* to seeing Ali and Bree together but I sure as shit didn't *accept* it.

I get used to being in the Underworld.

The Furies bring me fresh food and water. Grapes, plums, figs, pomegranates—fruits that almost never appear on the Island because it's so far from everything. Large, flaky flatbreads wrapped in thick linen napkins, fat green olives in olive oil, something I think is pickled samphire. At first, I try to ration it all, but stop when Megaera catches me trying to hide a pomegranate in my bedding.

"You don't have to do that. We can get more. Lots more."

"Where does it come from?" I ask. They don't eat, or at least not in front of me.

The three sisters exchange glances. "*His* table," Tisiphone says.

His. Hades's. "Does he know?"

Megaera shrugs. "Does it matter?"

Only that if he knows, it means he doesn't want me to starve to death. And that means there's hope he'll change his mind about sending me home once he thinks I've been punished enough. I ask Alecto to go to him again, to take me to him, but she tells me to give it time.

"How much time?"

There are no clocks, no seasons, no dusk or dawn in the Underworld, there is no sun to rise or set, so I don't know how long I've been here. I can't even use my period to figure it out; it never arrives.

Alecto shrugs. "He is the Unchanging One. He will only become more fixed in his cruelty if he feels pushed or if he knows he's hurting you. He'll relish that. But don't worry. We'll take care of you."

And they do.

With their bare hands, they carve a passage to a natural cavern with a small waterfall and stream running through it, to make me a bathroom. Then they hack footholds in the side of the rock with individual swipes of their talons when it becomes obvious that I can get down using the rope Alecto made but don't have the upper-body strength to haul myself back up. The whole bathroom-cave thing makes me grateful for my missing period, but it also makes me remember how once my period was late while I was with Ali and I'd cried my eyes out on Bree in the school toilets, imagining my dad's and Merry's faces when I told them I was pregnant. Halfway through my breakdown, Astrid had come in and Bree told her to fuck off, screaming in her face until she left. Then she'd ordered a pregnancy test for me online so we wouldn't have to get one from the Spar, but my period arrived before it did and the next month I was back to normal, in sync with Bree, and we never mentioned it again. I never even told Ali. I wonder if she did.

The Furies bring me quilts and pillows—presumably also stolen from Hades—to sleep on. Tisiphone even gives me candles and matches, the same brand we have at home, so I can see inside my bathroom cave. She won't tell me how she got them.

They bring me clean clothes, the same black shifts they wear, and I change them every three sleeps, which may or may not also be days, and wash the dirty ones in the waterfall. My jeans disappear while I'm asleep; later I think I see them woven into the ceiling. Alecto steals my tattered sweater and wears it as a kind of backward cardigan to keep her wings free when the others aren't around. I find it sweet, actually. The soles of my feet harden up pretty fast.

I get used to it.

But I can't accept it. When I sleep, I dream of snow; one by one, flakes bury me and I can't stop them. It never snows on the Island; it hasn't since before I was born. I wake up thinking I'm cold, but it's all in my head, the temperature here never changes. I fall back to sleep and dream of my dad and Merry scouring the Island, calling my name. I dream of them dredging the water in the lake looking for me; everyone in the woods, walking in a line, beating the bushes. Checking the caves and the beaches. By now the Oracle must have told them I'd gone to see her, and Connor's boat is in its dock, so they'll know I came back. And then I disappeared. On the day of my former best friend's funeral, I vanished into thin air.

Bree. I wonder what she'd say if she knew I was here in the Underworld too. I wonder if she misses the Island as much as I do. Bree-and-Corey. Corey-and-Bree. To the bitter end.

"I want to see the Underworld," I say, on the fourth/eighth/ fifteenth/sixteenth/twenty-third/forty-second day of my stay. I woke up with the idea that maybe if Hades hears I'm out and about, being obnoxiously alive in the land of the dead, he'll want me gone; historically he's been pretty keen to evict trespassers. "Is that allowed?"

The Furies look as if it's their birthday and Haloa all at once, beaming at me; even Megaera's snakes give excited little hisses, quivering atop her head. Alecto hugs me, pulling me to her so fast I end up with a mouthful of feathers and squashing a nectarine between us.

"We want to show you," she says in my ear, then nuzzles it. "We want to show you so much."

"Then show me." I laugh, puzzled and delighted, and she holds me tighter, before swinging me into her arms, making me squeal.

"Wait! I need to clean up first. Use my cave. Mortal things."

Megaera, Tisiphone and Alecto look between each other, talking wordlessly, and I wish that I was part of it, that I had that closeness with someone again.

"We'll see you there," Megaera says to me, and takes to the air, Tisiphone following her, leaving Alecto and me alone.

"See us where?" I ask Alecto.

"Hurry up and we can follow."

A few moments later, when I've washed the worst of the nectarine from my shift and cleaned the rest of me as best I can, Alecto lifts me into her arms and I cling to her, my heart trying to make a break for it when the ground peels away.

We leave Erebus, flying up and over the peaks of the mountains that act as a border between the Underworld proper and the outer lands. I realize then that the desert we flew over when I came here is hardly the Underworld at all, and I wonder what it's called and who is sent there.

We keep moving inland, following the path of a slim, silvery river that carves its way through the mountain range. As we fly, I catch the sound of ragged breathing and soft, wretched sobs. I make the mistake of looking for the source, my stomach lurching when I see the ground far, far below.

"It's the river," Alecto says in my ear as I tighten my hold around her neck.

"What is?" I speak into her shoulder.

"The weeping. The Cocytus is made from the tears of the shades in the Mourning Fields. They are what lie between Erebus and the Styx."

Oh. That answers that question. The Mourning Fields are where people who died in or of unrequited love go. Enough sadness between them to make a river.

The hairs on the back of my neck stand on end, and my throat tightens. I remember running home from the cove after Ali dumped me, tears streaming down my face, a hole in my chest.

Here's how I found out about them: I tried calling Bree the entire way home and she didn't answer. I went to her house, but the door was locked and it seemed like no one was home. I remembered then, Mick and Ella were taking the boys to the mainland to get new clothes and I figured Bree must have gone with them. I know now she didn't. I can picture her sitting on the stairs out of sight, listening to me trying to open the back door, hammering on it, watching her phone light up with my name, over and over, knowing exactly why I was there.

No one was home when I got to mine, so I went into the garden. I'd stopped crying, I was just numb. The next time I tried Bree, her phone was off; Ali was probably with her, so she knew what had happened—maybe not everything—and she'd turned her phone off. I went back inside, washed my hands and face, got changed, planning to go back to Bree's, figuring her family must be home by then. I put on makeup, because I was damned if I was going to let anyone see me crying, at least until I was safe at the Dovemuirs'. I got to the bottom of the stairs just as Merry came home, and when she saw me, her face fell.

She'd been walking back from a survey on the north of the Island and Cally Martin had come racing out of the Spar to ask what was going on. Bree and Ali had apparently just walked past, holding hands for all the world to see. Then they'd stopped by the postbox and kissed. Cally had called it *quite a show*.

We'd been broken up for two hours.

Alecto's arms tighten uncomfortably, her teeth snapping near my face, and I reel as I'm wrenched from my thoughts and find the only thing keeping me at her side is her hold. At some point I've stopped holding on to her and allowed my arms to fall to my side, my spine to bend backward, my body to fall limp. If she'd let me go . . .

I clasp my arms around her neck once more, shuddering.

"Thank you," I say. "Sorry."

She makes a soft, purring sound and heads upward, away from the river, until I can barely hear the whispering. I pull myself together. *It's all in the past.* Old news. Old pain.

A short distance later, we veer away from the Cocytus and follow the path of another river, this one live with currents I see swirling beneath the murky brown water. As the river widens, more and more streams and tributaries join it and the mountain range begins to taper away, revealing a vast plain.

And what can only be the gates to the Underworld.

They rise out of the river, stretching bank to bank, the filthy water slapping uselessly against them, barred from entry until they open. When we get closer, I see the gates are made from huge slabs of a matte black wood I'm pretty sure doesn't come from any tree that exists in my world, or if it ever did, it hasn't existed for centuries. They are as tall, and as forbidding, as the towers on either side. Those are built from gray stone and are crooked, with dozens of glassless windows, like something from a nightmarish fairy tale. The towers stretch high enough into the white sky that even flying far above the ground, Alecto and I still only reached their middles.

Any lingering melancholy evaporates as I imagine what it must be like to arrive here in the Boatman's small rowboat; coming to terms with the fact your life is over, buffeted by the currents, with only his silent company to comfort you. Approaching gates that, even if you craned your neck as far back as it could go, you still might not see the top of; the twin towers standing sentinel on either side, a hundred empty windows, like eyes marking your progress. Not knowing what was beyond, but knowing there was no going back.

I missed all of this when I arrived, and I'm glad of it.

I see movement in a window and stare. Alecto raises her free hand and waves and I see one raised in return; a pale arm, gold cuffs at the wrist.

"Who was that?" I ask as we fly on, looking over my shoulder at where the blurred shape stands in shadow, charting our course.

"Lady Strife."

It takes me a second, but then I remember: Eris, goddess of discord.

"Is she a friend?"

"More than. Once we lived in that self-same tower too, on the threshold of it all," Alecto continues. "She, we, and Lord War, and it was glorious."

"Why did you leave?" My curiosity gets the better of me. "Did you fight?"

"Not with she, nor with Lord War." Alecto's tone is dark. "It was decided after the Olympians threw down the old gods and the Underworld got its latest master that Erebus would home us better."

Hades, then. His arrival after he and the others had defeated the Titans must have caused problems with the gods and goddesses already living here. Having met him, I can see how that would happen. So he's the reason the Furies live inside a mountain far from everyone else, a place they carved for themselves out of stone—no wonder they hadn't been happy to see him there. *Latest master*. Weird to think that ruling the Underworld isn't necessarily a permanent thing, even if you are immortal.

"Do the others still live in the tower?" I ask. "Lady Strife and Lord War?"

"They do. And on the other side live Fear, Need, Death, Sleep and more besides."

"What about Hades?" He must have been in the same tower as the Furies, I guess. Maybe he'd taken their rooms for himself.

I'm wrong.

"The king of the Underworld built his own palace." Alecto clicks her teeth. "You'll see it soon enough."

We fly on. Below us the empty plain whips by in a blur of gray nothingness, and it starts to make me sleepy.

Then I catch sight of something that jolts me wide awake.

Hades's palace.

TERRAIN

IT CAN'T BE ANYTHING ELSE, ALTHOUGH *PALACE*
is maybe a generous way of describing it. *Fortress* would be accurate. *Prison* even more so. It's the ugliest building I've ever seen.

Unlike the towers, there are no windows, not even those
narrow ones for arrows, no turrets, no ramparts, no balconies.
Where the towers were crooked and had at least some personality, however sinister, the palace has none at all. No flags, no
ivy, no banners. The one deviation from cold stone is a set of
double doors carved from the same black wood as the gates to the
Underworld, on one side of the building, which I guess makes it
the front. But that's all. No ornate gardens, not even a basic, boring garden. Just a monolithic block of gray imprisoned behind
four matching walls, set on grounds of yet more ashy dust. He
couldn't have designed a starker building if he'd tried. Everything about it is forbidding, grim and impersonal.

It suits him.

I wonder if he's in there now, doing whatever he does. What would he think if I just showed up on his doorstep and asked him, begged him, to take me home?

I remember the cold look on his face as he told me to *stay*, to *enjoy it*.

Like anyone could find anything worthwhile here.

"Whereabouts are we?" I ask Alecto, unable to tear my eyes from the palace even as we fly away.

"Nearing the Asphodel Meadows."

Oh. Where I'd end up, when I eventually died. Where Bree will most likely be.

I forget Hades and begin to scan the ground, heart speeding, as I anticipate seeing her.

The first time I saw Bree Dovemuir, we were four. I don't remember it, but apparently I walked right up to her in the Spar while Mrs. Dovemuir was looking at cereal and took her hand. My dad had pulled me away, apologizing to Bree's mum, but all the way home I kept asking when I could see my friend again. In the end he'd invited Bree and Mrs. Dovemuir over for tea and so began the slow journey that would lead to her ruining my entire life and us both being here, in this dismal, monochrome land.

I can't understand where the *meadow* comes from in Asphodel Meadows. I think of meadows and picture long pale-gold stalks waving in a breeze, goosegrass burrs sticking to my skirt, fingers scattering the heads of bromegrass, taking one to stroke an arm, a naked back. Flowers. Grasshoppers. Sheep baaing nearby. Lazy fat bumblebees. Ants running over your toes. Your best friend making you a crown of daisies to wear while you make one for her. Buttercups held under chins. Cornflowers' he-loves-me-he-loves-me-not-he-loves-her-now-I-am-alone.

This meadow is nothing like that.

Like the plain we traveled over when I arrived, there's no real color in sight. Everything is washed out and faded, waiting-room beiges, ashy and faded grays. Even here, on the other side of the mountain, the light is dim—probably why Hades's palace has no windows, I decide; what's the point, with no view to look out on, no real light to let in. There's no sun in the whitewashed sky, so I don't know where the half-light even comes from, it just *is*. No grass. No flowers. If the ground had been orange, or golden, or even brown, you could have described it as a desert, but a wasteland would be closer to this dusty, cracked pale surface that stretches as far as the eye can see. For the briefest moment I think I can smell something rich and earthy, but then it's gone.

As we move away from the palace, I start to spot people—shades, I remind myself—milling about. They look up as we fly overhead; the realization that we're there travels through them like wind through wheat; heads lifting, faces turn, openly afraid, relieved when we pass by.

I search through them, trying to find Bree among them, looking for a snatch of her face, her brown eyes. A few times I think it's her and my heart both leaps and plummets at the same time, but it never is her.

Alecto flies on, and I twist my head to watch the shades as we pass. They don't hug, or even smile at each other. Just look at each other and nod, then continue milling about, the dust eddying in their wake the most exciting thing happening in the whole place.

I knew the Underworld wouldn't be like the Elysian fields, which is supposed to be some kind of eternal high-end package holiday; Ibiza for the dead. But I'd always thought the Asphodel Meadows would be a peaceful, content kind of place. Somewhere you could meet with the people you loved and catch up with them. Like a retirement village; lots of nice walks and plenty of benches for sitting and chatting. Duck ponds. Lawn bowling. Maybe golf.

Not this.

"Has it always been like this?" I ask Alecto.

"Since mortals started coming, yes," she says.

"And they're always like that? The people. The shades," I correct myself. "Just wandering about?"

"Yes."

Shitty kind of eternity. This place is so big, and there are so many of them, how would you find someone here? How would you be found?

Alecto banks sharply, and I look around. I'm surprised to see a roofless, bowl-shaped building, like a small amphitheater, in the distance, rising up out of the ground, the same dusty beige as the dirt around it. As we get closer, I see what looks like a line of shades waiting outside an arched opening, circling the building, but other shades are moving away from it, as fast as they can.

We fly over the rim of the amphitheater and descend, landing near the other Furies, who are each standing on a mound of earth: Tisiphone on the right, Megaera in the middle, with a place for Alecto on the left. There are no seats in the walls of the amphitheater, nothing at all except the mounds and the archway.

"What is this place?" I ask, my voice echoing faintly.

"The Prytaneum. Where we work. Stay close," Alecto warns as she puts me down and steps onto her mound.

"Don't leave our sight," Megaera adds, turning to me.

Unease stirs low in my abdomen. I move a few paces away, but stay within sight, wondering what they're afraid might happen to me if I stray too far. I can't imagine anyone would be stupid enough to risk doing anything that would make the Furies angry, but then again, the people they punish aren't exactly innocents.

I know what the Furies do, in theory, but I have no idea what that looks like in practice, and as Megaera calls, "Let the first of the guilty enter," I try to brace myself for whatever is about to happen.

A man comes through the arch. He's short, white, balding and clean-shaven, fiftyish when he died, so pretty young, all things considered. If I had to guess his job I'd say accountant, or manager of something in an office. He doesn't look like a criminal or a bad person, but I know from experience that looks can be very deceiving and for all I know this guy is Jack the Ripper. He approaches the Furies with no hesitation, ignoring me completely. He stops in front of Tisiphone with a resigned expression on his face, giving me the feeling he's been here, done this before.

I hold my breath.

Then, out of nowhere, Tisiphone has a mirror in her scaled hands, and she holds it out to the man, who takes it silently. He seems to steel himself, setting his shoulders and his jaw before holding it up and peering into it.

I wait for something to happen—I don't know what: a hand emerging and grabbing him by the throat; blood pouring from the frame and soaking him; for the mirror to start screaming accusations at him. But all that happens is the man looks into the mirror and his face slowly crumples, eyes squeezing together, mouth open in a silent wail. *He's crying*, I realize. He has no tears because he's dead, but he is crying nevertheless, sobbing silently at whatever he sees in the glass.

The Furies say nothing. Alecto gives me a swift glance, the slightest smile, then looks back at the man. They all watch him, bearing silent witness as he weeps for whatever he's done.

It goes on for a long time, and then as suddenly as it appeared, the mirror vanishes from his hands, and the man turns and leaves, his steps heavier and shoulders lower than they were before. I look at Alecto and she nods, letting me know it's over. For him, at least.

"Let the next of the guilty enter," Megaera says.

A young woman with brown skin and long, black hair walks straight up to her, her expression pained, and Megaera conjures a book, which she hands to the woman. The woman opens it and begins to read to herself and soon she, too, is crying without sound or tears, her hands shaking as she turns the pages. Twice she slams the book shut, as if repelled by what she reads, but she doesn't drop it or fling it aside, and I get the feeling she can't let go of it, that she has to hold it until she's finished, and sure enough she opens it again and reads on. She also walks away slowly when the book finally disappears, her feet dragging and sending dust storms whirling around the hem of her shroud.

It's all very *civilized*. I'd feared the Furies' punishments would be barbaric, physical ones; whips and chains and fire and needles. Not these subtle, custom-tailored ones that leave the dead even more despondent. I'm gruesomely curious about what their crimes were. And I'm desperate to know what the man saw in the mirror, what the girl read in her book.

It makes me wonder what Bree would have to do if she was being punished. Maybe watch a show reel of highlights from our entire friendship; all the times she told me I was being stupid and paranoid about Ali, spliced between scenes of her and him together behind my back. Betraying me.

Then I wonder what my punishment would be, for wishing her here. Maybe I'd have to watch her drowning alone in the cold and the dark, hearing her cry out uselessly for help, or worse, unable to scream as lake water filled her lungs? I shiver. It's a horrible image. A horrible death. I push it away and try to concentrate on the real punishments happening before me. Anyway, wishing someone dead isn't a crime.

The Furies stand as still as statues throughout, and though one or two of the shades look at me curiously as they approach them, they soon forget I'm there. It goes on and on, more shades arriving, accepting their punishments and leaving quietly, and though it sounds awful, pretty soon I'm bored and fidgety, drawing shapes in the dust with my toes, wondering why vengeance is so dull.

I'm trying very hard to stifle a yawn when I think I see someone I know approaching the Furies.

"Mr. McGovan?" I say. "Mr. McGovan, is that you?"

The Furies look at me as one, and I flinch at their cold, furious expressions. For a moment it's like they don't know me, and I want to run, put as much distance between me and them as I can.

Then Alecto's face softens and she shakes her head, warning me not to speak again. I lower my eyes to the ground, keeping them there until the Furies' attention returns to the man. Only then do I look back up, in time to see him push the hood back from his face.

It *is* Mr. McGovan. He died last year, in a fishing accident. There was a rumor on the Island that he'd never married because as a teenager he'd fallen in love with a Nereid, but she wouldn't give up the sea for him, so he became a fisherman so he could still see her. Bree and I thought it was so romantic. But after he'd died, it emerged—at his ekphora, no less—that he'd been sleeping with his brother's wife for the last fifteen years and the whole Nereid thing was a cover.

Alecto holds something out to him, a stuffed bear, tatty and old, and Mr. McGovan holds it away from himself like it's a tarantula. But slowly, reluctantly, he draws it closer, until he's cradling it in his arms like a baby, his face screwed up in misery.

I feel embarrassed, seeing him like this. He hasn't acknowledged me at all, so it doesn't seem to bother him that I'm there, but I feel awkward, being the audience to this moment that feels like it should be private. Then I feel shitty for being bored when it was people I didn't know, for shifting and fidgeting and sighing while they were going through this. I make myself stand tall and still, like the Furies.

I stay like that for the rest of the time, until they call no one else forward and instead crowd around me, chattering and happy.

"You did very well. Very well." Megaera sounds proud, and Tisiphone rubs my arm, smiling with all her teeth on show, and I'm glad I made them happy, that I didn't let them down.

"You mustn't talk to them," Megaera adds. "Not unless I tell you to."

"I'm sorry," I say, a little of the glow fading. "I didn't know. I won't do it again."

"No matter. It is past." She smiles.

I nod. "What happens now?" I ask.

The Furies look at each other.

"We will go back to Erebus so you can eat. You must be hungry," Alecto says, reaching for me.

My stomach growls in agreement and I realize I'm famished.

We don't fly back the same way we came; instead of going over the Asphodel Meadows we head away from it, and once again I see the river of fire on the horizon and I'm glad when we go no closer.

There are no shades here, and I understand why—it feels bleak, even bleaker than the meadow. Hopelessness radiates from the earth and I shudder in Alecto's arms. She holds me tighter.

We're halfway back when I realize we're alone in the sky.

"Where are Megaera and Tisiphone?" I ask.

"They have business elsewhere. So it's just us for now." She beams at me and I beam back. Honestly, I prefer it this way.

I've tried very hard not to have a favorite Fury, but Alecto is mine, and I wonder what it was like for her before I came. Three is a weird number to have with a group; no matter how close you all are someone always ends up a little bit on the outside. I get the feeling with the Furies that Alecto is the one on the outside.

She's different from the other two. Megaera always changes the subject if I bring up the mortal world, and my real life, and Tisiphone just watches me speak, not reacting at all. But Alecto is curious. She wants to know about the sea, and the sun, and the earth. Things she's never seen or known, because she and her sisters were born in Erebus. Not even born, she tells me, because they simply came into being one day, fully formed, knowing their names and their purpose, and they've been here, enacting it, ever since. She's never had a childhood, never grown up. I feel like Wendy from *Peter Pan* trying to explain life on Earth to her.

"The best thing about Earth is my garden," I tell her one afternoon, or morning, or middle of the night, when we're back from the Prytaneum and the others are off doing whatever they do while we stay here.

"How is a garden the best thing?"

I can't help smiling at how much she sounds like Bree.

"Because . . ." I close my eyes and picture it: eight beds, four on the left, four on the right. My shed, my compost bin. My little world that I build from scratch every year. How do I explain how *right* it makes me feel? I remember Ali saying it was boring, and scowl.

"What's wrong?" Alecto asks.

"Nothing. Just thought of something stupid. So . . . How is it the best thing? Well, everything in a garden starts from a tiny seed. They look like nothing at all, most of them." Then I remember my coat, and crawl to fetch it. I rummage in the pockets and pull some of the seeds that escaped my attack on the Oracle's table. "Like these." I show her the specks nestled in my palm. "Nothing special— What's wrong?" I ask.

Alecto has reared back and is staring at my palm like I'm holding a scorpion.

She doesn't tear her eyes from them as she says, "These are seeds, from your world?"

"Yes. They can't hurt you," I say. "They're not poisonous or anything."

"You brought them here?" She turns her stark gaze on me, and goose bumps rise at the intensity of it.

"Not on purpose. They were in my pocket when I came. Is that a problem?"

She shakes her head as she peers at them again, but her frown deepens. She surprises me when she says, "Go on."

"Are you sure?"

"Tell me." She says it so fast, like she wants me to talk before she can think better of it and stop me.

I swallow. "OK. They look like nothing, but they're everything. Every single plant grows from something like this. The food we eat, the materials we use to build houses and ships and

153

to burn when we're cold, to make fibers for clothes, for medicine, for fun, to make dyes and paper, they all start with a seed. There is life and potential in every single one of them. And that's the magic of it. You take this tiny thing and you make something new with it. With a seed, you can change the world. You can change everything."

Bree used to call me *Grandma Corey* when I talked about gardening, and I know what Ali thinks. I guess, like any hobby, it *is* pretty boring to hear about if you're not into it. But I was always excited for Ali when his hockey team was winning. I was happy because he was happy. And I went along with every scheme Bree ever had. It wouldn't have killed them to be nicer to me about my stuff. Like Alecto is. Maybe it's the novelty, but despite how she reacted when she first saw the seeds, she soon gets pretty into it.

"Tell me how they grow," Alecto says, holding a seed in her cupped hand and examining it. "Tell me how that happens."

I sigh. "I wish I could show you. It would be easier than trying to explain."

Alecto looks to the entrance of Erebus, then her black eyes narrow, sly and secretive. I watch, confused, as she begins scratching out a hole in the rock using the side of her talon, right there in my alcove. When the hole is around an inch deep, she scoops up a small black seed and gently tips it in, looking at me as if to make sure she's got it right. I nod, chewing my lip as I understand what she's doing.

"You do it too," she says, scooping out more rock, making more holes.

So I do, and we take it in turns to set up a little row.

When each hole has a seed, Alecto crushes more rock and covers them, then pours a little of my drinking water over them.

It breaks my heart. The seeds will never grow, because there's no sunlight here to wake them and no nutrients in the stone to nourish them. You can get a seed to sprout just by sticking it in a damp paper towel on a windowsill, you don't even need soil, but without some way to get nutrients to it, it won't ever become more than a sprout. It won't survive.

"Show me," she says, her expression determined.

"I can't. They won't grow," I say.

"Why not?"

"They need water and light to make food, so they can grow. Nutrients, from soil."

"You have light." She nods to the candles and matches. "And water. You do it all the time, you said, in your garden. You make them live. Try," she insists, taking my hands and placing them over one of the holes, keeping her own on top of mine. "Corey, try."

She always does stuff like that, reaches for me, touches me, strokes my hair as she passes, leans against me while we chat. At the end of every day she and her sisters groom each other, the routine so fixed, so essential to them. It makes my heart ache, and then that makes me angry because you shouldn't miss someone who hurt you. You shouldn't worry about whether they are sitting with someone on the other side of the mountain, or if they're alone in the empty vastness. You shouldn't wonder if they're thinking about you.

When Alecto places my hands over the hole, I let her, wondering what kind of seed it is—a herb, I think, maybe lavender or basil. I wonder if it will ever have a chance to grow, or will it stay here, dormant in the Underworld forever. And if it ends up back in the living world, will it still be able to grow after being here? *Will I?*

I shake my head. "It won't work."

"What won't work?" Both Alecto and I jump as Megaera lands beside us, Tisiphone a blink behind her, the sack containing my dinner in her hand. Neither of us had heard them return.

Megaera stills when she sees us, Alecto's hands still over mine. "What are you doing?"

"I'm just showing Alecto my seeds."

Megaera gives Alecto a vicious look and she flinches, releasing me.

"What seeds?" Megaera's jet gaze lands on me and I falter too. "Where did you get them?" she says, and though her voice is icily calm her snakes are coiled to strike.

"They were in my coat when I got here," I say. I don't understand what's wrong.

"Did you plant them?" she says.

I nod. I feel like I've done something wrong, but I don't know what. They're just seeds.

"You know they won't grow here," she says, and I nod again.

"I know. It was just a demonstration."

She looks at Alecto again and something dark passes between them.

"Eat," Megaera says, handing me the sack of food, and I do,

even though my stomach is knotted and tight, finishing it all under her watchful gaze.

That night when they groom each other, I see Alecto wincing under Megaera's hands, but she doesn't cry out or protest, just takes the punishment as stoically as any of the shades.

For once, I don't fall asleep first, too tense, my skin tight with the feeling that I need to be careful, that something is coming. Megaera returns to her nook, and Tisiphone to hers, but Alecto stays with me, and when I curl up in my blankets she lies down beside me so we're face to face. From this angle she looks human; her feathers could be hair.

Bree and I used to sleep like this, the two of us in my single bed. We'd start out back to back, then one of us would say something, usually something stupid or gross, and turn over and then the other would too and it would be carnage.

Listen. Would you rather kiss Thom Crofter with tongue or watch your dad take a shower?

Oh my gods, Bree, what is wrong with you?

I'd rather watch your dad.

Shut the fuck up, right now.

What? Your dad's hot. All-the-Way Allaway, that's what I call him.

I swear to Zeus I will slap you.

Can't believe you don't want me as your stepmum.

You are so sick. I can't even look at you right now.

It's dark, you can't see me anyway.

Your disgustingness glows in the dark.

You do.

I miss my bed. I miss my dad, and Merry, and the cottage. I miss my garden.

"Will you go to Hades again?" I whisper. "Tell him I'm sorry I was rude to him. That I'm sorry for everything."

"Don't worry," Alecto says, soft as a breeze. "It'll be all right in the morning. It will all be forgotten."

I'm not sure I believe that. I move my hand, holding it palm-up between us. Alecto looks at it curiously, then takes it.

Why was she so angry? I mouth at her, mindful that the other Furies are close by and there is no background noise in Erebus.

Alecto looks at me and shakes her head, just a little. I don't know if it means *I don't know* or *Not here, not now.*

Before I can speak, though, she does, pressing her mouth against my ear and whispering, "What would it be? If it grew?"

A miracle. Because nothing grows here. Nothing can thrive here.

EROSION

THE NEXT MORNING THE ATMOSPHERE IS AS BRITTLE and thin as sugar glass, and I know Alecto was wrong; things aren't all right at all.

It's Megaera who brings my breakfast, and she's all bright smiles as she hands it over, her snakes coiling amiably, languid-eyed and slow-tongued. She presents each dish to me like it's the first time I've seen it, even though it's just the usual fruit and flatbread. Her performance reminds me of Bree's mom after she and Bree fought; acting like everything was fine and weaponizing her attention and care. *Ah, Corey, I'm so glad you're here. Can I get you some juice? What about cake? I made it for Bree, but she's done with chocolate, apparently.* I never needed Bree to tell me they'd been fighting; it couldn't have been clearer.

"Eat up." Megaera's grin is all fangs.

I eat up.

After I've been to my bathroom for what Merry calls "a lick

and a promise," I wait for Alecto, who is still in her alcove, whispering with Megaera and Tisiphone, and again I have that weird sense that something is coming. They stop talking when they realize I'm there, and Alecto flies down, scooping me up on one wing and tearing out of Erebus.

"Is everything all right?" I ask her when we're clear of the mountains.

"Of course," she says, but she says it like it isn't, the way I said I was fine when Astrid or Merry asked.

I check to see the other Furies aren't within earshot when I ask her again why Megaera was so angry about the seeds. The only reason I can think of is the same reason Australian customs goes nuts if you try to take an apple off the plane: they're scared of invasive species devastating the ecosystem. But there is no ecosystem in the Underworld, there's nothing to kill, or dominate. There's nothing at all.

Alecto hesitates for a long time before speaking. "You have to understand, before this place was *his*, it was ours. We were here eons before even the Titans he and his siblings threw down. We came into existence when this *was* Tartarus—being and land as one and the same. There was nowhere we couldn't go before the Olympians carved the world into three. To the victors the spoils. Our home. Our world."

"I'm sorry," I say, then feel stupid because it's not enough.

Alecto inclines her head and sweeps low over the Acheron, and I look down to see our reflection in the murky water.

"When it was Tartarus, we moved with and through Gaia and Pontus and Nyx and Uranus. Then the Titans were born, and they took solid form, and their offspring did the same. After that—*because* of that—what we knew and could be was smaller and smaller, until it was this. Until we were us, bound to a form and a purpose and trapped in the land of the dead that was built on our bones."

"You weren't always the Furies?" I try to imagine them as she describes them, nebulous and changing, but they're so fixed in my mind as they are now—snakes, copper scales, and feathers—that I can't do it.

Alecto shakes her head. "We existed long before there were humans to punish. We are what we are now because the Olympians created humans. Our bodies were fixed with two arms and two legs, our home was remade to house their dead, and we were repurposed to right their wrongs. We once were masters and now are servants. So you see, it's best not to mention seeds again. Or anything from your world. It reminds Megaera of why we are as we are. How we lost what we lost. My sister will not be happy until there is justice."

Justice again. "Why does she like me if she hates things from my world?"

"You are different."

"What does that mean?"

She simply smiles and flies so fast that I can't draw breath to ask anything else.

We're the first to arrive at the Prytaneum for once, and I move to Alecto's left as she takes her place. Seconds later, Tisiphone and Megaera arrive and, without any fanfare, the punishments begin.

I watch Megaera out of the corner of my eye. I wouldn't have guessed she hated humans, or the human world, rather. She doesn't seem to take any pleasure in the punishments, and she's never been anything but kind to me, yesterday excepting, but even then, it was Alecto she was mad at more than me. She helped the others make my bathroom, gets my food. She's done so much to make me feel like I'm one of them. It's possible she's only nice to me to spite Hades; enemy of my enemy and so on. Still, I can get on board with that.

"Corey?"

I snap out of my thoughts and realize Megaera is talking to me. "Yes?"

"Come here," she says.

Something uncurls inside me as I approach her and stop in front of her mound.

"Come," she says, and I hesitate, wondering if she means I should get on the mound, until I realize she's not talking to me.

I turn to see a shade—young, male—walking toward us. He doesn't look much older than me, maybe nineteen or twenty. He's different from the other shades I've seen before. More vital, somehow. Not as faded. He's new, I realize. Only just arrived in the Underworld. My heart goes out to him, poor kid.

My sympathy doesn't last, though.

"Tell us why you're here," Alecto asks him.

Without any hesitation, he recites, "I stole from my parents. I took the money saved for their retirement. Now they have nothing and my father is sick. They can't afford the treatment he needs."

He says it all so easily, he could be talking about what he did on a holiday or on the weekend, and I stare at him, disgusted. What an asshole.

"How should he pay?" Megaera asks. She's talking to me now. "What is a suitable punishment for a feckless boy who stole from his parents and left them penniless in their greatest hour of need?"

I shake my head; I have no idea.

"Should we steal from him as he stole from those who gave him life?" Megaera continues. "An eye for an eye?"

"Well . . . Is he sorry?" I ask. "Does he have a reason for it?"

"It's too late for that." Tisiphone speaks—a rare occurrence. "He's here to be punished."

"But if he regrets it—" I begin, but Megaera cuts me off.

"The punishment is decided. The boy will bear witness to his father's suffering." An ornate mirror appears in her hands.

I don't understand. If the boy was still in the mortal realm, he'd go to prison if his parents told on him, but he'd get a trial first. What he's done is heinous and he should have to pay for it. But it's possible he had a reason for stealing the money. Someone might have been blackmailing him, or he might have been scammed. I look at the boy, trying to read innocence or guilt in his face, but his expression is blank.

Megaera holds the mirror out to me and nods to the boy. I feel uncomfortable as I take the mirror from her to him. He accepts it without protest.

When he peers into it, his mouth and jaw tightening, I look at Megaera.

"Well done," she says, smiling triumphantly, the awkwardness of last night all gone.

I watch the boy watching the mirror frown as the first cracks break his careful expression.

This isn't justice, I think. Justice would let him defend himself, let him offer an explanation if he has one. This is just hearing the crime and skipping straight to the punishment.

I remember the Oracle's cards. Myself, my path, my potential. Me, alone and sad, three dancing women, and then Justice. But this can't be it.

When the boy leaves, paler than when he arrived, Alecto urges me back to her side where I stay while the rest of the punished are called. Megaera doesn't call on me again, and I'm both disappointed and relieved.

"How long are they punished for?" I ask Alecto on the flight back.

"When they have paid, they no longer have to come to us."

"How long is that, usually?" I try.

"Until it is just."

"But what if the boy's father dies before it's just?" I ask.

"His punishment will continue. He will still see his father suffering, even if his father has joined the ranks of the dead. He will see it until it is just."

I don't understand. *I don't need to,* I remind myself. This isn't my world.

When we get back to Erebus, Alecto puts me down in my nook and I pause, because I can feel that something is different. But it's not until I sit down with my lunch that I see the gouges in the rock where we'd planted the seeds, the grit and stone scooped out, the holes left bare to make it clear they're empty. And when some instinct tells me to look, I search for the narcissus that brought me here, and find it's missing. So is my oilskin. My last piece of home. The loss of it brings me to my knees.

"She didn't have to do this," I say to Alecto, who watches me search with a sad expression that tells me she either knew Megaera had done this or at least expected it. "She didn't have to take my coat."

The Fury looks at me with wide black eyes.

"Will you go to Hades again?" I say. "Ask him if he'll take me home?"

She's still for a long time, then nods. "When the others are back, I'll go to him."

He says no.

I shrug, smile, decide to wait a few days, then ask Alecto to take me to him. I'll ask him myself. I'll get on my knees and beg if that's what he needs from me.

THE NEXT DAY, AT THE PRYTANEUM, MY MIND keeps wandering. As we flew over Hades's palace, I thought I saw him for a split second, standing in the doorway, looking up at the sky as if he expected us. But when I'd twisted in Alecto's arms, the doors were closed, the palace as desolate and still as ever. I find myself wondering what he does all day. Does he sit in the dark rooms of his fortress, brooding? Does he go to the Elysian Fields and spend time with all the heroes and celebrities?

Does he look at calendars of all the mortal festivals and decide which ones to go to?

He's the god we never speak of, never study, never pray to. Back when Bree and I had done our project on Artemis, this other kid, Eric, had chosen Hades. When our teacher found out, his parents had been called to the school and he had to start the project again, on Ares instead. Eric left, I remember, before we started high school. His family moved to the mainland.

"Corey," Alecto says in a low voice. "Another new one." She nods at a middle-aged woman making her way reluctantly toward us.

When the woman turns to look behind her, I follow her gaze.

To where Bree is standing in the archway, her mouth an O of shock.

ABSCISSION

I FREEZE, STARING RIGHT BACK AT HER.

This happened on the Island. Obviously, I knew she lived there and I knew it was possible—likely, even—that I'd bump into her if I left the house. But it was still a shock, every single time. It always hit me in the chest when I turned a corner and there she was.

Here she is.

Before I can say or do anything, she turns and runs, leaving me still locked in place, gaping at the place she used to be.

That's what she did on the Island too. Unless she was with Ali, whenever she saw me she'd turn and run.

I am halfway to the arch when Megaera lands before me, wings spread, her snakes hissing.

"Who is that?" she says, her black eyes narrowed as she looks between me and where Bree stood.

I can't speak, my tongue refusing to move, because I can't

quite believe it, can't get my head around the fact that was Bree, *she was right here.* Alecto lands beside us and answers for me.

"That's her, isn't it? The girl you told me about."

I manage to nod, then try to step past Megaera, but she blocks me.

"Where are you going?" she asks.

"I have to . . ." I find my voice, then stop, because I'm not going to be able to catch up with Bree if I waste time explaining myself. I try again to move past Megaera and her snakes hiss a warning.

"We have work to do," she says.

"I'm not a Fury," I say.

Megaera's eyes flash and panic races through me, but Alecto takes my arm, drawing me away, back to the mounds.

"Corey, please," she says.

"I need to go after her," I reply, but the urge to follow has gone and I don't know what to do, or what to think. I knew she was here—gods, of course I did—but I realize I'd stopped expecting to actually see her. I'd assumed this place was too vast, too crowded for it to happen. Does she know she's here because of me? Does she hate me for it?

I hope so. Because I hate her.

I stare at the archway, willing her to come back so I can tell her so.

Alecto bumps against me, in comfort, I think. "Let us finish here. We'll talk in Erebus."

I nod, ready to go along with it, at least until we draw level with the shade Bree had come with.

"Do you know her?" I stop, ignoring Alecto pulling at me and ask the shade, "That girl. Bree Dovemuir. Are you friends with her?"

The shade is silent, clearly terrified as she looks in horror at my and Alecto's linked arms. And when Megaera joins us, the shade's eyes stretch so wide I can see a ring of white around the iris. I'd forgotten how frightening the Furies look when you first see them.

"Leave," Megaera says to the shade. "Go."

I watch the shade hurry away, my eyes trained on the archway.

"Why did you do that?" I ask Megaera, . "I just wanted to know if she knew Bree."

"I told you not to talk to them unless I said you could. We have work to do," she repeats, then stalks to her mound and takes her place. "Alecto, now," she commands, and I feel a vicious bolt of dislike for her.

From the look on her face, she isn't feeling all that fond of me at the moment, either.

It's for Alecto's sake that I keep my mouth shut and let her lead me. She keeps my arm tucked in hers, pinning me at her side. I'm half on the mound, which isn't big enough for us both, while the rest of the guilty approach and accept their punishments. I stay silent as the dead come and go, my eyes locked on the arch. My heart is vibrating in my chest as I watch and wait, trying to decide what to say if Bree does come back.

I'm sorry.

I'm not sorry.

It was an accident.

You deserved it.

I wish I could take it back.

I'd do it again if I had the chance.

I love you.

I hate you.

I always will.

But she doesn't return. And I know Bree well enough to know that if she wants to avoid me, she'll be as far away from here as she can get. And maybe that's for the best. It's not like I came here to rescue her, and I have no idea what I'd say to her nor why I'd even want to. She's not my problem anymore.

When it's finally over and Alecto releases my arm, I turn to her, ready to be taken back to Erebus for lunch, but it's Tisiphone who scoops me up. I didn't even know she was behind me.

"What's going on?" I ask, twisting in Tisiphone's arms to look at Alecto.

When she keeps her eyes on the ground, refusing to look at me, alarm fizzes in my veins.

"It's time you learned all of what we do," Megaera says. "So you understand why we cannot afford for you to break the rules."

"What does that mean? Isn't this it?" I nod at the Prytaneum. "This is what you do."

"This is the least of what we do."

Tisiphone springs into the air, making my stomach swoop, and soon we are flying out, away from the Prytaneum and the palace, toward a stretch of the Underworld I haven't seen before.

The Phlegethon glows crimson on the horizon, and every hair on my body stands on end.

"Where are we going?"

Tisiphone inhales, and I think she's about to answer, but then Megaera and Alecto join us, flanking us. I turn to look at them, to gauge how much trouble I'm in, and what I see makes my heart stop.

They are monsters.

Their lips are pulled back over their needle teeth, mouths open wide—wider than should be possible—to expose dark, cavernous insides; black eyes alight with violence. Megaera's snakes are reared to strike, their fangs elongated. Alecto's plumage has risen, making her look twice her usual size, a giant in the skies.

But it's their hands that frighten me most. Their left hands are curled like claws, talons extended. And in their right, they each hold a cruel-looking whip, dozens of brass-spiked lashes splaying out from the center. My insides turn to liquid with pure, animal fear at the sight of the whips, because they could only have been designed to hurt. To flay.

Then Megaera turns to me, her mouth yawning, big enough to swallow me whole, and I scream.

"Now you will see what we do," she says.

Alecto calls out a name and a short distance away a group of shades begin struggling with each other.

"He's here!" one of them calls, finally shoving the shade of a middle-aged man away from him, the others immediately closing ranks. "That's him."

171

"He's lying!" The accused shade turns wild, wide eyes on the Furies, hands held out in supplication. "I'm innocent."

"You lie!" Tisiphone roars, the sound like thunder inside her chest breaking against my ear, and I whimper, but she pays no attention. "You lie and you deny us our divine right to exact justice."

"You should have come to the Prytaneum," Alecto says in the harsh croak of a rook, a sound I would never have imagined she'd make. "It was a mistake to make us come to you."

And now I know what Megaera and Tisiphone do while Alecto and I wait in Erebus, and what happens to those who try to avoid the Furies and their punishments.

Alecto and Megaera dive. The shade tries to run back to the safety of the others, who're backing away, trying to get clear.

Because it's too late.

I hear the squeal of lethal whips cutting the air and then my scream is joined by the desperate shrieks of the shade. I close my eyes, I can't watch, though I have no way to stop listening as he wails and begs for mercy, his voice a broken burble of words. Tears began to leak from my eyes and I feel sick, my insides churning; what could he have done to deserve this? Surely no one deserves this?

As though in answer, Alecto begins to intone a list of charges against him: *broken marriage vows, raised a hand to his wife, raised a hand to his mistress, forced her to terminate her pregnancy, lied about his wife during their divorce, lied about his income so he wouldn't have to support her.*

He sounds like a piece of shit.

But I still can't quite reconcile that with what they are doing to him.

It's the absence of the sound of snapping whips that makes me realize they've stopped. I crack open an eye to find we're rising, flying away. In Tisiphone's arms I turn to see the shade still facedown in the dirt. The ones he was trying to hide among are drifting away from him, some watching us leave with clear relief that the ordeal is over.

The fallen shade doesn't rise.

"You did better than I thought," Tisiphone says, her breath tickling my neck. She sounds *pleased*.

I retch.

"The next one will be easier."

No. "Take me back," I say. "I want to go back to Erebus."

"When we are done. You have to know, Corey. You have to learn."

No. I can't watch more. I can't witness more.

Ahead of us, Megaera and Alecto have stopped and once again a group of shades below cower.

"Please, I can't," I beg as Megaera calls a name.

Below us a shade wails, high and bestial, and those nearby flee.

I catch a glimpse of a young woman, not much older than me. Her hair is the same color as Bree's, long and wavy, like Bree's used to be. I turn away as Alecto and Megaera head for her, whip hands raised.

This time Megaera reads the charges: *jealous of her friend's relationship, attempting to break them up, lying, stealing.* The sound the shade makes as they thrash her pierces me, I can't bear it, my fists clenched so tight my nails cut my palms. She looks like Bree; what she's done is like what Bree did. And the Furies saw Bree, she was right there. . . .

I won't open my eyes again. Hearing it is bad enough; I don't want to see it too. Instead, I try to tune it out, the names, the crimes, the screams. On and on it goes, the Furies taking turns to serve the lashes or indict the guilty, until it all becomes one violent, never-ending howl in my head, turning me inside out.

"COREY?" A MALE VOICE. "CAN YOU HEAR ME?"

I blink, and the world comes into focus.

I'm back in Erebus, atop my blankets. A man—no, Hermes—is looking at me with shadowed hazel eyes. I haven't seen him since I arrived on the beach, however many weeks or months ago that was. His skin looks like moonlight in the glare from the candle in the alcove. Someone has lit it.

"Hello," he says. "Welcome back."

I frown at him, trying to remember how I got here, but nothing comes to me, only what I'd seen, what I'd tried to turn away from. My stomach lurches and I heave.

Behind him, the Furies move toward me, reaching out, ever eager to touch. They look like themselves again, beautiful and serene, but I flinch from them, bile rising.

Hermes gives me an assessing look, then turns to the Furies. "Perhaps if I have some time alone with her, to explain?"

I can't see his expression, but whatever it contains makes

them consult each other silently, darting their eyes toward me then back to each other.

Megaera looks at him. "No tricks, Messenger."

"On my honor."

"We'll return."

I shiver under the weight of her words, and Alecto slips me a small, sad smile, but I just stare at her until Megaera takes her by the hand, urging her away. I watch the three of them fly out of Erebus, leaving me alone with Hermes.

"I'd ask if you're all right, but if you were then I wouldn't be here," Hermes says, his voice easy and bright. "You scared them."

I look at him, upper lip curled with disgust. *Me*, scared *them*?

"I could have told them you weren't ready," he continues, as casual as if we were sitting side by side at a bus stop and he was commenting on the weather or a sports score. "But that would require someone to actually talk to me about what's going on." He looks at me from the corner of his eye.

"What happened to me?" I ask, the words scratching my throat. My voice sounds gravelly, a twenty-a-day habit with a petrol edge to it.

"You fainted."

"How long was I out?"

He gives me a look. "A while."

"How long is a while?"

"Trust me, you're better not knowing right now. You have enough to deal with."

I don't like the sound of that. "Why are you here?"

"The options were limited and I'm guessing I was preferable to the alternative," he says.

"Taking me home?" I say.

"Taking you to the one whose realm you're in."

Hades.

"Why—" I halt. There are a lot of ways I want to end that question, and at the same time I don't think I want the answers.

Hermes gives a sad smile. "I am sorry this is happening."

"If you'd helped me on the beach, it wouldn't be. I'd be safe, at home, in my world. In fact, if you'd left me alone the first time we met—"

"I didn't know who you were, then. I thought you were simply a mortal who'd seen something they shouldn't have. I was just doing as I was told. This isn't my realm. I can't interfere with things here. Not without causing a lot of problems. You know what I am, don't you?"

"A god?" I say it with as much disdain as I can.

"Yes." He laughs. "But I'm also a psychopomp." He looks me in the eye. "I'm one of the very few beings who can move between the land of the living and that of the dead at will. It's a very privileged position, and one I am not willing to forfeit. Someday you'll understand why."

I strongly doubt it.

"Why do they do that? Whip them, I mean," I ask after silence has stretched thin between us.

Hermes exhales slowly. "They're bound to scourge the shades that don't go to the Prytaneum to accept their punishment. They're fair game if they try to avoid it."

I shudder. *Fair game.* "No one deserves to be tortured. It's inhumane."

"*We're* inhumane," Hermes says. "By definition. And it doesn't hurt them. Not physically. They don't have bodies, Corey. They feel no real pain."

"Well, I suppose that makes it all right," I say.

Then I start crying.

I bow my head to my knees and wrap my arms around them. A strong arm comes around me and I'm gathered into a chest that could belong to a statue if it wasn't for the immense warmth of his skin.

He doesn't rub my back annoyingly, or tell me to *hush, there there* or that *it will be OK*, which I appreciate because it definitely won't be OK. He just holds me while I cry, salt water flowing from me like I'm the Cocytus. I imagine my tears pouring down my face, making their own river of sadness and flooding Erebus, until I have nothing but dry sobs and gasps left.

"Corey?" Hermes says, an edge to his voice.

I shake my head, not ready to unwind myself and face the mess I'm in yet.

"Corey?" he says more urgently, nudging me. "What's that?"

I peer up at him, embarrassed, but he's looking away, at a corner of my alcove, and I follow his gaze, my jaw dropping when I see what he's staring at.

From the stone floor, a small green shoot with two tiny leaves is growing.

COTYLEDON

I CRAWL OVER TO THE SHOOT, MY TEARS— everything—forgotten.

The first seed I ever grew was a tomato plant. I don't really remember it, I was six, but my dad likes to tell the story every year when I harvest the first of the tomatoes. It's kind of a tradition; we eat my tomatoes, and bread Merry makes, and mozzarella my dad imports, and he tells the story of how the seeds were in with a bunch of them my mom left behind. They were old, too old to be viable really, but I wouldn't be told. I planted them, and against all odds they grew into the sweetest tomatoes he'd ever tasted.

Seeds want to grow. They won't, unless the conditions are right, but like all living things they want to be alive and will fight for the chance if they get it.

"Corey, what is it?" Hermes asks again.

It's one of the seeds I planted with Alecto, the ones that had made me feel shitty for going through the charade of sowing, because I'd known—*I'd known*—they'd never sprout. They'd just sit under the piles of stone dust we'd heaped over them, forever, because there is no sunlight here. There is no soil. And Megaera dug them all up. There is no possible way the plant can be here.

And yet it is.

I look at Hermes, trying to figure out if he's done it in some weird attempt to cheer me up, but he is looking between the sprout and me, his face a mask of shock.

"You did this," he says, and all I can do is shake my head because this isn't possible. It just isn't. Every hair on my body is standing on end.

Hermes moves to my side, on his hands and knees, staring at the green sprout. It's so bright, so *vivid*. It hurts my eyes to look at it. I've forgotten green, I realize. Forgotten how beautiful it was. I haven't had a favorite color since I was ten, but if I did, it would be green.

I reach out and stroke the shoot. It's so delicate. So fragile. My fingers tingle as I brush the tiny leaves. Seed leaves. *Cotyledons*. That's their proper name. They come in first, before the true leaves, the first sign that germination has happened, that it's started.

It's a miracle. A real, true miracle.

Then I remember Megaera's face when we told her we'd planted my seeds. The rage writ across her features, her fingers curled, eyes blazing. Alecto's silent suffering when Megaera had tended to her that night, *punished* her. All because of my seeds. She won't think this is a miracle. She won't like it at all.

Before I can change my mind, I crush the tiny thing under my thumb.

"Corey, no!" Hermes says, but he's too late.

I feel sick for killing it, but I swallow the guilt. It was for the best. Too much has gone wrong already. And it won't happen again. It can't; I don't have any more seeds. I dig in the hole for the roots and crush them too, grinding them under the stone, my stomach aching as I do it. There. No one has to know.

"Things don't grow here," I say to Hermes, who's staring at me, mouth open.

"Apparently, they do now," he says. "For you, anyway."

I shake my head, fixing him with sharp eyes. "I didn't do anything," I say firmly.

"Corey—"

"It's nothing."

"It's not—"

"It is," I insist. "There were a bunch of seeds in the pocket of the coat I was wearing when I got here. It must have sprouted in there and fallen out."

It hadn't been sprouting then. It had been a tiny, brown sleeping thing, no bigger than the head of a pin. Smaller than some of the flakes of rock that we'd put over it.

"And it grew."

Blood pools in my cheeks, the heat searing. "It didn't grow.

180

How could it grow? There's no sunlight, there's no rain, no soil. I told you, it must have started in my pocket."

"Do you keep sun, rain and soil in there?" Hermes asks.

"Of course not." I bite off the words. He stares down at my hand and I rub the green away. "It would have died anyway."

"Would it?" he asks, his eyes bright on me. Then he turns to the entrance and makes an impatient sound. "I hear them coming back."

"Hermes, don't tell them. Promise me." I feel like I did before the lightning strike, that terrible, charged moment when the air changed and I knew something was about to go wrong. When I inhale, I half expect to smell ozone. "Please," I beg. "Please don't tell them. Please, Hermes. You said you can't interfere with anything, so please, please just leave this alone."

He gives me a long, inscrutable glance and then sighs. "All right."

"Thank you." I stand and kick the floor smooth, tidying up the dust that moved when I pulled the sprout free.

Seconds later, the Furies arrive.

Alecto is carrying a sack, which I guess from the size and shape holds food and water for me. But as she shifts its weight I remember the scourge in her hand, the flick of her wrist as she brought it down. I can't look her in the eye as she holds the bag out to me.

"Thanks," I say, my voice stiff, my fingers trembling as I take it.

The atmosphere is thick enough to choke us all.

"Mind if I join you, ladies?" Hermes asks, his voice loud with false cheer. "I'm in no rush to go back to my duties. Or my pleasures, for that matter. What could possibly compare to your company?"

"Corey may decide," Megaera says. I glance at her to see her watching me with a fixed expression I can't interpret. "If she wants you here, you can stay."

It feels like a test, but I don't want to be alone with them. I shrug. "Stay if you like, I don't mind either way."

"Charming."

The Furies keep back, watching me keenly as I sit on the floor and open the sack, and I hesitate, struck by the irrational fear I'll open it and find Bree's head inside, staring back at me.

I don't, obviously. They've brought the same bread, oil, grapes, olives and figs as usual, but there are other dishes too. White beans and fennel in a herby, garlicky sauce, a flaking pastry with spinach exploding from it. Fat, rum-soaked raisins, candied nuts, another pomegranate.

I look up at the Furies and they smile, three matching sets of sharp teeth in half-moon crescents. And I realize the new food is an apology. This is their way of trying to make up for what happened. An unexpected jolt of pleasure rushes through me at the idea that these women—these monsters, these goddesses—feel they had to make it up to me. But I don't let it show on my face. They're not getting away with it that easily.

"Help yourself," I say to Hermes when he sits opposite me.

The Furies look at him sharply, as if daring him to. Pretending not to notice, and curious to see if they'll stop me, or him,

I hold out a fig. He takes it with a flourish that suggests he's noticed their behavior too, splits it deftly in two and eats it. The Furies don't say or do anything, and I feel another thrill of satisfaction. They must really want to make me happy.

Their expressions darken every time Hermes takes something, even a grape, even a single raisin, but they hold their peace, and between the two of us we polish the meal off.

"I didn't know you ate mortal food," I say to Hermes as I wipe the last of my bread around the olive dish, soaking up the dregs of the peppery oil. "I thought it was ambrosia for the gods."

He raises his brows. "It's both," he says after a moment. "Either. And it seems the Receiver keeps a fine table."

You wouldn't have thought so, from his palace. I try to picture Hades at the Thesmophoria, a burger in his hand, but the image shifts and I see him lit by the fire, smiling down at me. "Do you eat with him often?"

Hermes barks a laugh. "I've never been invited for dinner. He prefers to keep things professional between us." Again I see that hint of bitterness, just at the corner of his eyes.

The Furies begin to stir, glaring at Hermes, reminding me of Bree's mum, yawning and sighing as soon as it turned nine o'clock if I was still there. Fear kindles in my belly; I'm not ready to deal with them yet. I sneak a glance at my hands; there's no trace of the shoot.

"Do you see him a lot?" I ask Hermes.

"No more," Megaera says suddenly, her voice harsh. "It is time for us to retire. Leave, Messenger."

One of the bowls slips from my grasp, cracking on the

stones before splitting into three long, jagged pieces. The Three of Swords card flashes across my memory. At the same time, Alecto leaps across the alcove, as if to scoop me into her arms, and I hold up my hands, keeping her back.

Her feathers droop as she halts, her face falling. Before I can stop myself, I reach out and give her a swift pat on the arm, heart aching when she makes a soft, grateful sound and smiles at me.

When Hermes toes the largest shard carefully with a winged sandal, Megaera gives him a dark look and picks it up; for a second I think she'll stab him with it.

Instead, she crushes the glass to a fine powder and blows it over the edge of the rock to join the insect shells and fragments on the ground below. Then she turns back to Hermes.

"I'm leaving." He speaks before she can. "I won't outstay my welcome. Ladies, it's been a pleasure. Corey, I'll return soon."

"You will not," Megaera snaps.

Hermes shrugs lazily. "I might not have a choice. *He'll* want to know what happened. And if he's not happy with my report, he might come looking himself." He leaves the threat hanging in the air.

Megaera's face darkens. I bet she wishes she had stabbed him now. The Furies look at each other.

"Return then, if it pleases him," Megaera says, turning to the silver-skinned god. "But go now."

"Come." Alecto stalks toward me and gently hooks an arm through mine, drawing me away from Hermes, toward my nest of blankets. When I sit, I see Hermes has gone.

"We will soothe you," Alecto tells me.

Panic sprints through me and I stiffen. "No, I'm fine. Actually, I'm tired. I don't feel well."

"Be with us," Megaera says, her tone making it clear it's not a request.

I remember her face, her teeth, her talons. The scourge in her hand. The sounds it made.

I fold my shaking hands in my lap as Tisiphone and Megaera settle onto my bed. The snake-haired Fury sits in front of me, Tisiphone behind, and then their hands are on me.

Alecto kisses my temple and then begins combing through my hair, gently scratching my scalp in loose, lazy circles over and over. I have to admit it feels nice. Tingly. Little shivers of hot and cold travel up and down my neck, blossoming out over my shoulders as she works the knots carefully out of my hair. I've been finger-combing it daily, and I thought I'd done OK until I feel her talons catch time and again teasing the strands free and smoothing them down.

I stretch my legs and arch my feet in pleasure, my eyes flutter closed. They fly back open when Megaera takes my left foot in her hand and I watch as she kneads the sole and heel with firm, sure fingers, careful not to scratch me, then extends the massage along my ankle and calf, sending tremors of bliss through me. And just as I've got used to the twin pleasures of the head and foot massages, Tisiphone starts drawing on my back, one talon extended to cast shapes across my skin, whirling spirals and sweeping lines, pictures and words in a language I don't understand. They touch me differently from the way they touch each other, changing to accommodate my human body. To make me fit with them.

Megaera looks up at me and I smile at her through half-closed eyes.

"It will be better next time."

And I'm so lulled, so sedated by their hands, that I catch myself nodding along before the words make sense.

"What? No!" I say, pulling my legs away from her and shifting out of Tisiphone's reach. Megaera's snakes are startled by the sudden movement and rear up, opening their mouths and spitting. Alecto's talons get caught in my hair, and I yelp, wrenching myself free, leaving blond hairs tangled in her fingers.

"No?" Megaera asks.

"There won't be a next time," I say, scrambling to my feet and staring down at them. "I can't do that again. You can't take me to do that anymore."

"But how will you learn?" Tisiphone asks.

Learn. "Why would I need to learn?"

"For when you join us."

The Furies rise, forming a wall of nightmares.

"What do you mean?"

"It's why you came here," Alecto says. "We felt your power. It called to us."

"I didn't come here; it was an accident. And I don't have any power," I say, taking a step back.

"You do." Megaera looks at me as if she can see inside me. "Great power." She says a word in a language I don't understand.

"What does that mean?" I ask, my voice cracking.

"It's what brought you here. It's what you are. Like calls to like, *Bringer of Death*."

That's what the Oracle said. I shake my head. "No."

I'm a gardener. I give life. I grow. I don't destroy.

My thumb itches where I crushed the shoot.

"You are going to make things right for us," Alecto says. "Justice."

"No," I say again.

"You're like us. One of us. It's why you're here."

Alecto takes a step toward me and I take one back, shaking my head from side to side. No, that's not what it was. That's not what this is.

"Corey, stop," she snaps in a way she's never spoken to me before, spooking me enough that I move even farther away.

I realize my mistake instantly, as my stomach drops away with the ground and there is nothing beneath me. I have a horrible flashback of the earth opening on Lynceus Hill and I know I am going to fall again, this time onto rock that will shatter me.

But before I can, Alecto has plucked me into her arms, wrapping them and her wings around me. I fight her for a moment and then give up, terrified and confused.

The others join us, sandwiching me between scales and feathers and cold, leathery skin, stroking me and caressing me and even though right then I hate them a little bit, it feels nice and I know I'm safe.

"We need you," Megaera says so softly that I'm not sure I'm supposed to hear her. So softly I can pretend I didn't.

I turn in Alecto's embrace, and through a gap in the arms and bodies and wings I see the spot on the ground where the seed grew.

Great power, Megaera said. I think of how my fingers tingled when I touched the shoot.

None of the seeds from my pocket should have been viable. I don't even know what it was, and I have no idea how long it had been in there. Then there was the spell in the sea—not the sea, the Styx—and, as I pointed out to Hermes, the fact that seeds didn't grow without three fundamentals: good soil, sunlight and water.

Yet it had grown.

And I wonder, even as a warning sounds inside my head, if I could do it again.

I *want* to do it again.

NATIVE

I WAKE IN A TANGLE OF FURIES, OUR LIMBS, hair, snakes and wings all twined together. It's Tisiphone wriggling an arm out from beneath my neck that pulls me from sleep before I'm ready. She murmurs in my ear she'll get my breakfast, then kisses my forehead with cool lips.

"My sister," she says on a breath as she leaves.

And I remember everything: Bree, the hunt. Hermes, the shoot.

The Furies' belief that I'm one of them.

Fighting the feeling someone's walked over my grave, I unravel myself from the others, who're already awake and watching me with glinting, fond eyes. I paste a smile on my face, then struggle out of the blankets and grip a candle and a few matches in my teeth, before making my way down to the bathroom cavern.

When I return, marginally cleaner, slightly more awake and

infinitely more worried about what the day will hold, Tisiphone is back. To my relief, so is Hermes.

He sits cross-legged in Megaera's alcove, along with the three sisters, and from the way they all turn to look at me—Megaera with a scowl—I get the impression I've interrupted something. Again.

"Good morning," Hermes calls, sounding cheery. His hair is falling in perfect curls that frame his face, his white shift spotless, silver skin lustrous with health and vitality. It makes me acutely aware I've been wearing this shift for a lot longer than three days, and the only reason my hair isn't matted beyond rescue is the Furies' grooming last night. *Turning feral*, a voice in my head says. *Or Fury*, comes the dark reply.

"Hi," I say, too loud, trying to drown out the whispering inside me.

All four of them give me a puzzled look before returning to their muttering.

I watch them as I pick at my food, four immortal heads bent close together, talking too softly, too swiftly for me to hear anything, though my ears burn. And so does my thumb; a hot, itching feeling exactly where I squashed the shoot. I expect it to be red, blistered, when I look, but it seems fine. When I surreptitiously check the patch of stone where the shoot grew, that looks fine too.

I'll have to come up with a proper plan for next time. Maybe try in my bathroom, where the Furies don't go. And I need to think of some reason why I need my oilskin back; there are bound to be seeds caught in the seams of the pockets. I'll ask Alecto, I decide. I glance over to see her watching me, and we both smile quickly, then look away, like we caught each other doing something we shouldn't. I'll have to get her alone. Maybe later, when we're back from—

I stop. I don't know if they're going to take me with them while they work. I don't know if they're going to make me watch the scourging again. I push the food away, nauseous. I can't do it again. I can't.

The Furies fly to me as I pack up my dishes, and my heart starts to beat hard and fast behind my ribs.

"You haven't finished," Alecto says.

"I'm not hungry," I say.

Megaera looks at me. "We must attend to our duties," she says, and my stomach swoops. "But you will remain here today. Hermes is to stay with you, so you will not be alone. There will be time for us. Lots of it. And he has been warned," she adds ominously.

We both turn to where the god stands with a beatific smile. I'm so relieved I feel dizzy.

Alecto steps forward and runs a cold, gentle finger down my cheek, then she leans in and kisses it.

"We'll bring you more delicious food when we return," she says. "And tales of our glories to inspire you. I will miss you," she adds quietly. "Sweet, soft sister."

The three Furies give me warm looks, then leap from the alcove and fly away, leaving me and Hermes alone. He walks on thin air, over to me.

"You didn't tell them, then."

"I promised," he says.

"What did Megaera mean, when she said that you've been warned?" I ask.

A funny look passes over his face. "Simply that if I try to take you out of the Underworld, their retribution will be both swift and relentless." He pauses, running his tongue across his teeth. His eyes focus on some point behind me as he says, "Apparently, they've never tested their scourges on god flesh before, but they're eager to know what the result is. And while I'm not their preferred victim, if I cross them, they'll see my ichor water the Asphodel Meadows."

I blink at him, shaken. "Wow."

"Indeed." He looks back at me. "Paints quite the vivid and detailed picture."

We both fall silent, and I try not to imagine it.

Then something else dawns on me. "Did Hades tell them not to take me out again?"

A wicked smile spreads across his perfect face. "Why don't you ask him?" Hermes nods behind me.

I turn, and my entire body bursts into flames.

Hades stands behind me, perfectly upright, perfectly still, his hands and his shadows held close to his sides. One eyebrow is raised, but then his face smooths back to that benign, front-of-house expression he seems so fond of. He's in mortal clothes again: black trousers, a black shirt buttoned all the way to the top, shoes, hair swept back from his now-impassive face. Next to Hermes he looks even less like a god; he could be some mainland city boy dressed for a night out with his friends.

I'm mortified, even more aware that my shift is filthy. That I'm filthy. I wish the earth would open and swallow me.

He speaks before I can.

"What happened?" Hades's voice is sharp. "Your arm."

His attention is fixed on the scars the lightning strike left. The marks have faded from red through pink to silver. I've gotten used to them.

"Oh—they're old," I say, tracing the lines. They're patterned like the roots and branches of trees. I kind of like them actually, for that reason.

He looks troubled. "Do they hurt?"

"No. Not anymore." I look down at my arm again. "Like I said, they're old. Remember the day with the lightning? When I was on the hill?"

His throat bobs, and he nods.

"It happened then," I say.

Hades frowns so deeply that his thick brows almost meet, but when he speaks again, his polite-stranger voice has returned. "How are you otherwise?"

Fine. Two can play this game. "I'm very well, thank you," I say with a small, impersonal smile. "Really, just splendid. And you? Are you well?"

His mouth twitches, like he knows what I'm doing. "I'm well. And glad you are too."

"Good. Great."

I feel another blush blooming and look back at Hermes, who's literally glowing with amusement, his skin emitting a soft, silvery light while he grins so broadly that his dimples are ravines.

"Do the Furies know about this?" I ask him.

"They do not." It's Hades who answers but I don't turn, far

too conscious of my flushed face. "All being well, this will be a singular occasion and there will be no need for them to know I was here."

"Why are you here?" I still can't look at him.

"Because of the shoot."

Betrayal burns through me. "You promised!" I glare at Hermes.

He holds up his hands, still grinning. "I promised not to tell the sisters, and I didn't. Besides, I didn't tell my uncle, either."

"This is my realm," Hades says. He sounds closer. "Nothing happens in it without my knowledge. Nothing," he repeats.

I turn and find he's directly behind me, less than an arm's length away. I avoid his eyes as I say, "I don't know how it happened."

"I want you to try again."

"I told you, I don't know how it happened," I protest, despite the fact this is exactly what I want too. I look at the ground. "I'm not even sure it was me."

"I'm sure enough for us both." His voice softens, but when I glance up, Hades's gaze is level. "Hermes will remain here while we're gone. Should the sisters return, he will alert me and I'll bring you back without them ever knowing you were away."

"No." I seize my chance. "I'll do this, at least I'll try, but only if you swear to take me home afterward. Please. I don't want to come back here, I need to go home. If you'll do that, today, if you'll promise, then I'll try my hardest."

"I . . ." He pauses, then nods. "I promise," he says. "Today. As soon as we're done." He hesitates, then holds out his hand.

By the time it dawns on me that he's not trying to hold my

hand, that he wants to shake on our deal, he's already lowering his, and I end up half yanking him toward me when I grab his fingers. Hermes doesn't bother to hide his laugh, and Hades and I give him twin scowls.

"All right." I release Hades and fight the urge to wipe my palm on my shift. "Let's go."

Hades pauses in the act of folding his arms, trying and failing to make it look like he was merely crooking his elbow for me. Hermes snorts, and when I look at him, he gives an exaggerated, lascivious wink.

"Have fun," he says.

Stomach churning, skin burning once more, I hook my arm through Hades's as loosely as I can. The world instantly turns inside out.

When it rights itself, I stumble into the god at my side and he reaches to steady me with his other hand, momentarily locking us in an awkward embrace, chest to chest.

I recoil before he can, slipping my arm out of his and stepping away, trying to get my bearings and my composure back.

Looking around, I see we're inside a sort of roofless enclosure, about the size of my garden back home, made from the Underworld's gray stone. There are no windows, but also no doors. No way in or out. My mouth dries.

"Is this some kind of prison?" I turn to him.

His hands are in his pockets, to keep me from molesting him again, I assume. "No."

"Then what is it? It looks like a prison. No windows. No doors."

He turns to one of the walls and as I watch a door of black wood appears right in the middle. I look at him, mouth open in astonishment, then walk to the door and press my hands against it. It's cool to the touch.

There's no handle, but no sooner have I thought it than one appears, made of some cool, dark metal. I turn it and open the door a crack. A few shades are standing nearby, staring, so I close the door and turn back to Hades.

He's watching me with a strange expression on his face. "I want you to try growing something here, in the Underworld proper," he says. "The walls are to keep it from prying eyes."

"The Furies can fly," I remind him.

"They don't come this way." He pauses. "We're near the Elysian Fields."

"I don't have any—"

Before I can finish, he pulls his hand out of his pocket and opens it. Nestled in the palm are a dozen small black and brown flecks. Seeds. He gestures at me and I hold my hands out, cupped beneath his as he pours the seeds into them. He's careful not to touch me.

"Will these suffice?"

I shrug. Maybe. Moving the seeds into my left hand, I drop to my knees and run my right through the cracked gray dirt. It's dry and lifeless, like everything else here.

Every year, in early spring, my dad and Merry would take me and Bree to the garden center on one of the bigger islands so I could stock up on all the things I needed for the coming year. Replacement tools, new seeds and seed trays, netting, canes, compost, soil mix. The soil mixes came in huge bins and you filled your own sacks with as much as you needed. It was the part I loved best, so while Bree went off to the café to get a sandwich and flirt with the staff, and my dad and Merry went off to look at the outdoor cooking stuff, I would dig my hands into the dirt and feel it. You were supposed to use a trowel, or at least gloves, but I never did. Always my bare hands, clutching the loam. I don't know how, and it was probably all in my head, but I could tell just from crumbling the soil between my fingers if it was good. If it would grow things. Which is how I know the soil here won't grow anything.

And yet a seed grew from rock, a voice whispers inside my head.

I examine the seeds. A few small black ones, like the one I planted in Erebus—basil, I think. Maybe lavender. Rounder, brown ones that could be coriander. I stand and begin to walk around the space, trying to decide where to plant them. All of the things I normally consider—the position of the sun overhead, which part of the garden will be in shade at what time of day—none of it matters. There's no time of day here. There's no shade, because there's no sun.

"Fuck it," I mutter, marching to the center of the garden.

On my knees, I use my fingers to dig into the dirt, making holes a couple of inches deep and depositing one of the little black seeds inside each, then covering it over. I shuffle away, leaving space, then do it again. I don't do it in any kind of order, bother to keep to neat lines, or think about root space. It seems pointless given all of the other obstacles the seeds face. I just make holes, seed them, cover them, and move on, until all the little seeds are gone.

When I stand and look down at the ground, you can barely tell where I've put them. I peer around for a rock or something to mark the space, then stop. Why bother? If they grow, we'll see them. They'll be the only spot of color here.

"Now what?" I turn to Hades.

"I suppose you do what you did to make it happen."

I recall the day before and my cheeks heat. "I cried," I say. "It grew after I cried."

Hades looks away and frowns, like he's embarrassed by my answer. "What made you unhappy?" he asks.

"This place," I answer. His jaw clenches. "The way it is. The way it works. The Furies took me with them on their punishments."

"I know," he replies. "I told you, I know everything that happens here."

I scowl at him. "And you're OK with me seeing that? Or do you think I *enjoy* it?"

From the tension in his expression, I know I've hit my mark.

"I thought it was what you wanted," he says stiffly. "To work with them."

"No, I don't want that. They don't even listen to the shades; they just punish them. I like them, they've been great to me, but . . ." I trail off.

"But that's not how you'd do it."

"It doesn't matter how I'd do it. I shouldn't be here. I should be with my family."

"They don't mourn you," Hades says.

"Excuse me?" I stare at him, outraged.

"Corey." Hades says my name softly. "They know you're not dead. That's why they don't mourn you."

I shake my head. "Where do they think I am?"

"With your mother. They believe you needed some time away from the Island after what happened, so you went to her."

"How is that possible?" But I already know the answer. "You did it. Why?" Why would he help me? Why do something kind for me?

"It wasn't fair for them to worry about you."

"Oh, but it's fair to keep me here?"

His eyes flash. "You choose to stay. You could have asked me anytime to leave."

"I have!" I glare at him.

His voice is low when he says, "I think I'd remember if you'd come to me."

I force a blush down. "All right, so not me personally, but Alecto has come to you at least half a dozen times to ask you to take me home and you've said no to every request."

Hades stares at me. "Corey, Alecto hasn't come to me. Not once."

"Yes she has."

Even as I say it, I get this creeping, familiar feeling in my gut. The same one I felt when I rushed away from the Oracle the second time, because she'd told me something I didn't want to hear. The same one I fought when I was running home from the cove the day Ali broke up with me and Bree wouldn't answer her phone.

"Why would I lie to you?" Hades steps closer, his eyes boring into mine.

"Why would she?" I say. But I know why. They told me why last night. Because of this great power they think I have that's going to make me one of them.

My hands rise to cover my face, my chest so tight I can't get any air inside.

She lied to me. She pretended to be my friend. They all did.

It happened again.

My eyes and throat burn with tears. I can't breathe. I'm shaking so hard it feels like the ground beneath my feet is moving.

It happened again.

ithappenedagainithappenedagain

"Corey," Hades says, reaching for me, and I shake my head, staring at him, begging him silently not to touch me, because if he does, if he of all people is nice to me, I think I'll shatter. Then his gaze slips past me and he makes a face I've never seen on him before, open and careless. He looks like a human boy.

He takes me gently by the shoulders and turns me around.

"Look, Corey," he says, his breath ghosting over my ear. "Look at your garden."

I forget that I'm upset. I forget everything.

Twelve green shoots push their way out of the ground as I watch, tiny leaves unfolding and extending outward as the stems slowly reach for the empty sky.

"You did it," Hades says, and when I look at him, his eyes are bright and fierce, fixed on me.

I did this.

GERMINATION

I APPROACH THE SHOOTS ON SOFT FEET, SCARED that if I'm too loud or heavy I'll send them retreating back into the earth. I kneel down carefully.

I'm good at growing things. It's my skill, like how some people can pick up new languages, and some can draw, and others can sing. I can't do any of those things, but I can grow stuff. Nothing I've planted has ever failed. Ever. I always thought it was just because I got the timing right, and did the research, and paid attention.

Now I wonder.

Hades comes to kneel beside me, the legs of his fancy trousers right in the dust.

"Nothing like this has ever happened here before?" I whisper as I look down at the shoots.

"Never. Not even y—" He stops, and swallows. "I can't do this. I can't give life. There has never been life like this here, before you."

He looks uncomfortable, his shoulders stiff, almost by his ears.

"Has it happened to you before? On your Island?" he asks.

I'm about to shake my head, when I remember the day before Bree's funeral. I'd thought Merry's cabbages looked small, and then I'd sat on the side of the bed and put my hands in the dirt while my dad talked. I'd been angry with him, fighting not to lash out, and when I looked at the cabbages again I assumed I'd been mistaken, that they were bigger than I'd realized. When I accidentally fell asleep in the garden a few nights after Ali and Bree left me, I'd woken up the next morning to find all my so-called winter squashes had ripened overnight. Everything had, in fact. I hadn't thought it was because of me. Why would I?

"How can I do this?" I ask him. "How is it possible? Is this a gift from one of you?"

Hades says nothing, watching me carefully.

I look at the plants, trying to make sense of them. Then something else occurs to me, and I start to laugh.

"What's funny?" Hades asks.

"The Furies," I explain. "They said I had power; they could feel it. That's why they want me to stay here so much, why they lied, because of my *great power*. What are they going to do when they find out it's just this?"

"Just this?"

"Growing things." I keep laughing, but it's not really laughing. "My superpower is gardening." I push my hair out of my face with both hands. "Megaera's going to be furious. Ha. Furious. Fury."

202

"Corey . . ."

"And my ex thought it was such a stupid thing to do. *Boring.* That's why he cheated on me with Bree. Because I was boring." I turn to Hades. "She didn't care about it either. If I ordered some new seeds or something and told her, she'd fake yawn until I—"

Hades suddenly lifts a hand and pushes a strand of hair behind my ear, stunning me into silence.

"I think being able to grow flowers in the land of the dead is quite special, actually." His black eyes meet mine, his fingers lingering behind my ear.

I look away and clear my throat, frowning intently at the plants as he withdraws. "They have thorns," I say.

"Are they roses?" he asks, reaching out with long fingers to touch one of the thorns. I watch, transfixed, as he presses one finger against it, hard enough that it should pierce his flesh, but no bead of blood appears. *Ichor,* I remember. The gods don't bleed. Golden ichor flows through their veins. If his flesh was pierced, molten gold would bubble up.

"The seeds you gave me weren't roses. What were they?" I ask.

I am horribly aware of his eyes on me, scanning my profile.

"I don't know. Hermes brought them."

"You're staring," I finally say.

"Forgive me," he replies, but he doesn't stop.

Irritation sparks. "What?" I turn to him, biting out the word. "Seriously?" I say through gritted teeth. "What do you want?"

He won't look away, he keeps on *staring*, and so I stare back, refusing to back down first. My eyes are burning—I feel like I could cry fire—but his go on for eternity, deep black pits with no bottom, no end. If I fell into them, I'd fall forever.

He turns away first, but I don't feel like I won.

"Now I understand," he says. "Look."

And I look.

The plants grew again while we had our staring contest, the leaves now level with my eyes. The thorns have vanished, disappearing as if they never were, and now each plant has a long green bud.

I rise to my feet, and Hades rises too, turning to me. "You're blocking yourself. Or something is blocking you. When you lose control of your emotions, it unblocks you and your power is freed."

"Wait. You were staring to make me angry? It was for this?"

He ignores the question. "If you get past the block and learn to control it, you'll be able to grow things at will. Anywhere. Everywhere."

Everywhere . . .

I suddenly see myself taking the flowers out into the Underworld and showing everyone what I've done. I want to open the door and invite them all in. I want to give all of the shades a flower, tuck them into their hair, behind their ears, give them this color and this life. *Never*, Hades said. This has never happened before; nothing has grown here before, and yet it did for me. I've brought life to the land of the dead. I could change this whole place and no one could stop me.

I walk away from him, back to the door, and I brace my hands against it, wondering if I dare. It's not cool anymore but the same ambient, unchanging temperature everything is here. Overhead the sky is the same old gray.

"Why is it like this?" I mutter to myself.

"Why is what like this?" Hades says, appearing beside me.

I jump.

"This place. The absence of everything. No sun in the sky, but it's light all the time. No clouds, no nighttime. No wind, not even a breeze. No trees, no plants, except those." I nod at the still blooms behind us. "No houses, no shelter. Does it ever rain? Snow? Hurricanes? Why? Why is there nothing?"

"What use do shades have for weather? Or houses? Or trees?" Hades asks.

"Because . . . they're part of life. I know no one here is alive," I snap, before he can say it. "That's not the point. The point is there's nothing here. An eternity of nothing. Could you exist like this?"

"I do."

Pity prickles. "So your palace is as barren as everywhere else?" I ask.

"Would you like to see it?" he replies, surprising me.

Yes. "No. That's not where I'm going with this. I'm talking about people spending eternity in a glorified version of a car park," I say. "It's hateful, don't you see that? Torture." I stop, thinking of the Furies, who are out there now, meting out their justice. "I know you can't grow things, but why did you make it like this?"

"I didn't."

"Then who did?"

"The Old Ones. I didn't build this place, I inherited it. Three straws, three kingdoms."

I know this. Zeus got the Earth, Poseidon the seas and Hades the Underworld.

"Why don't you change it?"

He looks at me as if I'm being stupid.

"Things here don't change," he says. "Until now." He looks back at the flowers. I still don't know what they are. "Until you."

Then he reaches for my hand.

"What are you doing?" I snatch it away.

"Making changes," he says, holding out his hand. "Trust me."

It's shocking to realize he's the only person here now that I do actually trust. I take his hand.

He lifts our hands level with our eyes, then presses them together, lining up our palms like we're children having a contest to see whose are the biggest, whose are the widest. He's the victor—the tips of his fingers are a whole joint longer. He slides his fingers between mine, and I curl mine in response. His skin is cool and soft, how it was when he held me at the Thesmophoria, and I taste honey in the back of my mouth. I watch him watching our joined hands, fascinated, as though he has nothing to do with what's happening, as though our limbs are acting of their own accord and we're just the audience.

Then he steps closer again, until only the width of our hands is keeping us from being chest to chest. It's my turn to stare now, my mouth dry, my heart fluttering behind my ribs like a bird.

"Your hands are different," he says.

"What?" I look up at him.

"At the Thesmophoria. Your skin was callused. Hard."

I try to pull away, but he doesn't let me. "Well, not all of us sit in a palace all day, giving orders. Some of us use our hands."

"It isn't a bad thing. I'm just saying they're softer now," he says, eyes meeting mine, his eyebrows drawn down into a frown. "You're flushed," he says.

"Side effect of being alive," I reply. "And stupidly pale."

"Again, I didn't say it was a bad thing."

I swallow, my blush brightening, and look away, over his shoulder.

And then I gasp as one of the blooms opens, before my eyes, and I see what they are.

Narcissi, but red.

I know what he's doing too.

"You're manipulating me." I wrench my hand from his. "Messing with my emotions to see what works. We've done sadness, anger and frustration. So you thought you'd try . . . *this.*"

He looks stricken, then shrugs. "I'm sorry. I had to be sure my hypothesis was right."

"Well, congratulations." I shake my head. "You're as bad as the others."

"I just wanted—"

"To use me. Like the Furies," I cut him off.

"No. That was—"

I speak without thinking. "Shut up."

I'm surprised when he obeys, pressing his lips together, hard.

I walk over to the sole flower, staring down at it.

They don't exist. Red narcissi. Not true crimson. Not in my world, anyway. I'd bet anything they only grow here. Underworld flowers. I wonder what would happen if I tried to grow cornflowers here. Or marigolds. Or roses. What would they look like, in the Underworld?

"Corey," Hades says, his tone urgent enough to make me turn. "The Furies have returned. I need to get you home." He reaches for my arm.

"No," I say.

He stills. "You don't want to go home?" He speaks carefully.

"I do, obviously." I pause.

"But?" he prompts.

I look at the flowers and my heart gives a funny little skip.

"You want to do more," he says, his eyes glittering.

"Well, now I know my family is all right, and you're not keeping me a prisoner here out of spite . . ." He raises an eyebrow. "Maybe I could stay a bit longer, to see what else I can do. Can you get more seeds?"

He nods.

"Then should I stay a little longer? Just to see what happens next."

"You can stay as long as you wish," he says hurriedly.

"I have conditions."

"Of course you do."

We both fight not to smile. *He's Hades,* I remind myself. *Not your friend. No one here is your friend.*

"Condition one is that as soon as I ask you to take me back to the Island, you do. No matter what's happening here."

He reaches into his pocket and pulls out a coin, handing it to me. His face is carved in profile on it.

"Say my name while you hold this. I'll come straight to you."

I look down at the coin. "All right. Number two, you don't mess with me to make me grow things. No tricks or manipulation. No mind games. Let me figure it out. If you're right about it being a power blockage, I have to try to get past it without being influenced. Otherwise, it's useless."

"Of course. Anything else?" His gaze intense, eyebrows slightly raised.

It's on the tip of my tongue to ask to see Bree. To say . . . I still don't know what I want to say to her, if anything at all. Although, she ran away from me, so maybe I should take the hint. I'll have to figure it out before I go home.

The garden has always been the place I've done my best thinking.

I shake my head. "That's all for now."

His expression smooths once more. "All right."

Before I can ask how he plans to smuggle me back into Erebus without the Furies knowing, he takes my arm and there is that sickening feeling of rushing and contraction and the next thing I know we are standing in the pitch-black cavern I use as a bathroom.

His lips move against my ear. "I'll be back."

I nod, my mouth too dry to speak.

"You asked once why I was at the Thesmophoria," Hades says on a cool, salt breath. "I was there for you."

Then he is gone, blinked away, and I am alone.

MAIDEN TREE

I WASH MY HANDS IN THE STREAM, PICKING Underworld dirt out from under my nails. When I wipe them on my shift, they're trembling.

I play with the coin Hades gave me, turning it over in my hand, moving it along my knuckles like a magician, before holding it in my palm. I can't see it in the darkness of the cavern, but I feel it, rubbing my finger over his profile; haughty, arrogant even. Some people might say it's a stretch to read arrogance into a silhouette carved onto a piece of metal, but it's there. I turn it over and feel the other side. A circle, connected to a long ridge, two smaller circles at the end. A key, maybe.

"Corey?" Alecto's voice echoes through the passageway. "Are you well?"

I suck in a deep breath as my temper flares. *She lied to me. To my face.*

"Fine," I say, harsher than I'd like. "I'll be out in a minute," I add, forcing myself to sound soft.

To sound ignorant.

She told me to trust her, to be patient, and she'd help me. But she never went to him. She used what she'd learned about me and Bree and tried to suck me into their world. She made Hades out as the villain and that she was my friend and I *believed* her. Again. I growl softly. That's the thing that gets me. Again I trust someone and think they're on my side and again I'm taken for a ride, made a fool of. I must be the worst judge of character in the whole world. And now I have to go out there and pretend everything is all right.

I grip the coin tight in my fist and breathe deeply. I can do this. I've survived worse. I just have to get through the rest of the day, then Hades will come back and I can test my power. And if it gets to be too much, I can use the coin and go straight home. I have choices. I'm in control now.

"Corey?" Alecto calls again.

"Coming," I say.

I push the coin into a corner so it won't catch any light.

I'm shaking when I leave the cavern.

Alecto is waiting for me, a soft, welcoming smile on her lovely face, and something cracks inside my chest.

"I'll carry you," she says, stepping forward as I reach for my rope and it takes everything I have not to push her away, to scream at her that I know what she did, what she's been doing.

I'm grateful Megaera dug up the other seeds. They'd be sequoias right now if she hadn't.

"Thanks," I say, and even manage a smile as she scoops me up. Nestled against her chest, I smell her familiar scent of dust and girl for a second, and then she's lowering me, beaming at me, and I didn't know a heart could be so broken and still work.

"We were beginning to think you'd fallen in," Hermes says, a slightly panicked look on his face before he turns away. "I hope you're feeling better."

I stumble into my blankets, pulling them up and over me as a shield, unable to stop trembling. I can feel them all staring at me and I look down at the fraying wool, scared they'll see on my face that I know the truth.

"What's wrong?" Megaera asks. "Something ails you?"

"No. I . . . Yes," I say, when Hermes gives a slight cough. "I don't feel well."

"You don't feel well?" Megaera repeats, an edge to her voice.

"I have a headache. I'm human. It happens," I snap.

"I should go." Hermes's voice is look-at-me loud, but I keep my face lowered. "It was good to talk, Corey. I'm sure I'll see you again. Tomorrow, perhaps?"

"Sure," I say.

"Tomorrow then," he says.

Ironically, the thing I want most in the world right now is *my* garden. I want to dig. I want to work until I'm sweating, until I stink and I'm starving. I want to sink into a deep bath and let the water soak away every ache and pain. Then I want to get up and do it again. I wonder what's happening in the other garden right now. Whether the plants are still alive. Whether they'll make it.

The Furies pull me from my thoughts.

"What ails you?" Megaera frowns, crouching in front of me, forcing me to look at her. "You're not right. Did the Messenger touch you without leave?"

"What? No!" I say. "No, not at all. Why would you think that?"

"He's a god, you're a girl," Tisiphone says, and Alecto nods.

"You're both behaving strangely," Megaera says. "Both skittish, both distracted."

"Not because of him. I'm a bit ill, that's all. It happens." They keep looking at me. "He didn't touch me, I promise."

"You will tell us." It isn't a question, but a command. "If anyone touches you," she continues. "Anyone at all."

I swallow, my mind skipping back to my fingers twined with Hades's, his face close to mine, his words before he left, and my stomach flutters.

They've never asked about the kiss with Hades. Maybe Alecto never told them, though I doubt that. I suppose it's another mortal thing they don't understand. There's no way I could explain that I still feel weird about it. Weird*er* after today.

"Corey?" Megaera's voice is serpent soft. "You must tell us."

I've never been a great liar, despite Bree trying to teach me for both our sakes; she could look her mother dead in the eye and swear we hadn't done whatever it was, and the second Mrs. Dovemuir looked at me I'd blush, giving us away.

It's all right for you, Bree would say. *Your dad isn't like my mum. If I didn't lie, I'd never be allowed to do anything. It's a necessary evil.*

And I'd agreed, until I was the one she'd lied to.

"Because you're ours now," Megaera continues. "Our sister. Insult to you is insult to us. Assault on you is assault on us." Her eyes bore into mine, as if she can read the truth across the back of my skull, carved into the bone.

My blood turns cold.

"There can be no secrets, Corey."

"No," I say. "No secrets. And no lies."

A shadow crosses her face, but she nods. "No secrets and no lies," she says, then moves to sit behind me, pulling me into her embrace. I let her, because it feels safer than looking directly at her.

"What did you do with the Messenger?" Megaera asks, stroking her talons down my arm lazily.

"Not much," I say, working to keep my voice calm. "I felt ill almost as soon as you left. We chatted, mostly."

"What did you talk about?" Megaera enquires, her hands moving to my shoulders, massaging them, thumbs rubbing circles on the back of my neck.

"Nothing really. Humans and gods," I improvise, aware of how close her hands are to my throat. "How different I am, from him. From you."

"No, you're the same as us," Megaera corrects.

"You're one of us now." Alecto joins us, sitting at my side and taking my hand, stroking the palm with her fingers. "A sister."

"I'm not, though," I say, my voice sharper than I mean it to be. "I can't ever be. Look at you. And look at me. Look how different we are."

"You will have wings," Megaera's breath tickles the nape of

214

my neck, sending a chill down my spine. "You will fly, as we do. You will be as we are. Soon."

I open my mouth to ask how, but stop. I have a flash of some future version of myself, reptilian wings exploding from my back, my nails elongating and thickening, curving into talons. Green, leaf-shaped scales covering my skin like armor. My eyes as fathomless and black as their own, all my humanity gone. I shiver, and the sisters resume stroking me, hands running over my shoulder blades and down my back. I think of what I left behind in the walled garden. Suddenly, growing wings doesn't seem like such an unlikely thing.

Eventually, I pretend to fall asleep so I don't have to speak anymore, and they lay me down, tucking the blanket around me before they go.

I can hear them talking over in Megaera's nook, but every now and then they pause and I feel them look at me, three pairs of black eyes watching possessively. They think they have me. They think I'm theirs, and the really awful thing is, if it had gone on much longer, I might have been. I don't like feeling that it was Bree who saved me, but if it hadn't been for seeing her and what happened after that, then they'd still be drawing me into their web, and I'd be lost.

Eventually I fall asleep for real, because the next thing I know, Alecto is shaking me.

"You need to eat," she says, smiling gently, nodding to where food has been laid out for me.

And I smile back, because in that moment I forget she is a liar, and that was always the worst bit after Bree too.

I'd wake up in the morning and reach for my phone to message her about the weird dream I'd had or to see if she'd messaged me, but then I'd see the photo of my garden that replaced the one of us, and it would all come flooding back. I'd open my apps to check if she'd updated about the life I was no longer part of. For some reason she never blocked me and I never blocked her. Ali, yes. Bree . . . no.

Alecto's face falls when I lean away from her. "What is it?" she asks.

"Will you go to Hades again?" I ask her. I can't help it. "Actually, will you take me to him? I think this time I should ask him myself. Maybe that's what he's waiting for. Maybe that's why he keeps saying no. It's worth a try, isn't it?"

She hesitates for long enough that I think she's actually going to agree.

"That will only make him angrier," she finally says. "You don't know him as we do."

And the crack I feel inside my chest widens. Because if she'd said, *Yes, I'll take you, let's go,* then it might mean Hades was the liar and I'd got it all wrong. It might mean I'm not a fool. It might mean that I hadn't put my faith in the wrong place, the wrong people. Again.

"Let's try it," I press. "I mean, he's already furious with me. What else can he do?"

"This is his realm," Alecto looks behind her to where Megaera and Tisiphone are watching us. Both of them are perfectly motionless.

"But you have the treaty," I say. "And you said I'm one of you, so if that's true, it should cover me as well, right?" My voice is too high, and I know they know something is wrong when Megaera and Tisiphone glance at each other. My pulse speeds up.

"If you're one of us, why do you want to leave?" Megaera asks.

"Because . . . I'm worried about my family."

She looks at me with abyssal eyes. "They'll come here sooner or later."

For a moment I don't quite understand what she's saying, as if she thinks they too might pick a flower and plummet into the Underworld, but then it falls into place and the hairs on the back of my neck stand up.

"When they're dead?"

"It happens to all mortals."

I can't bear the idea of my dad and Merry here. In those awful shrouds, in a world without color and texture and sound and flavor. No birds for Merry to get excited about. Nothing for my dad to tinker with and break more before he fixes it.

Alecto makes a soft sound and puts an arm around me. I push her away. "Don't," I say.

"Corey?"

I can't stand the confused, hurt look on her face. It's a lie, it's all a lie.

I scramble out of the blankets and grab a candle, the matches and a spare shift. "I have to wash," I say.

"What happened with the Messenger?" Megaera asks again.

"I told you, nothing," I reply as I grip my rope and climb down. "Everything's fine."

In the cavern, I light the candle and melt its base to the rock. Then I pull out Hades's coin. I was right, it is a key on the other side. I wonder what would happen if I called him to take me away now. If I asked him to hide me inside the stark walls of his palace while we test the limits of what I can do, would he do it? Would I start a war?

I put the coin back under the rock. No. I need to find another way out of this. One that won't get anyone hurt.

I pull the shift over my head and wash myself, scrubbing at my skin with my hands, letting my body dry before I put the cleaner shift on. I finger-comb my hair. I haven't seen my reflection properly since I got here; I have no idea how I look. Like a maenad, I guess.

I can't hide in the cavern forever.

When I climb back up to my nook they're all waiting for me, sitting together. Tisiphone is toying with Megaera's snakes, stroking their noses and letting their tongues flicker over her fingers, and Megaera is combing Alecto's feathers, smoothing them down. Alecto holds out her arms for me and I pause, wondering what will happen if I refuse. Then I swallow the lump in my throat and join them.

I look at them, the three Furies, and wonder when exactly they stopped scaring me and if that was my biggest mistake. That I humanized them, edited them, let myself believe we were all just girls thrown together. Megaera, her fierce heart, her unflinching gaze; Tisiphone, scales like burnished armor, always listening. And Alecto, who I'd almost opened my soul to, who I'd thought could be the other half of me. I forgot there were only three women in the Three of Cups, and that the sad woman in the Three of Swords was still alone. That Justice was alone, too.

"We know something is wrong," Alecto says as she combs through my hair. "You should tell us."

"You shouldn't keep things from us," Tisiphone adds.

I swallow a choking laugh and Alecto's fingers still. "It's . . . it's just Hermes was talking about the mortal world, and it made me miss my home. My old home," I add.

Megaera makes a sound through her teeth. "I knew he'd said something to upset you. Foolish god."

The three of them call him names, insult his parentage, his powers, his behavior. I stay silent and seethe while they rail against him, satisfied to have solved the puzzle of what's wrong with me.

Look, Bree. I can finally lie.

DEAD HEAD

MY RESPECT FOR HERMES GROWS THE NEXT DAY when he comes back and the Furies immediately surround him, raging at him for upsetting me. To his credit, he doesn't even try to protest, just goes along with it all, head hung in contrition while he apologizes, promising not to do it again.

There is a moment where I think it's not enough.

"Perhaps you should come with us," Megaera says to me. "We can keep watch over you at the Prytaneum."

No. I have to go back to the garden. I have to see what else I can do.

"My head still hurts, that wasn't a lie. And I don't want to cause trouble with you and Hades," I say.

"Him," Megaera says, her eyes narrowed.

"I could stay, instead of the Messenger," Alecto offers, but Megaera shoots her a dark look.

"I think not."

Alecto lowers her head, pulling her wings in and making herself small, as Megaera stares at her. Alecto whimpers softly under her sister's terrible gaze and I can't help feeling sorry for her.

Megaera looks back at Hermes, then at me, her snakes following the movement of her eyes, back and forth between us. I raise my hand to my forehead and try to look as frail as I can.

"You will stay here today, to rest," she says to me finally. To Hermes she hisses, "You will not upset her again."

"Of course not," Hermes says airily. "Corey can sleep. I'll occupy myself."

Megaera gives us searching looks. "Corey will come with us next time," she says to the god. Then to me, "You still have much to learn. And we have so much to teach you."

Stomach dropping, all I can do is nod.

Megaera gives me another long look, then launches herself into the air, Tisiphone following.

I reach for Alecto as she walks past me, taking her hand and squeezing it. Then I wink, like she did, the first time Hades came here. She gives me a sad little smile and then leaves.

"What was all that about?" Hermes turns to me.

"I had to pretend you'd upset me and that's why I was in a weird mood yesterday."

"No, I understood that. I mean the tension between them."

"It was Alecto's idea to plant the seeds that became the shoot you saw. Megaera caught us sowing a bunch of them and wasn't happy; she dug them all up. Almost all," I amend. "I don't think she's forgiven Alecto."

Hermes laughs. "And that's why you didn't want them to know the shoot had grown. I see. You've stirred up quite the hornets' nest."

"I didn't mean to."

"Still . . . It's impressive work. Dividing the sisters, beguiling Hades . . ."

"I haven't . . . ," I begin, then stop. I turn around, scanning the nook.

"He isn't here yet." Hermes looks delighted with himself, and I don't know if I believe him, so I turn again, scouring every part of Erebus I can see. When I'm satisfied we're still alone, I look back at Hermes, who's watching me with a shrewd, expectant expression.

"Have you asked yourself, sweet Corey, why exactly is it that the Unchanging King of the Unchanging Realm is suddenly interested in gardening? Why has he not forced you to leave his kingdom?"

"It's his kingdom, he can do what he wants," I say, feeling oddly defensive.

Hermes licks his lips, looks behind me, opens his mouth, then hesitates. When he speaks, he's slow and deliberate, so unlike his usual breezy self. "Would that it were so simple. I told you I go between here and there, remember?" I nod. "And that I'm one of only a few who can." He pauses, waiting for me to speak, but I don't know what he wants me to say.

He gives me a small, soft smile. "It's hard enough for me, Corey, just going between. I can't imagine how hard it would be to live in two worlds and not truly belong to either."

"Enough."

Hades's voice rings through Erebus, and Hermes and I both turn to him.

He looks furious, shadows lashing at his sides, his jaw square with anger. He strides to my side, eyes burning into Hermes.

"We'll discuss this later," he says to the other god. "Call me when they return." Then he takes my arm and before I can say goodbye, before I can say anything at all, we're gone.

I stumble again when we arrive in the garden, and he steadies me, immediately walking away once I find my balance. He marches to the far end of the garden, then turns and walks back, coming to a halt a few paces away, hands clasped behind him.

I'm stunned when he says, "I owe you an apology."

"Just one?" It slips out before I can stop myself, and I clamp my mouth shut.

His eyes glitter. "Make a list for me. This particular one is for not checking on you. For leaving you with the Furies and not returning to ask how you fared. I relied on secondhand information and that was wrong of me."

"For the record, they took really good care of me. Until the punishment thing." My heart aches. "I should thank you for the food, actually. It's nice. So, thanks."

He gives a slight bow. Then, "I know you mislike when you think I read your mind, but please don't listen to Hermes."

I falter, because I'd been about to ask him what Hermes meant.

"He means well. But don't listen," he adds.

"All right," I say. I'm amused when he looks surprised, both eyebrows rising. "I can argue if you want," I add.

"I know you can." He meets my eyes and I swallow.

I look away.

"So, what's the plan today?" I say, examining the rows of narcissi. None of the others have bloomed yet. "Do you have any more seeds, or shall I try to make the others flower?"

"I have seeds, but think perhaps you should try with the others. If you want," he adds.

"Works for me."

I walk over to the flowers and kneel in front of them, expecting Hades to come and kneel beside me. When he stays back, I turn to him.

"Are you going to stay over there?" I ask.

"I promised I wouldn't influence you."

Right. I look back at the buds.

Self-conscious, I close my eyes and try to clear my mind. I breathe steadily, in and out, thinking of the flowers, the petals unfurling. Then I picture Hades standing behind me, watching me, and my eyes snap open.

"When you made the door in the wall, how did you do it?" I say.

"I wanted a door there."

"That was it?" I turn to him. "You just willed it to exist."

He nods.

All right. I turn back to the flowers and will them to open.

I become aware of something inside my chest, a kind of pressure, right in the center, between my navel and my heart. I think of the flowers, urging them to change, and it feels as if my ribs are vibrating, rattling, something behind them wanting to be free. I focus harder, gritting my teeth, holding my breath. *Open,* I think. *Come on. Open.*

But when I finally exhale and look, the narcissi are all still in bud; there is no change.

"I can't do it," I say, placing my hands on my stomach. "I can feel where it is, but I can't make it open."

Hades joins me, lowering himself at my side.

"There's no rush. You can try for as long as you want. As long as it takes."

I shake my head. "Megaera won't let me stay in Erebus again. She almost didn't today. She wants me to go back to the Prytaneum with them. To continue learning to be a Fury."

"But you don't want that?" Hades asks. "You don't want to join them."

"I love how you all talk like it's even possible. Like you can be a Fury *and* mortal."

He's silent for a moment. "It's not entirely unprecedented. Medusa was a Gorgon, and mortal. Sometimes when gods have children, things are complicated." He frowns as he speaks, reaching for a bud and brushing his fingers over it.

"If I was a Fury, I'd be your enemy," I say.

"I would not like that." His voice is soft.

"Me neither," I say, just as quietly, sitting back on my heels.

"Another apology," he says, at a normal volume. "For the way

I behaved when you came here. I was taken by surprise, and I am not often surprised. I reacted badly. I was ungracious and I'm sorry for it."

"It's all right. I wasn't exactly nice to you."

He's silent for a moment, and I try willing the buds again. "You could stay with me," he says carefully, breaking my concentration. "If you wanted to stay here a little longer, that is. I have room to spare. I could keep you safe."

"They'd hate you." I turn to him. "They already hate you."

"I know," Hades says.

"I don't want them to hate me." Despite the lies and the scourging, despite everything, I don't think I could stand it if they turned on me.

"I know," he repeats. "I suppose I should take you home."

I nod. I want to go home. It's what I've wanted ever since I got here, to go back to Dad and Merry, the Island and my garden, Astrid and Lars and Manu and school. Back to my real life.

So why do I feel like crying?

"Tell me about it," Hades says. "Tell me about your Island."

"You were at the Thesmophoria, you pretty much saw everything." I hesitate. I want to ask what he meant by he was *there for me*, but I'm too embarrassed. Maybe in the cavern, in the dark, I could, but not here, in the open. From the way he stiffens when I say "Thesmophoria," I get the impression he feels the same.

"There are twelve hundred people in total on the Island. Which means everyone knows everything about you. People leave sometimes, but not often. It's a forever kind of place. It used to worry Bree . . ." I stop. When I go home, Bree will still be here. She hated the Island, but I think maybe she would have liked it more if she'd known this would be where she came next.

"What worried her?" Hades asks, drawing me back to the conversation.

I kick my legs around and cross them, arranging the shift to cover myself, facing him. He does the same, mirroring me.

"That it's a forever place. It was too small for her. She wasn't happy there."

"But you were?"

I nod. "I loved it. Love it," I correct myself. "It's home, you know? It's who you are. I am the Island. I'm the salt and the soil and the hawthorn. I'm the beaches and the fields and the woods. It's me."

"So, this is what I am?" Hades gestures to the ground, then the sky. "I'm a desert. I'm sunless, seasonless, barren and empty. I'm death and the dead and lonely, hopeless eternity."

"You're dramatic," I say, and to my surprise he laughs, a low, free sound from deep inside him that makes me smile.

He looks shocked by it. I wonder when he last laughed. When he last actually talked to someone, other than me. Whether he has friends. Whether he has anyone at all.

"And you're to blame," I say. "If this place is barren and empty and lonely, change it. You keep telling me it's your realm, so do something about it."

"I cannot do what you can."

"So do something else. And . . ." I pause. "If I can figure out how to unblock myself, maybe I could help a bit, before I go. A few trees, or something?"

227

He looks at me, his eyes wide, but then his gaze becomes unfocused and his eyes turn white.

"The Furies are back." He blinks, and he looks like himself again.

"Already?" I say. "But we only just got here." I look at the tightly budded flowers and feel the sting of disappointment. *I'm not finished yet.*

Hades stands and offers me a hand, pulling me up. "If I take you to the hill, is it easy for you to find your way home from there?"

"One more day." The words come in a rush. "Let's see if they'll leave me in Erebus tomorrow. I'll pretend to be really tired. I've hidden the coin in the cavern, and if they don't buy my excuse, or they don't care, I'll call you when they think I'm washing."

Hades is staring at me. "Are you sure?" he says. "Corey, be sure."

"I am. One more day won't make a difference to Dad or Merry. One last try."

He nods, then we're gone.

He doesn't say anything when we get back, just presses his fingers against mine, then vanishes, leaving behind a cool, salt breeze that's quickly drowned by the water in the cavern. It's only then I realize we'd still been holding hands. I wash mine, then press my cold palms to my face to calm my burning cheeks.

I emerge from the cavern to find Alecto pacing.

"There you are. Come, we must go," she says, crossing the floor to me.

I step back. "Go where?"

"To the Prytaneum."

"But I'm staying here. Megaera said. My head still hurts." I peer up at Hermes, who sits on the edge of my nook looking down at us, and he gives a faint shrug, a swift shake of the head, no closer to understanding what's happening than I am.

Alecto gives me an exasperated look. "Everyone's there. We must hurry," she says, lifting me unceremoniously into her arms, and then we are airborne, leaving Hermes behind.

We avoid the Asphodel Meadows, taking the faster route near the Phlegethon. I'm still not recovered from traveling with Hades, and my head spins as we fly. The journey is swift, each wingbeat full of purpose, and when I ask Alecto who "everyone" is, she doesn't reply. My heart is heavy in my chest, my stomach clenching with worry.

Outside the Prytaneum the shades are waiting; they look up as we fly over. I scan them all for Bree, but don't see her, and I'm relieved by it.

Alecto lands in a cloud of dust and deposits me beside Megaera, then crosses to her mound.

"What's going—" I begin, but Megaera silences me with a look.

"Enter," she calls above my head.

My heart stalls as the woman Bree had been with approaches the Furies. I glance at them, wondering if they recognize her too, but their faces are serene.

I look at the arch, shifting to see if anyone is hovering just beyond it, and a taloned hand grips my shoulder, holding me fast. So they *do* recognize her. That's why they sent Alecto back for me. Because she was next, and they wanted me here for this.

"Why have you been sent to us for justice?" Megaera asks the shade, whose eyes are fixed not on the Furies, but on me.

"I killed my mother," she tells me.

"Matricide," Tisiphone and Alecto hiss together, and the shade and I flinch simultaneously.

Megaera bends low to my ear, though she speaks loud enough that I know the shade can hear. "Matricide is one of the worst crimes of all. To take the life of the one who gave you yours, who carried you inside them, who nourished you with their own blood and vitality. To steal their life from them . . . Think carefully on what that means. What it deserves." She straightens and then says, "Corey, what should we do with this creature?"

They brought me here to punish her.

I look at the shade, whose hair is streaked with gray at the temples, whose knuckles are red and raw, even here, in the afterlife. Her shoulders are stooped and rounded; she looks like someone who has worked, and worked hard, all their life.

Bree came here with her, waited with her. I want to know why she thought this woman was worth that.

"Why did you kill your mother?" I ask.

I feel Megaera stiffen behind me, feel Tisiphone and Alecto turn to me.

"The why does not matter, only that she did," Megaera says, and I hear her snakes hissing in agreement.

"It matters to me," I say without turning. "People have reasons for doing things. If I have to choose the punishment, I want to be sure it fits the crime. Tell me," I ask the shade. "Why did you kill her?"

The shade keeps her gaze lowered as she answers. "She was dying. She had been sick for a long, long time. She begged me to help her, but I said no, and I kept saying no. Until I said yes." She looks at me then. "And I don't regret it. Zeus help me, I should have done it earlier."

"Zeus cannot help you now," Alecto says. "She is like the boy. She is unrepentant of her crime. She said so herself."

"There is blood on her hands," Tisiphone says. "And she must pay."

"Choose, Corey. Choose how she should be punished for her crime," Megaera urges.

The shade lowers her face once more, resigned to her fate, which rests in my hands.

An eye for an eye. That's how the Furies operate. But it's a stupid way to live.

I know what to do.

"She will leave this place and find the shade of her mother. They will be reunited and must apologize to each other. Your mother placed a great burden on you by asking you to deliver her death, knowing this would be your fate," I say as the Furies stir behind me. "And you should apologize for taking her life, even if she asked you to. It is still a crime. If you forgive each other, the punishment is done."

The shade looks up at me, eyes wide with hope. When her gaze moves behind me, she flinches, and I gather my courage and turn too.

All three Furies are staring at me, onyx eyes glittering.

"Is this because of the girl?" Megaera asks. "The one you look for, even now. You go easy on this shade on her account? Though she betrayed you, you would grant a boon to her companion?"

"No," I say honestly. "It's nothing to do with Bree. This is justice. Real justice."

"She took a life." Megaera steps down from her mound so we are eye to eye.

Around her head, her snakes coil and weave, tongues flicking out to taste the tension in the air. Tisiphone and Alecto step down too, moving to flank their sister, and my legs turn to jelly but I lock my knees and put my shoulders back.

It's as if I'm seeing them again for the first time: Megaera, pale-green skin darkening where it meets the serpents that grow from her scalp, diaphanous wings folding behind her as she crosses her arms, watching me. Tisiphone, face half-shadowed by the hood that frames it, bronze scales covering every part of her, dust settling on her feet and ankles from the landing. And Alecto, with her mane of feathers that rise when she's angry or confused, risen now, her crow-black eyes fixed on me. Their talons, their mannerisms. Their *otherness*.

Still, I hold Megaera's gaze steadily as I say, "It's not that simple. It wasn't cold-blooded, or hot-blooded." I'm painfully aware that the shade is still behind us. "It wasn't an act of anger, or vengeance, or jealousy. It was mercy." When Megaera says nothing, I continue. "You asked me what I think the punishment should be, and I've told you. If you disagree, that's your choice. I'm not a Fury. I keep trying to tell you that."

For a long moment no one says or does anything, the stillness echoed by the Underworld beyond the Prytaneum.

"Go," Megaera suddenly spits at the shade. "Leave this place. Do not let us see you again."

The shade does not need telling twice and hurries from the Prytaneum.

"What has the Messenger been saying to you?" Megaera asks.

"It's nothing to do with him."

"Don't lie to us."

"Don't lie to you?" I say. My temper surges, and I try to keep a grip on it, but they're all looking at me as if I've disappointed them, when I'm not the one who lied. I'm not the one who kept them prisoner and isolated them and tried to make them become something they're not.

It bursts from me. "How about you don't lie to me? How about that?"

Alecto steps forward. "Let us go back to Erebus," she says, always the peacekeeper.

"I don't want to go back to Erebus. I want to go back to the Island. Take me to Hades. I want to ask him why he keeps refusing my requests. Because he always does, doesn't he, Alecto? Whenever you go to him and ask, he says no, doesn't he? He's the reason I'm still here, right? Not you, lying to me."

"Take her back," Megaera snaps at Alecto. "We'll deal with this later."

Alecto hesitates, as if she expects me to fight, but Erebus is exactly where I want to be. I'll grab the coin and call Hades; I'm done with this. Done with all of them.

"Corey?" Alecto says, holding out her arms, waiting for permission.

Her eyes are big and round, questioning, and I nod, once, allowing her to lift me up.

"Alecto." Megaera speaks before her sister can take off. "Put her in my hollow, not her own."

No.

Alecto nods and then her wings spread.

"It was for your own good," Alecto says as we fly, whipping through the air so fast I feel nauseous. "Everything we've done was for you. You'll understand soon. You're one of us."

I don't reply, turning my face from hers.

In Erebus, Alecto takes me to Megaera's hollow, as she called it, instead of my own, and I back away from the edge. There is no rope here. No easy way down. I have to get that coin. I have to get to Hades.

"I need to use my cavern," I say.

Alecto shakes her head.

"I need to," I repeat, allowing some of the desperation I feel to creep into my voice. "Human, remember? Alecto?" I say when she keeps shaking her head, refusing to look at me.

She leaps backward off the ledge and lands silently on the ground. I take two tentative steps forward, enough to see her slipping inside the cave she helped make, her wings brushing against the walls.

There's nothing to worry about, I tell myself. I hid Hades's coin under a stone. Unless she overturns every piece of rock and rubble in there, she won't find it. And even if she does, it's just a coin. It could have come from anywhere.

I take another step toward the edge, wondering if I can climb down.

Alecto emerges from the cavern and looks at me.

In her hand is a crimson narcissus.

"Where did this come from?" she asks me.

Fuck.

BLOOM

I STAND WITH ALECTO IN THE WALLED GARDEN, looking at the narcissi. They seem forlorn now, just two thin rows of green in an expanse of dust. I see the gap where the missing one came from, the only one that had bloomed.

I walk to it and bend to stroke the broken stem. Sap wells under my touch, oozing from the break, and the tips of my fingers tingle.

"What is this place?" Alecto asks. She stays near the wall, has since we got here, legs bent to make a fast escape if she needs to.

"It's a garden. My garden," I say, straightening to look at her.

"Who brought you here? Hermes?"

I shake my head slowly.

The Fury changes, her fangs elongating, her plumage rising. But for once I don't flinch.

"*Him?*" she growls.

I nod. "Megaera didn't get all the seeds we planted in Erebus. She missed one. And when you left me with Hermes the first time, after the scourging, I was so upset I made it grow. That's the power you think you can feel inside me. I'm not a Fury; I just make flowers grow. So all the lies and schemes were a waste of your time. It was only ever this." I spread my hands over the flowers.

Alecto is shaking her head. "This isn't what we wanted for you," she says.

"It's all I have."

She doesn't say another word, springing into the sky, leaving me staring after her.

She'll go to the Prytaneum, or wherever her sisters are, to tell them. And then I guess they'll come back here. I look at the door, I bet it's a long walk to Hades's palace from here. I don't think I want to run anyway. I want this all to be over.

I crouch down in front of the snapped stem and touch it. Again, sap wells up, spilling like milky tears, and again my fingertips tingle, as if the stem is electrified, sending jolts of energy out to me. Or perhaps it's the other way around. No. It's both. We do it together.

As soon as I think it, I feel something relax and loosen in my chest, a twist like the turning of a doorknob, and I know that whatever was blocking me is gone now.

Once again, I close my eyes and will the flower to grow.

A spider can grow a leg back if it loses one. A slowworm can regrow its tail; in fact, it can choose to break its own tail if it needs to escape. With plants you can take a cutting and put it in soil or water and it might root. A perennial will grow back. An annual won't. A narcissus is a perennial, but once you cut a flower, you usually have to wait a year for it to regrow.

I don't.

Inside my chest, in that spot between my navel and my heart, something chimes, a bell that has finally been rung after hanging silent for too long. A great rushing fills my body, something waking and trying to fight its way out, beating against the bars of my ribs.

Just when I think it will smash through the bones and burst from me, someone blows into my face; cold, sharp salt air. I gasp, sucking it into my lungs and opening my eyes.

"You did it."

I'm only a bit surprised to find Hades is here. We both look at the narcissus. It's a little smaller than the others, and there is a small join where the new stem grew, but if you weren't looking for it, you'd never know. The others have opened too, a blaze of red against the green.

I can still feel the echoes of the ringing in my chest spreading through my body. As they subside, a steady feeling of calm takes their place. I'm dreamy and content as I say, "How did you know to come here?"

He frowns and ducks his head; if I didn't know better, I'd think he was embarrassed.

"I was already here. I saw Alecto bringing you."

"She found the flower you left."

He winces, his expression pained. "I'm sorry. It was . . . I'm sorry."

I shrug. "Honestly, it's for the best. I'm tired of all the lies and tricks and machinations. And at least when they see this, they'll have proof that this is my power. That I'm not a Fury, that I'm . . . a gardener."

He smiles, lips together. Then he reaches into his pocket. "Care to test the limits of your power while you wait?" he asks.

He pulls out packets of seeds from my world, dozens of them: asters, pansies, geraniums, violets, foxgloves, hollyhocks, poppies, dianthus. He holds them all out to me.

I take them, fingers brushing against his cool skin, and tear the tops open before handing half of the packets back to him.

"What should I do?" He peers at them.

"Scatter them. Spread them around. However you like. You take that end"—I nod behind him—"and I'll take this one, and we'll meet in the middle."

He nods and turns, then pauses. He moves his hand in the air and a pomegranate rests in his palm. Its skin is wrinkled and withered, and he looks at it for a long moment before meeting my eyes.

"It's from Erebus. You hid it. It has seeds in it, does it not? I thought it might mean something."

"It meant I was afraid of you cutting off my food supply and me starving. I forgot about it. Wait . . ." Something occurs to me. "It was in my blankets. You creep," I say.

I'm joking, but vivid scarlet rises from inside Hades's buttoned-up collar and paints his face.

"I was trying to find somewhere to hide the flower."

"You're as bad as Hermes."

"What does that mean?" he asks.

"Ask him about the time he perved on my underwear."

Hades's expression immediately changes from embarrassed to outraged. "He what?" he says in a flat, clipped voice.

I nod slowly, holding my hand out for the pomegranate, and

Hades tosses it to me. I tuck it under my arm as I turn from him, scattering the seeds as I go. A few seconds later, I hear him moving too.

Last time I dug holes, but this time I shift the dirt with my bare feet, plunging my toes into the ground and kicking dust over once I've the planted seeds as I go. I check on Hades to find him using his pristine shoes to copy me and I grin. He catches me and smiles too, sheepish, shy.

We meet in the middle, and I take out the pomegranate. I'm not sure it's edible anymore. I plunge my thumbs into it and tear it in half, then again, careful not to spill any of the seeds. Though the skin is leathery, the innards are all right. I give it a tentative sniff and pass two pieces to Hades.

"One in each corner," I say, and we both go to the limits of the garden. My hands are covered in juice and I poke my tongue out, tasting it as I walk back, then sucking it from my fingers when I find it's OK. Hades looks at me and does the same and we meet once more, red mouths and sticky fingers, on either side of the row of narcissi.

"Close your eyes," I say, and he does, immediately.

I steal a moment to look at him while he can't see me, amused by the slight frown wrinkling his brow. I want to reach out with my thumb and smudge it smooth. As if he can tell I'm looking at him, his frown deepens, and I start to smile.

Then I close my eyes too, and turn my thoughts to the seeds.

I feel as calm as a spring day as I reach out for every single one and, like before, urge them to grow. For the husks to split and the life inside to spill out, bear down and rise up at the same time, root itself in the earth and anchor to the dirt. I urge the stems to reach for the endless pale sky, to pull themselves toward it. And again, I feel that chime inside me, a clear, perfect toll.

We open our eyes at the same time and look at our garden. A real, unreal garden.

The red narcissi have been joined by other plants. Dozens of them. Against a wall, tall vines with heart-shaped leaves grow from what I thought were broad beans but are obviously not. These plants have long, gauzy white blossoms made from dozens of tiny flowers; they look like wisteria spun from candy floss or spiderwebs. Purple dahlias-meet-peonies with frilled petals grow on thick stalks between small indigo cabbage-like plants with honeycomb leaves. Rows of lush silver-leafed herbs that fill the air with a horrible sweetness when I brush past them, nine-petaled flowers that look as if they've been dipped in liquid copper. Orchids patterned with skulls, a row of perfectly spherical flowers that look like a model of the universe, deep-blue flowers speckled with long orange stamens raining pollen onto the ground.

Save for a few narrow paths cutting through the growth and around the outside, the entire space is now full of plants. Everything is the color of jewels or precious metal: amethyst, sapphire, ruby, pearl. None of it existed before today.

But the trees are the most incredible part. A quartet with corded trunks tower, taller than the walls, thick, waxy foliage such a dark green it is almost black; the garden isn't a secret anymore. They would be astonishing enough, the trunks so thick that if the two of us reached around them our fingers would scarcely meet. That alone would be enough of a miracle.

Were it not for the golden fruit glinting between their leaves.

Fruit, growing in the land of the dead.

I did this.

Delight bubbles up inside me, sparkling through my veins, and I laugh, spinning around to see it all, then spinning some more because it feels good to spin. All of this has grown from some hybrid of mortal seeds and immortal land. And me. My desire. My power.

I did this. Mine. My garden. My land.

I can feel *everything*. I can feel the plants. I can't explain it, but as I look around, I know exactly which ones need a little extra coaxing, can find the ones that haven't fully woken, even if they're hidden by the leaves of others. I know where they are and what they need from me.

I look at Hades, his eyes wide with astonishment, and I wonder what he'd do if I did this across the whole Underworld. Would he be angry and tear them up, or would he throw himself into them?

Would he pull me down with him?

"Corey," he breathes, then shakes his head, speechless. He turns on the spot, looking at the garden.

I go to the closest tree, reaching for one of the fruits.

It comes away easily in my hands, the skin a gold somewhere between the color of lemons and the juiciest apricots. As with the original pomegranate, I pierce the flesh and pull it apart, smiling when I see the seeds inside. They look like little chunks of amber, little chips of topaz, and I scoop a few out, lifting them to my mouth.

"Don't," Hades says.

I pause. "Why not?"

"Because it seems unwise to eat a thing that grew here, in the land of the dead."

"But I grew it," I say. "It's mine."

"Corey," Hades warns. "You don't know what will happen."

I give him a long look and then eat a seed. It doesn't taste like pomegranate. It tastes like salt and honey. I eat five more.

Nothing happens.

Hades looks almost sad, and he reaches out, but then his head snaps upward and he looks to the skies. He grabs my hand.

"The Furies are coming. Let's go."

"No. I want to see them. I want closure," I say. "You go."

"I'm not leaving you."

My stomach dips. "Hide then. If they see you, it will go badly."

He nods.

"Stay close," I add.

He gives a closed-lip smile, then vanishes. His hand stays in mine for a second longer, then he lets go.

I look up and watch the Furies, black spots against the pale sky, getting closer.

It's only as they get close that I realize there's something wrong with Alecto's shape—she looks bulky, arachnid, as if she has extra arms or legs.

"Corey," Hades breathes.

But I've seen.

Bree.

Parasite

The Furies land. Alecto drops Bree, then pushes her, roughly, unkindly, so she's right in front of me. For a long moment, Bree keeps her head down. And then she looks right at me.

She's washed out, like an old photograph, or curtains faded by the sun. Her chestnut hair is dull, the curls limp. Despite it, her chin is raised mutinously, her eyebrows arched with disdain, and she meets my eyes without blinking. Looking at her, anyone else would think she couldn't care less about what's happening, but I *know* her. She's terrified.

She should be.

This is the first time we've really faced each other since the day before Ali broke up with me. I'd gone to her house, even though she'd been avoiding me, which I'd thought was because she was tired of me talking about Ali. I'd gone there without even messaging her, in case she told me not to, but I still let myself in the back door, because I always had. I'd called "hello" to her brothers, who were glued to something on the TV that looked inappropriately gory, and then I headed up to her room.

At the last second, I decided to knock on her closed bedroom door, only because she wasn't expecting me, and things had been so awkward with us that just going in like usual felt like the wrong thing to do. When she barked "Just a second!" I waited, weirdly panicked about seeing my best friend of almost thirteen years. I didn't think about why *she* sounded panicked.

"Corey!" She'd opened the door and her face had dropped, then turned from red to a weird, sickly gray. "What are you doing here?" She stayed in the doorway, keeping me on the landing.

"Just wondered if you were free?" I remember I'd smiled. I was trying to be normal and fun.

She opened and closed her mouth like a fish, and then shook her head. "I'm babysitting the boys."

"I can stay if you want?"

"Let me just . . . I'll meet you downstairs in a minute."

I'd nodded and gone down to the kitchen to wait, pouring myself a glass of juice. Of course I noticed she was being weird, but I was so relieved she hadn't told me to go home that I didn't care. She came downstairs and hustled me into the back garden with its patio paving stones and begonias in pots.

"Your dress is inside out," I said, noticing the tag flapping in the wind.

"Is it?" She reddened and reached behind her, feeling it. "Weird. So, what did you want?"

I didn't talk about Ali.

I wanted to, because the night before he was supposed to come over while Dad and Merry were at a pub quiz and he never showed up. I was humiliated, because I'd made pizza for us—I even used dairy cheese on Ali's half because he'd started complaining when I just used my cheese—but worse than that, because I'd worn *lingerie* I ordered online after reading a stupid magazine article in line at the Spar about putting the fire back in your relationship. Even though I knew dressing in cheap red lace solely to please him was awful, I didn't care; I just wanted things to go back to how they were. But he never showed up. I called his phone and it was off, and when I walked down the lane, the lace on the knickers chafing my inner thighs, his mom said he was out; she'd thought with me. If not, she didn't know where he was, and I didn't know where either and you'd think on an island of precisely twelve hundred people someone would fucking know where he was, wouldn't you?

So I didn't say a word about him. I asked Bree if she fancied heading to the mainland to go shopping before we went back to school; I made up a stupid story about something I'd seen online; I asked if she was going to Astrid's beach party that night; I asked if she wanted to take the boys swimming in the cove. She said no to everything and then said she had to check on her brothers and she'd message me later, and I *still* didn't get it.

Not until the next day, when Ali dumped me in the cove and Bree didn't answer my messages. Not until I spoke to Merry and then Little Mick and wee Aengus showed up at my door with a list—an actual fucking list—of stuff to get back from me.

Not until I remembered the inside-out dress and how fast she'd hustled me out of the house.

And now here she is, in front of me again.

I know the Furies are manipulating me. I *know* it.

All the rage I'd felt toward them for lying, all the rage I'd felt toward Hades, toward the Oracle, toward my dad, and Ali, and the Islanders. And to her. Bree. All of it comes back to me. Hades touches my hand—a warning—and I snatch it away.

Or did she break your heart?

Yes.

Yes, she fucking broke it. She broke *me*.

The place in my chest where my power comes from fills with hate.

I address the Furies. "What is she doing here?"

An expression crosses Bree's face that I recognize from the last few weeks we were friends, when everything I did annoyed her, and that stokes my fury; the nerve of her being annoyed by me when she was the reason for it all.

"Well?" I step forward, and when she recoils, her defiant expression cracking, something inside me howls in delight. "Why are you in my garden?"

She hesitates. "I—"

"What?" I cut across her. "What could you possibly have to say to me?"

She falters, and I feel another stab of triumph. I wanted this so badly on the Island. I wanted this moment where I'd take her down and pay her back. I imagined it every single night before I went to sleep, my own lullaby.

Alecto, Tisiphone and Megaera are watching us with hungry expressions.

"We found her for you," Megaera says softly.

"She hurt you," Tisiphone tells me.

"You wished for her to die," Alecto says.

I could have lived a thousand lives without Alistair Murray. I lived half of one in the months without Bree.

And I can't forgive her for that.

"Corey . . . ," Bree says.

I shake my head.

Alecto and Tisiphone come to flank me, each taking one of my hands, while Megaera rests her head on my shoulder, making us a many-headed beast. I'm still furious that they lied and that they manipulated me, but as I watch Bree's terror when the snakes nuzzle me, tongues flickering over my temples, I love the Furies again, could almost forgive them. I turn and kiss one of the snakes on its serpent nose, made bold by Bree's terror. They all squirm in delight, clamoring for more of my kisses, which I grant.

"You're *our* sister," Alecto says to me in a soft, deadly voice. "We were there for you. We *are* there for you. You're one of us."

"Almost," Tisiphone says. "There is just one thing she must do."

"You have to choose," Megaera says.

And I understand then why Bree is here; it all slots into place. This is what it comes down to. I have to choose. Will I be the boring little gardener, sweet and naive and hopelessly stupid? Or will I be like them, powerful and fierce and untouchable? Will I be what Hades wants me to be, or what they want me to be?

What do you want to be? something inside me says.

I want to be what I was. I want to be happy with my best friend and my boyfriend and my life, but I can't have that. I can't have the thing I want, and it's because of Bree Dovemuir. She killed the old me, long before I wished her dead.

And I wasn't sorry. Not then.

Not now.

I kiss Alecto's cheek, then Megaera's, then Tisiphone's.

"I'm sorry," Bree says. Her voice is high and choked and it warms my bones. "For what I did."

"They always say they're sorry when it's time to pay," Megaera whispers to me, loud enough that Bree can hear. "I'll tell you a secret, sister: if they'd said they were sorry before they got here, we would have no rights to them. If she'd apologized to you before, if she'd atoned, you wouldn't see her now. She'd be one of the legion dead, nothing more."

I turn to Megaera, and she leans forward, kissing one eyelid, then the other. When she pulls away, her black eyes are gleaming. And when I look back at Bree and she screams, a pure high cry, I know mine are black too. That the choice is made.

"I'm sorry," Bree says again, beginning to sob even while her eyes stay dry. "Corey, I'm sorry."

"They're sorry when it's time to pay," I say in a voice that isn't yet mine, but could be.

"Please don't. Please," she begs. "Corey, I'm sorry. I'm really sorry."

Then she steps back and I feel the snapping of the stalks like a plucked string inside me. *My plants.* Bree looks up in horror as she realizes what she's done, but whatever she sees in my face makes her step back again, trampling more of my flowers, and something inside me roars as I feel them break.

There is a burst of white-hot pain at the ends of my hands and I look down at them to see talons stretching out from the skin. I bite my lip to keep from crying out and my teeth, newly sharp and longer, pierce the skin, and I taste blood, hot and salty.

I smile.

Bree screams again and tries to run, but Tisiphone shifts one way and Alecto the other, blocking her in.

My shoulders start to ache, a crawling sensation across the blades, a stretching and unfolding. I wonder idly if they'll be the dragon wings from my fantasy, and I hope so. Right now, I feel like I could spit gobs of flame at her. Right now, I want that more than anything.

"Here." Megaera slips something into my hand and I look down once more, and this time see a scourge fitted with bronze balls.

It fits right inside my taloned hand and, like Hermes said, it doesn't really hurt them. . . .

"Corey."

A voice rings out behind me like a thunderclap and we all turn, all us Furies, to where Hades stands, visible once more.

His shadows lash at his sides, rising up and behind him like wings, and he is no longer wearing his human clothes, but a long robe that shows broad, muscled shoulders and powerful arms. His eyes are as black as ours, a circlet of cypress leaves woven through his hair, a two-pronged fork in his hand. He towers over us, taller than before, his skin has taken on the sheen of pearl. *Finally,* here he is. The king of the Underworld.

"You may not interfere, Receiver," Megaera says. "It is our job to have justice."

"This isn't justice and she's not one of you." He nods at me.

"Is she not? See her eyes, her hands. See her teeth. Look at her. Ask her if she's owed justice. Will you deny her if she says yes?"

Hades's attention shifts, onyx eyes raking over me, and I stand tall and proud, gripping my lash as he grips his fork. We match. Something in his eyes flickers.

"Receiver, if you try to take her from us you will have war," Tisiphone says. "We have claimed her."

"She's not yours to claim."

"Stop talking about me like I'm not here." My voice is loud and sonorous, and from the corner of my eye I see Bree cover her ears and flinch. "All of you."

The Furies turn to me; even they look surprised, black lips parted.

Hades is the only one who doesn't.

"What you are is not one of them," he says, speaking only to me.

My back aches where the wings still haven't come through and I wish they would. *Let's just get this over with.*

"And punishing this girl won't make you feel better."

I look at Bree cowering with the snapped stems of the flowers I grew from my will around her and the urge to strike rises again.

"It's worth a try," I say, smiling when Bree whimpers.

Hades looks at me for a long moment. "Then go ahead." He leans back and his shadows become a throne, forming around him. He sprawls across it, raising a lazy hand and waving at me. "Do it. Water your garden with her pain, if it pleases you."

I turn to Bree and tighten my grip on the scourge, feeling my palm slick with sweat. It won't actually hurt her, I remember again. She doesn't have flesh or nerves. It's the fear of it. That's the punishment. The terror.

She's already terrified.

Bree's eyes are squeezed shut and I remember the day we had our ears pierced. That for all her big talk she'd gripped my hand with painful tightness, and she'd closed her eyes so the piercer wouldn't see she was crying. And I knew if I told her to forget it and let's just go home, she would have, but I didn't. Instead I pretended to be afraid, really, truly afraid. Because sometimes you can only be brave if you think there's someone else more scared than you and that was the price I'd pay because we were Bree-and-Corey, Corey-and-Bree, until the bitter end.

And what a bitter end it was.

The scourge slips from my hand and disappears before it hits the ground.

"Corey?" Alecto says.

"What are you doing?" Megaera takes my face in her hands. "You have to punish her, Corey. You have to finish this."

The tips of her talons press into the skin along my temples. Long nails are no good if you're a gardener. I peel her fingers away gently, looking at my own claws as I do. My hands don't look like my hands anymore. No calluses. No sign of who I am in them.

She's right. I do have to finish this.

I turn to Hades.

"I want to go," I say.

"I promised," he says, reaching for my hand.

Then we are gone.

Annual

WE APPEAR ON A LONG, DESERTED DOCK NEAR the towers by the gates to the Underworld. Hades looks like himself again, no robe, no circlet, no fork, and I—

I don't know what myself is. I don't know what I am. Who I am. What I want. Where I stand.

Hades brushes his thumb roughly over my mouth, and when my tongue snakes out to lick my lips, I find my teeth are back to normal. When I look down, my hands are too.

"And so, you're finally leaving," he says.

"What will happen to my garden?" I say, even though it's not what I mean. Not completely.

"I'll keep it safe." He smiles, lips closed.

"What do I do back there?"

"What you did before, I suppose."

I let out a humorless laugh. "I was miserable before."

"I know."

I look at him. "How do you know?"

He half turns, looking past me. "I told you I came to the Thesmophoria for you."

I nod, my pulse speeding.

"The Furies weren't the only ones who *felt* you," he says. Then, to my absolute shock, *he* blushes, two pink spots high on his cheeks. "During the summer. One moment nothing, and then . . . you." He pauses again and clears his throat. The color in his skin fades. "So I decided to come to the festival to find you. But you were not ready to be found, so I chose to let you be. But first I allowed myself one dance. A kiss I should not have stolen."

"It wasn't stolen," I say. "It was freely given. I hadn't even had any wine then."

He smiles again, and this time it reaches his eyes. "I'm glad to know."

"And now?" I ask. "Am I ready to be found?"

"I don't think that's for me to decide." His hand rises to cup my cheek.

I hear footsteps and Hades releases me, turning to nod to someone. I see the Boatman walking toward us, the shade of a young man following him.

The shade looks at me first, eyes wide, then he spots Hades and folds in on himself.

"Go," Hades tells him, and he darts past us. "Charon will take you back to the Island."

"Will everyone be all right?" I ask. I don't want to care, but I'm painfully aware we left Bree in the garden with three very angry Furies and I'm worried about them too. All of them. None of them deserve it, but you can't turn love off. I wish you could.

"No real harm can come to any of them," he says, but we both know that isn't an answer. "Goodbye, Corey." Hades leans forward and kisses my cheek. I feel his coldness and for a second I want to lean into it and stay there forever.

Then he turns and walks away, his shadows hurrying after him like courtiers.

The Boatman is silent as we make our way along the deserted dock and I'm grateful; I don't have the energy for even basic small talk. When we reach the lone boat moored at the end, he offers a hand to help me aboard, and I only realize after I'm settled in the stern that the old me would have recoiled from his skeletal fingers or forced myself to take his hand out of politeness, then shivered at the feel of his cold, papery skin.

But I guess it would be hypocritical for me to flinch from the inhuman now, wouldn't it.

The tips of my fingers still hurt from where the talons—*my talons*—pierced through them. There's no wound, the skin isn't even red, but when I press my fingers together, the pain is as bright and hot as a burn. My shoulders ache too, and I roll them, trying to work out the pain like it was nothing more than a kink from sleeping badly. I run my tongue over my teeth, then over the punctures they made in my lower lip. Then I do it again, where Hades's thumb was.

"Ready, Lady?" the Boatman asks, voice rustling like wind through wet leaves.

Yes. No. I grip the sides of the bench, sending a jolt of pain through my hands, and nod. Ready as I'll ever be.

The Boatman uses an oar to push away from the dock. Ahead of us the gates to the land of the dead swing inward on silent hinges, causing waves to slap against the boat, and I realize with a dull, distant start that—the Boatman excepted—I'm the first person in the history of everything to be rowed *out* of the Underworld. There's no joy in it, though. No thrill or triumph that I'm finally going back. Only a dull ache that feels a lot like heartbreak.

As we pass beneath the towers, I hear a low, rumbling growl and turn to see six red, glowing eyes high above us in the shadows, following our path. I know what it is. It falls silent when I meet its gaze, and I watch the eyes move lower, imagining three heads coming down to rest on giant paws. The eyes stay on us, watchful, until we've passed, and I keep my gaze on them.

When we're clear of the gates, I turn to see them close. My heart thuds heavily in my chest, speeding up when something moves in one of the windows in the tower on the left, catching my attention. I see a sliver of pale cheek and forehead framed by shadows, a single dark eye. I don't raise a hand, and neither does he, but I don't look away until he blurs into nothingness. Then I face front again, and watch the horizon as it comes to us.

We follow the Acheron between the mountains, and I think of Erebus and wish we'd pass it, even though that's stupid; it's not like the Furies would be sitting out on the tiny spit of a landing strip, waiting to wave as we passed, to wish me a safe trip. I picture them swooping down from the skies and mobbing the boat to spirit me back home, pulling me into the tangle of them and us, feathers and scales and claws. I'd let them, that's the thing. Even after everything. Thanks to them I've literally seen the monster in myself, and it liked company. We liked *their* company.

Then we're clear of the mountains, the river spitting us out to sea, and I watch as the water surrounding the boat changes from the brown of the Acheron to the slate gray of the Styx, which surrounds the Underworld. Then, finally, it becomes a deep, inky blue. At almost the same instant, goose bumps prickle over my entire body. Not from fear or apprehension, but because I'm cold.

My breath catches in my chest.

I'm cold, and there's color. And that means—

We passed through no fog or barrier, but at some point we'd crossed the unseen line between the realm of the dead and the land of the living. When I turn to look behind me, the Underworld is gone, only dark ocean all around as if it had never been there at all.

I wrap my arms around my shivering body, look up and see stars.

I let my head fall back, gazing up into the moonless sky. Hundreds of thousands of tiny white lights dot the sky, the Milky Way a pale ribbon weaving between them. Orion's Belt. Ursa Major. Calliope. Perseus. They are the ones I know, the ones I can always find, and so I do, searching for them, tracing them with my eyes; the same reliable old stars in their same old, familiar places.

A lump forms in my throat because it's beautiful, so beautiful, and I hadn't appreciated it before. The thing about growing up somewhere like the Island is you stop marveling at things like the stars and the Milky Way, because unless there are clouds you see them every night; they're always up there, always waiting. You can get used to beauty, have a surfeit of it, stop looking—not because you're ungrateful but just because you're so used to it. You'll take anything for granted if you think it's always going to be there. It's only when you lose it that you realize how much you wanted it.

"Are you well, Lady?" the Boatman asks, his voice carrying easily over the water.

"Yes. I think so." I lower my head to look at him and find I'm crying, but I don't know why. I wipe the tears away with the back of my hand and clamp my jaws together.

He lowers the oars and shrugs off his cloak, then holds it out to me. "Take this. It's cold for you on this side."

"Don't you need it?" I ask.

"No, Lady. Please," he says, pushing the cloak toward me.

I take it and swing it over me. It brings none of his warmth with it, because he has none to lend, but it keeps the cold night air from my skin. The lump in my throat returns and I swallow it down.

"We're almost there."

As he says it, a shaft of bright light sweeps out across the sea and I twist to see my father's lighthouse, high on the rocks, the beam passing over the dark water and then moving on.

"Won't he see us?" I ask, not sure. "My father. He's one of the lighthouse keepers."

"No one sees me until they're meant to."

I'm relieved only for the split second it takes for the double meaning of his words to sink in. It would be so like the other gods to allow to me to finally come back, only for it to be a trade with someone I love. It would be so very them to have me disembark and have to watch my father, or Merry, or someone else I care about take my place in the stern of the boat.

The Boatman reads my mind. "Be easy, Lady. I have no collections planned tonight." His voice is solemn, but his red eyes are kind when they meet mine. I give him a weak smile, which he acknowledges with a nod.

As we round Thetis Point, I see a sleek gray head emerge from the water a few meters away, strangely human black eyes following the boat. A seal. I wonder if it's the same one Bree and Ali saw last . . . I stall when I realize I don't know how long I've been gone.

"What month is it?" I ask the Boatman. "What year?"

"I don't know, Lady. I don't keep mortal time."

A shiver spills from the base of my neck all the way down my spine. For all I know, time in the Underworld passed like time in a faerie kingdom; a day there is a month here, a week is a year. Maybe I'll arrive back on the Island to find that everyone I love and know is already in the Underworld and has been for decades, that I flew over them with the Furies and never knew.

The seal vanishes silently beneath the surface, and then I see the harbor, and the same old fishing boats I knew as a kid, the *Elizabeth*, and the *Kahana*, and *Our Mutual Friend;* so many mornings spent harassing tired fishermen with Bree to find out if they'd ever seen mermaids or even sirens. If they're still here, still working, from the looks of the lobster crates piled up in the back, then I can't have been away long. It's a splinter of hope.

The Boatman rows us right into the dock, to the mooring beside Connor's boat, then rests the oars and rises, walking smoothly to me, hand outstretched. Once again, I take it, let him help me from the boat onto the solid dock.

I am back from the land of the dead.

"Farewell until we meet again, Lady." The Boatman returns to his bench and reaches for the oars.

"I . . ." I falter, suddenly not wanting him to go. I try to think of something to keep him here, but nothing comes except: "Your cloak. Do you need it?"

"Keep it," he says as I begin to pull it off.

"Are you sure?" I'm stalling, and I don't know why. "Because if you wanted to wait, I could fetch a jacket?"

"You'll be all right, Lady," he says quietly. "I am certain of it."

I'm glad one of us is.

I stay on the dock and watch him pull away, rowing back out of the harbor to wherever he goes next. Then I exhale, and a small sob that had been hiding in my throat comes out too. I close my eyes and stand, listening to the sound of the ocean, the car-alarm screams of seagulls somewhere nearby. The Island. I'm back. *Where I belong*, I tell myself, trying to ignore the way it has the hollow ring of a lie.

My legs feel rubbery as I turn and begin to walk through the deserted harbor, up through the boatyard and past the boat sheds to the bottom of the high street.

Even in the dark, everything is too bright; the orange glare from the streetlamps, the red postbox at the end of the lane, the green paint around the windowsills and door of the pub, the whitewash on the buildings; all of it hurts my eyes after the ambient blankness of the Underworld.

I turn onto the high street and stop, staring along it, drinking it in. There's the Spar, Cally Martin's ancient silver Fiesta parked outside. The pothole in the center of the road is still there; the sole traffic light on the Island, at the crossroads opposite the doctor's, is still dented from when Astrid's older brother drove their dad's car into it during a driving lesson three years ago. A familiar battered black bicycle is chained to the lamppost outside the butcher's. When I get closer, I see a note has been cable-tied to it. I open it to see a typed police notice signed by Constable Moretide warning the owner to move it or they'll be fined. Declan has added a handwritten part, telling Thom Crofter he's on his final warning and he really will be fined if he does it again, this time Declan means it.

Nothing has changed.

The scrappy ginger tom that sometimes belongs to Lars's family slinks along the wall, turning to hiss at me as I pass, and I hiss back without thinking, stunned when the cat pelts into a garden, fur on end. I cross the road and peer into the window of the bakers, half expecting to see a monster looking back. I stare at myself, raising a hand to touch my cheeks, my mouth. They feel soft and warm. They feel living.

In the street beyond, the town clock chimes, making me jump out of my skin. I count: three chimes, and as the last one fades away a light comes on in one of the upstairs window in a cottage further down the street. I remember who lives there; Craig McGovan, the brother of poor, punished Mr. McGovan, and his sons, fishermen, they're waking up to begin the day.

I hurry past, heading for my dad's house—*my home*, I remind myself—slinking along the lane in my borrowed cloak and bare feet. Another reason I'm lucky I've arrived in the dead of night—how would I explain what I was wearing if anyone saw me?

As I turn onto my road, my heart starts to speed up, my palms turning sweaty. I wipe them on my shift, my mouth dust dry. *This is where I belong*, I tell myself firmly. *This is my home. All my things are here. My life is here.*

I skirt around the side of the house, not quite ready to go inside, opening the squeaking gate and entering my garden.

It's dark, with no moon to guide me, the streetlight doesn't reach this far, but I know this place better than any other and my body remembers it, so I don't smash my shins or stub my toes or stumble into or over anything. I sit on the side of one of the beds and wait for my eyes to adjust, then I survey my former kingdom. Most of the beds are still covered over with the black sheeting I put on them; the only one still uncovered is the one I left that way; the garden is like Sleeping Beauty's kingdom, frozen in time waiting for a princess to wake. I walk over to the uncovered bed and look down in dismay at the decaying remains of the parsnips and cabbages I'd been growing. It looks like Dad and Merry left them to die, and that sends a bolt of annoyance through me, that they couldn't even be bothered to try to care for them, or even to pick them.

I push my fingers into the earth, sucking in a sharp breath at how warm and moist and alive it feels. It's a living thing and little jolts of electricity travel along my arm, up and down, like my nerves are communicating with the soil. And as soon as I think that, I whisper into the night:

"Grow."

Almost immediately the life begins to return to the poor dead plants. I watch the withered tops of the parsnips turn smooth and plump, new fronds growing tall and strong, and I know if it was light enough I'd see they were a deep verdant green. The cabbages fill out, thick leaves blooming and folding tightly on each other. Within a matter of seconds, they look how they had when I left; a minute more sees them swollen to a size that would win prizes if I took them to the summer fair.

Nothing I grow here will be unexpected, or new. The seeds I scatter will grow into whatever's on the front of the packet. I will never again wonder what will grow from the strange alchemy of myself and the soil of the Underworld, and I hate it, because I never knew it was possible before, and now I don't want to give it up.

I pull the vegetables from the earth and carry them up to the house.

The back door is open, as always, because no one on the Island locks their doors. I tiptoe inside.

It smells like home.

I'd never noticed how it has a smell, because I'd never been away for more than a night or two before, but now I know it does. It smells like mechanical oil from my dad, and coconut oil from

Merry. It smells like cumin and garlic, metal, and coffee, clean laundry and something warm I don't have a name for, but it's ours, a mix of all three of us.

I put the parsnips and the cabbages on the draining board and open the fridge. There's a lone bottle of water in there and I open and drink from it, not bothering to get a glass. It tastes flat, almost stale, after the water in the Underworld, even though I know it can't be because I just broke the seal. I leave the fridge open for the light, planning to check the cupboards for snacks, when I see the *Island Argus* on the table.

I lift the paper and check the date: *Week 11, March 20.*

Stomach swooping, heart racing, I take the paper with me, closing the fridge and heading to the living room, where I find the remote on the arm of the sofa and turn the TV on. I mute it, flinching away from the sudden, bright glare as the screen comes to life, and squint at the date on the TV guide, my mouth falling open.

March 22. Tomorrow is my birthday. I've been gone for almost five months.

I hear a creak above me and startle, turning the TV off and freezing in place. I listen to Dad and Merry's bedroom door open, slow, shuffling footsteps on the landing, the bathroom door clicking closed. Then I hear a muffled male cough and tears spring into my eyes. *Dad.*

That's my dad; my lovely, kind dad, who raised me alone for so long, and who I've missed so much without really knowing it until now, doing what Merry calls the *shuffle of shame* to the bathroom at four a.m. because he'll have insisted on taking a cup of tea to bed with him. I have to stifle a laugh, because it's all so familiar; I've heard them have the same exasperated conversation so many times—even made jokes about it with Bree when she stayed over, mock bickering about waking each other up if we got one more hot chocolate, one more soda.

It makes my heart soar and sink all at once; because they're still the same old Merry and Dad, doing the same old things. And I'm . . . not the same.

I daren't move as I hear the flush, then the running tap and the door opening once more. . . . Every nerve in my body is stretched taut. . . . And then the footsteps return to the bedroom, the steady tread of the half-asleep, not even hesitating, completely unaware there is someone else in the house. I wait for the bedroom door to close, and when it does my bones turn to liquid, the paper still clutched in my hand shaking. I stay where I am, a living statue, long enough for my pulse to get back to normal, and then I creep to the kitchen, return the paper to the table, then scrawl a note: *Surprise! I'm home. I caught an early boat from the mainland and I've gone to sleep for a bit.*

Then, edging up the stairs like a crab, I sneak into my bedroom and shut the door behind me.

It smells of me, of the me I used to be. The curtains are open, letting light in from the streetlamp that falls on my neatly made bed and the pile of clean clothes at the end of it. I have a vision of Merry or my dad tidying up, airing the room, wanting it to be nice for when I came back, leaving the clothes on the bed so I'd know they hadn't gone in my drawers, had respected my privacy even as they cleaned up my mess.

I wonder how bewildered they'd been by my sudden departure *to my mother's*, how much it hurt them, whether there were moments when they knew something about it was wrong. Then I wonder how they'll feel about me being back, strolling in in the dead of night with no warning. I hadn't considered *they* might feel as weird about it as I do, that I'm not the only person who might have changed. Too late now, though. I suppose if they're against my return, I could really go and find my mum.

I pull off the Boatman's cloak and my shift, and drop them to the floor, then hesitate, guiltily picking them back up. I hang the cloak in my wardrobe and drop the shift into the empty laundry basket, finding clean underwear and pajamas in the stack of fresh clothes and pulling them on. The rest I move neatly to the floor, close the curtains over, then crawl into bed.

Everything is too smooth and too soft; the fabric of my pajamas feels weird against my skin, the mattress beneath me yields too much under my weight. It all smells wrong too; floral and chemical, and I roll onto my back to get away from it.

You're home, I tell myself. *This is where you belong. Here, in this room, in this town, on this Island. This is where your people are.*

But I don't believe it. I lie there, staring up at the ceiling I've stared up at my whole life, and I don't believe it. It's only when I finally get out of bed, retrieve my shift, wrap it around the pillow and press my face into it that I'm able to fall into an uneasy sleep.

STASIS

I WAKE UP TO MERRY WATCHING ME, A CUP OF coffee cradled in her hands.

I sit up, gasping, pulled from some dream that slips away within seconds of me waking, and there she is, leaning against the doorframe.

"Merry?" I say, and with three steps she's beside me, the coffee spilling on the bedside table when she puts it down and pulls me into her arms.

She holds me tightly, her hands pressed against the tender part of my back, but I don't squirm away. Instead, I wrap my arms around her, just as firmly. She smells the same.

"Why didn't you say you were coming?" she asks my hair, then squeezes me. "Why didn't you call us?"

"Surprise," I say, voice muffled by her shoulder.

She pulls back then, keeping my arms in her hands. "Is everything all right? Did something happen with your mom?"

"No, everything's fine," I say. "Seriously," I add when she raises her eyebrows. "I just . . . I wanted to come back."

"What time did you get in?"

"Oh, around five, maybe?" I fudge. "I got the first boat over."

"I wish you'd said you were coming. We've got nothing in for you."

"That's OK, I don't need anything. Where's Dad?"

"Work. He missed your note, you know. And the veg on the side. He walked straight past them. You know what he's like first thing, as bad as you before you've thrown three mugs of coffee down your throat. Talking of which."

She picks up the cup she brought, frowning at the ring of liquid it leaves behind. "I'll clean that later. What's wrong?" Her voice is sharp when she turns back to me.

Tears are streaming down my face, and I shake my head, not able to explain them.

"Hey." Merry puts the cup down again and pulls me back into her arms. "What's going on, Cor?"

"I just missed you," I choke into her shoulder, tips of my fingers on fire as I press them into her, which reminds me what lurks underneath my skin and makes me cry harder, because she wouldn't want to comfort me if she knew there was a monster in me. "So much."

"We missed you too." She rubs my back like I'm a little kid. "I didn't even realize how much until I saw your note, came up here and there you were." Her voice sounds tight, and when I lean away I see tears in her eyes. "Look at what you've done," she laughs, wiping them with a sleeve. "What a pair."

"Sorry," I say, feeling wretched because it's such a small word and it has to hold so much and I can never, ever explain to her or anyone else the half of it. But there is something else I need to say, out loud, to someone who counts. "I have to tell you something."

"OK." She looks at me, her expression wary.

I take a deep breath. "I wished Bree dead. The night she died. I wished for it, and it happened."

Merry stares at me.

"Oh, Corey." Her eyes fill again. "Is that why you left? Because you thought you were responsible? Oh, pet." She embraces me again. "I want you to listen to me, and listen carefully. You did not kill that girl. Even if you wished for it."

"You don't understand—"

"Corey, you can't wish someone to death."

But I did. And I shouldn't have. I especially shouldn't have been happy about it. It's not who I am.

Merry lets me cry, and sits with me until I'm out of tears and my head throbs with weepy pain. "Better?" she asks, and I nod, because she needs me to. "And you're sure nothing happened to make you come back—not that I'm not over the moon you are," she says. "You're not in trouble, you didn't have a fight?"

I almost smile. "No."

She gives me a long, searching look. "All right," she says finally. "Well, how about I go and make fresh coffee?" I nod, and she continues. "And you should have a shower, because honestly, Corey, you look filthy, and you kind of reek."

A surprised laugh bursts from me at the unexpected parenting. I must be an absolute mess if she's calling me out.

"What's that?" She reaches behind me for the shift still wrapped around my pillow.

I shove it away. "Nothing. It's nothing. I'll be down once I'm clean."

Merry gives me another piercing glance. "OK," she says slowly, suspicion lacing her voice. "Don't be long."

I am long, though. I get under the shower and I stay there, letting the hot water fall on me, beating against the sore spots above my shoulder blades until the ache is finally gone. I wash and condition my hair, comb it and then repeat the process two, three times, until my hair squeaks and my scalp hurts. I pumice my feet, sloughing off all the hard skin that served me so well as I climbed to and from my alcove and in my secret garden. Then I wash my body again and again, using almost an entire bar of soap as I scrub away at months of Underworld dust and crud that turns the water brown before it swirls away, leaving me disgusted and fascinated. I really was filthy.

Hades didn't seem to mind.

Stop.

By the time I get out of the shower I'm dizzy from the heat and the steam. I open the window and watch as the cool outside air seems to suck it away, then wipe the mirror to look at myself. I look older; the planes of my face are sharper, cheekbones more prominent, eyes warier. I peer down at my body, turning this way and that. I still have the scars, and way more muscle than I used to, but otherwise I am still myself. Whatever I am, or am not, I look human.

As I walk back to my room to dress, my newly smooth feet tender against the floorboards, I hear Merry talking and pause, for a second thinking someone else is here before I realize she's on the phone. Talking about me.

". . . got a T-shirt or something wrapped around her pillow," I catch, and strain to hear the rest. "I guess she must have started seeing someone new and it ended. Poor kid. She was such a wreck last time. Right before her eighteenth too." A pause. "Yeah, tomorrow. I know, me too, completely slipped my mind. And Craig hasn't mentioned it. I don't know what we'll do."

So, she thinks I've come home with my tail between my legs because I've been dumped. Again. And I suppose I kind of have; except it's not a boy, it's a god, and he didn't dump me, I kind of dumped him, and the Furies, and my other garden, and everything to do with the Underworld.

I can work with that.

It stings, though.

I dress in jeans and a sweater, but the denim chafes and feels constricting, my legs not used to being covered anymore, so I end up pulling on a loose cotton dress, not a million miles away from the shift, which I hide at the bottom of my wardrobe. I dig out a pair of soft pumps to protect my feet, twist my hair—which is darker now, no longer wheat blonde but ashy, like the Underworld has leached the color out of it—into a knot on top of my head. I pause long enough to vaguely neaten my bed, then go downstairs. Merry is still on her call, though by now she's moved on to talking about work, something about volunteers and a team briefing. I wave as I pass her pacing the living room and head into the kitchen to pour myself a coffee.

The caffeine hits me like a freight train, sending me into a full-body shudder. With no milk I can drink in the house, I add water from the fridge, diluting the coffee until it doesn't feel like I'm drinking lightning. Then I open the back door and step outside.

It *hurts*.

The world is green and blue, saturated in color that takes my breath away. The fields beyond my garden, the emerging leaves on the trees, emerald and bright, a cerulean cloudless sky above. Yolky sunlight, coming from behind the cottage and bathing the garden, the warm red glow of the terra-cotta bricks in the walls. There are birds singing, and it seems so loud to me; hard to imagine that once, not so long ago, I wouldn't have noticed it for more than a moment unless I'd tried to. Now it's a riot and it makes my head ring.

"It's colder out than it looks." Merry joins me, arms crossed over her chest. "We didn't know what to do with it." She nods toward the garden. "Still, I suppose it's early enough in the season for you to get stuff going. If you're sticking around," she adds, unsure.

I stay silent.

"We'll order in for tea, if you want?" Merry continues, glossing over our uncertainty. "I can order at the Indian place you like, and have it brought over on the seven o'clock boat. A birthday treat."

"That'll be nice." I try to sound like I mean it.

"Cor, I've got to confess, we haven't got you anything, for tomorrow," she continues awkwardly. "I'll be honest, it completely slipped our minds, and then I saw your note . . . I'm really sorry, pet. We'll make it up to you."

"It's fine," I say, though it hurts to have been forgotten. I suppose I deserve it. "I didn't expect anything."

"It's your eighteenth, Corey," she says. "I can't believe we didn't remember. But work's been so busy, and you know what it's like." She frowns, obviously confused that she could have forgotten something so important. To be honest, I'm confused too. I was gone for five months, not five years.

"It's fine," I repeat, turning to her and pulling her into a hug. It's not her fault. "Seeing you again is more than enough."

"Aye, well." She laughs, squeezing me and letting me go. "Listen, I've got to go out to the cliffs to meet some of the volunteers for the nest count," she says. "Do you want to come?"

"I'll be all right. I'll go and see Astrid."

Merry gives me a sideways look. "She'll be in school. It's Tuesday."

School. "Right, yeah. But's it's almost lunchtime. I'll just pop by."

Her eyes narrow. "How's school down south? You settle in OK?"

I shrug. "Fine. Boring. School's school."

She isn't fooled for a second and I'm only saved by her phone ringing. I follow her inside, listening as she tells whoever's on the other end that she's on her way.

"We'll talk later," she promises me, grabbing her bag from the table.

"Sure." I smile. "See you when you're back."

"Corey . . ." She hesitates in the doorway. "I love you. You know that, don't you? I know you're not mine, but I love you like you are."

"I am yours," I say immediately. "Yours and Dad's. And I love you too. Both of you, more than anything."

Merry rushes back to me and pulls me into her arms, and I hold her, tightly, breathing her in.

"All right, I'll see you later." She kisses my cheek, like the Furies did, then leaves.

I exhale, feeling dangerously close to tears again.

I SHOULD SPEND THE MORNING WORKING OUT the details of my cover story, coming up with something convincing about the mother I couldn't actually point out in a crowd and our made-up life together on the mainland—fake school, fake friends, the fake ex-boyfriend who's my excuse for showing up out of the blue. I even start, opening my laptop and logging in, fingers automatically tapping out the password I barely remember. But then I close it, instead heading downstairs and grabbing a jacket before leaving the cottage. I want to be outside. I want to use my legs.

If I'd thought the world was too bright the night before, and the garden was a riot, it's nothing compared to how bad it is in full sunlight. How do people live like this, how do they not constantly have migraines from it all? The colors of everything assault me; I barely get to the end of the path before I have to run back to the house and rummage in a drawer for sunglasses, jamming them onto my face. They help, a little, muting the worst of it, making it bearable as I walk to the center of Daly. Where I find they do nothing to disguise me.

"That's not Corey Allaway?" Cally Martin barrels out of the Spar to stare at me. "When did you get back?"

I guess I'm finally forgiven for telling her to piss off.

"This morning," I say over my shoulder, not wanting to stop. "Sorry, Cally, I'm running late."

"You stop by on your way back," she shouts. "I want to hear about life on the mainland, if you're not too important for us Island folk now."

I almost turn around and say it again. *Almost.*

It's the same all along the high street, people call after me, gaping like I have horns, the idea of which makes me laugh to myself, because it's about the only thing I don't have lurking somewhere inside me. In the end, I duck down the alley by the tearoom and walk along the back lane, dodging bins, heading toward the school in peace. I hear the bell toll twelve, and realize I actually could go and see Astrid at lunch, if I wanted. And it's not like I have anything else to do.

The Island school is a pair of squat stone buildings on the east of the Island, one for reception and junior pupils, and the other for seniors. A few years ago, the council had considered merging our school with two others, but the motion didn't pass, because it would mean us having to get a boat over to another island and back each day, and if the weather was bad—which it is, in winter—we'd end up missing loads. So we stayed here, in our little school.

I hang back, hiding behind a thick oak, waiting, watching the doors open and children flood the playgrounds.

I see Wee Aengus and Little Mick—Bree's brothers—come flying out, coats done up only at the top button, flaring like capes behind them as they race down the lane, heading home for the hot lunch Mrs. Dovemuir cooks every day for them. More follow, then the doors for the senior school are thrown wide and amid the small crowd of teenagers that stream out I spot Astrid, chatting animatedly to Hunter, followed by Lars and Manu holding hands. That makes me smile; I'm glad they're still together. I'm about to call out to them, when I stop.

My heart stutters, but in a reluctant, shadowy way, like a dog doing an old trick for a new owner, as Ali comes out and leans against the wall, clearly waiting for someone. It does it again when a girl comes out and walks straight toward him, calling goodbye to her friends. It takes me a few seconds to place her: Mirielle Mason, from the year below us. She looks up at him and smiles, he bends to kiss her, and I brace for it to hurt, but it doesn't, not even a little.

When he breaks the kiss, he looks up, in my direction, as if he senses me watching, and I duck behind the tree, heart racing, trying to come up with a reason why I'm lurking there, wearing sunglasses, that doesn't make me sound insane.

But he doesn't come over, and I move around the trunk, watch him walk toward his house the way he once had with me, and then with Bree, perfectly in step, one arm slung loosely over Mirielle's shoulder, hers tucked under his blazer, around his waist. They'll be going to his house, where Ali will start to make them toasted sandwiches, but stop to kiss. They might not eat at all, or she might end up finishing them off and they'll stuff them down as they race back to school to beat the bell. I know it, because it's how I spent lunchtimes, once upon a time.

Part of me wants to know when he started dating Mirielle, how long it took him to stop mourning Bree. Did he wait for his hair to grow back, or was he already looking around at Bree's perideipnon, deciding who his next victim would be.

I realize as I think it that I don't actually care, that I'm not even curious enough to ask someone, and it surprises me. It happened without the rites or the rituals or any of the stuff I thought it would take. With just a bit of time, I am over my first love.

First romantic love.

I watch Ali and Mirielle, and for a heartbeat I want to call after him, catch up with them, just say hello, like I would anyone else. But the urge goes, and I turn away.

"Corey?"

Mr. McKinnon is standing with his bike, smiling at me.

"You're back?"

"Yes."

"Coming back to school?" he asks.

I guess so. I nod.

So does he. "Good. We've missed you. How are things on the mainland?"

"Oh, you know. Different."

"Were you waiting for someone?"

"No. Just passing, on my way somewhere."

"I'll let you get on with it." He begins to wheel his bike away, then pauses, turning back. "It's your birthday tomorrow, isn't it? Happy birthday for tomorrow if I don't see you."

"Thanks. Bye, Mr. McKinnon."

Bree's birthday is exactly a month after mine. A whole month of *Listen to me, I'm older and wiser than you* and *Don't worry, Grandma, I'll take care of you.* And now, never again. I'll always be older and wiser and she'll always be seventeen, barely even getting the best summer of her life.

I start walking in the opposite direction of the town, not wanting to see anyone else from school. I only realize where I'm heading when the hill looms above me and I see the temple, and then it feels inevitable. I pull the sunglasses off, squeeze through the nekrós gate, and follow the path around to the graveyard.

Bree's grave is easy to find, even if I hadn't seen the plot from Lynceus Hill on the day of the funeral, it's one of just two new ones added since the last time I was here, which was with her and Ali, funnily enough, before everything went wrong.

I stare at Bree's gravestone. I'd have thought Mrs. Dovemuir would go really in, something massive and ornate in the shape of a heart or with columns, maybe even with a photo of Bree on it, but it's just a simple, clean white rectangular stone, with pink roses and celery flowers in a vase on one side, a lekythos on the other. I pick up the lekythos and pour some oil onto the grass.

Bree Dovemuir, cherished daughter and beloved sister, taken too soon.

She should have got to be eighteen. At least.

"Don't they say every criminal eventually returns to the scene of the crime?" A crow voice croaks and I turn, mouth open, to see the Oracle winding her way between plots toward me, her black dog trotting at her side, a midnight-colored scarf fluttering like wings behind her.

FLOWERS

"WHAT ARE YOU DOING HERE?" I ASK, TOO shocked to be polite. "I didn't think you left your islet."

"I heard a rumor a girl had returned from the Underworld and I had to see if it was true," she says, smiling wickedly at me. She's old right now, her back bent, her face wrinkled like a walnut. "And so it is. Here you are, returned from the place no one usually gets to leave. Why, I can count on my hands how many precede you. You must have made quite an impression. Or you were thrown out for bad behavior. With you it could be either."

She cackles at her own joke, then walks right over Bree's grave, moving to stand behind it, the dog settling at her feet. I watch, scandalized, as she pulls two metal cups, a small flask and a plastic bottle of something red from her apparently bottomless pocket and lines them up on top of Bree's headstone, making her own minibar.

"That's sacrilege," I say.

"I doubt she'd complain and I don't see why you are, unless everything's all fixed now between you?"

I shake my head.

She looks up at me and frowns, reaching towards my mouth. "Now, what have you been doing?" she asks. "Eating what you shouldn't. Well, that's that then."

I slap her away gently, and touch my lips, expecting to see gold, but my fingers come away clean.

It seems unwise to eat a thing that grew here, in the land of the dead.

The Oracle opens the flask and pours a clear liquid into both cups, then tops it off with the red juice. She holds a cup out to me and I lean forward and sniff it, smelling something sharply alcoholic, and something sweetly familiar.

"What is it?" I ask.

"Vodka and pomegranate juice." She gives me a cunning look. "Normal pomegranate. Not your fancy golden ones. Take it," she continues, before I can refuse. "You owe me for tidying up the mess you left behind."

"I really am sorry about that—"

"I don't mean the tantrum you threw before you stormed off my islet. I mean the mess you left behind here when you went gallivanting off to claim your destiny."

"I didn't go off to claim my destiny. I picked a flower and got sucked into the Underworld," I tell her. "I didn't do it on purpose."

She gives me a look.

"I didn't," I repeat. "And I thought Hades had fixed every-thing."

The Oracle leans over the gravestone and lifts my hand, put-ting the cup into it.

"Yes, by telling me to. It was me that made sure your father and Meredith thought you were safe with your mother, and not missing or drowned. Me that convinced their thoughts to drift away like smoke whenever they wanted to call you. I had them—all of them—think there was nothing unusual in their not hearing a word from you, nothing strange about you vanish-ing between one moment and the next, leaving your phone and your laptop and all your clothes behind. I had my work cut out covering for you, Corey Allaway. So you will accept my hospital-ity when I offer it."

She glares at me, her face shifting from old to young, then settling in the middle, maternal and fierce.

I raise the cup to my mouth like I'm sealing a bargain. The first sip is all juice, the second mostly vodka, and it stings the wounds on my lip from my teeth, then burns my throat all the way down. When the cup is empty, I try to hand it back to her, only for her to fill it again.

"I'm still underage until tomorrow."

"It hasn't stopped you before." She grins.

"How did you do it?" I ask, swirling the vodka and juice to mix it this time. "Make everyone forget. With the nepenthe?"

"No need." The Oracle smiles again, sly and clever, and for a second she reminds me of the Furies. "Not when the Island's water is contaminated by the Lethe herself."

My mouth falls open. "Seriously? The Lethe's in our water?"

"Not much, not much. A mere trickle. Oh, don't look so po-faced," she snaps, and I adjust my expression, though I'm not entirely sure what po-faced is. "Were it not for the Lethe making things nice and easy, no mortal would be allowed to stay on the Island. Not with it being so close to the Underworld, with all the comings and goings. Too many questions otherwise. Too many unexplained things here at death's door. Bad enough you kids telling each other to climb the hill and look over your shoulders, keeping the rumors going. No, it's best they drink the water and forget the things they see."

So *that's* why Hermes had been upset when I wouldn't drink the tap water. He thought that would solve the problem. All this time . . . I think of my poor dad and how he'd replaced the pipes. And I suppose it explains why Merry forgot my birthday is tomorrow.

"Why?" I ask. "Why is it foul to me but no one else?"

"It's not just you. I don't like it, either. Nor does Hermes . . ."

She grins, and for a split second I see all three of her faces at once, superimposed over each other: the gap-toothed grin of a maid, the tolerant smile of a mother and the knowing leer of a crone. Three in one.

"How do you do that?" I ask, then redden realizing how rude the question is. "Sorry, I just . . . Most people only have one face."

She huffs. "Most people have two faces. If you haven't learned that by now, there's no hope for you."

At the Oracle's feet, her dog gives a long, almost-human

sigh, then lowers its head onto its paws, looking up at me with glowing red eyes. I take a sip of my drink.

"Let me ask you a question. Why did you come back, Corey?" the Oracle asks.

"Because this is my home."

"Is it? Still?"

Home is who you are. That's what I said to Hades. But I don't know who I am anymore.

I consider everything I know about myself. Everything I love and care about. I play no instruments or sports, I can't sing or draw. I can grow plants; that's my one skill. My one gift.

"I had a garden there," I say slowly. "In the Underworld. Only for a day, but I grew it. In the land of the dead, where there is no rain and no sun, I made flowers. I made fruit too. Golden pomegranates, like you just said. The first and only ones of their kind. They tasted . . ." I pause as I remember. Salt and honey. "I'm the only one who can grow things there."

The Oracle stays silent and tops up her drink.

"But I'm something else there too. I'm different." *Claws, fangs, almost-wings. Darkness in my veins. In my heart.* "The Furies said the same thing as you: Bringer of Death. That's what they called me too. How can I be the Bringer of Death when I grow things? That's the opposite of death."

"How can I have three faces? How can Hermes walk in dreams?" She downs her drink and then tries to refill it, hissing when the flask yields no more. I offer her my cup and she takes it.

I shrug. "I just want to know which I am," I say.

285

"Can you not be both? Can you not have two faces? Can you not belong in two worlds?"

"Hermes said it was hard enough, just going between. That you couldn't really belong in two worlds."

"I manage just fine. But then, unlike our quicksilver friend, I've *accepted* my lot in life."

She gives me a pointed look, then knocks back my cup of vodka, draining it before dropping the cup, her own and the flask and bottle back into her pocket. The dismissal is clear, our drinking session is over.

"What do I do now?" I ask anyway.

"I told you, you'd have your answers when you paid your dues. Are they paid?"

No. Not yet.

The Oracle doesn't say anything else, silently rearranging her scarf around her shoulders, and her dog stands, reading the cues of her body. She gives me a deep bow before she goes, and I watch her leave, walking straight over the graves with the dog trotting behind her. She casts three shadows and I think of the Three of Cups. Then of the Three of Swords. And finally, Justice.

When the Oracle is out of sight, I sit down on Bree's grave and pluck the roses out of the vase. They're limp and loose, soft when I squeeze the heads. A single petal falls onto my knee and I brush it aside. This time I keep my eyes open as I leak a little bit of my power into the roses. I watch them straighten, the flowers tightening, the color deepening. It's strange to see, like a video speeded up, but real, and happening in my hands. When the roses are perfect, I put them back in the vase and fluff the celery flowers around them, giving them a little brightening up too. Mrs. Dovemuir will get a nice surprise when she comes to replace them.

I push my fingers into the ground, just a little bit, aware that somewhere beneath me is Bree's coffin. Not that she's in it in any way that matters, but still. I think of how she looked in the Underworld, delicate and wan in her shift, and it strikes me it's kind of similar to the shapeless dresses her mom bought for her. I bet she's noticed it too, and she hates it, and I wait for the vicious stab of glee that something's bothering her, but all I get is a weak little pinch of something that might be vindication, but might be something else. Then I think of how scared she looked when I'd changed, like she didn't know me at all, and I wonder again what I am. What happens next for me.

Across the Island a bell tolls, calling everyone back to school. I stand up, intending to go home, only to freeze as I see Mrs. Dovemuir.

She's standing at the entrance to the cemetery, an armful of flowers, talking to Priestess Logan, and I immediately duck, palms clammy, my heart racing. I can't see her; I can't speak to her. Not after everything that's happened.

I lower myself to the ground and crawl as fast as I can toward a line of cypress trees, ducking behind them and slowly standing. I peep around the trunk to see the priestess embrace Mrs. Dovemuir and then release her.

Bree used to mock her mother, asking where she was when feminism happened, because Mrs. Dovemuir likes to wear dresses, heels and makeup every day. The woman making her way to Bree's grave is wearing a dress, but it's crinkled, there's a stain on the skirt. Her hair isn't blown out, but pulled back in a ponytail, and there's not a scrap of makeup on her drawn, gaunt face. She looks older. She looks crushed.

She leans against her daughter's headstone and my stomach twists when I think of me and the Oracle, drinking vodka on it mere minutes ago.

I watch Mrs. Dovemuir examine the flowers in the vase and hold the ones she's brought next to them. She takes out the ones I fixed and adds them to the new bunch, mixing them all together. She has a tough time getting them all back in the vase, but she manages. I watch her top up the oil in the lekythos, then pour a little onto the ground.

I watch her break down.

She crumples from the middle, folding in on herself until she's kneeling on Bree's grave. At first, she doesn't make a sound, and it reminds me of the shades and how they cry, but then I realize she's started saying something, and a second later I hear it properly: *Sorry.* She's saying she's sorry, over and over, chanting it into the ground over Bree.

I can't bear it. I can feel her grief—her desolation—from here. I wish I could tell her that I'd seen Bree and she was all right, but it wouldn't be true, and it wouldn't help. I leave, carefully following the tree line along the side of the hill. I turn for my dad's house, then stop and walk the other way.

First, I go to the lake where Bree died. Someone is fishing on the far side; Thom Crofter, I think, though it's hard to tell under all the fishing gear. Whoever it is raises a hand and hails me, and I wave back, because I'll know them, will have known them my whole life. I walk to the spot where Bree was found, and you can't tell she died there. There's no mark, no sign, no plaque, no flowers. The reeds are green and tall; when I look into the water, I see frogspawn. We put some in a jar once. It never hatched.

I walk up to the field where we have the Thesmophoria, but I don't go in, dissuaded by the herd of cows that all turn to me when I freeze on top of the steps leading into the pasture. I heard once that the reason cows freak out if you go in their field is because their depth perception is rubbish, so you have to walk slowly and stop often so they can figure out where you are. We tried it out, me and Bree, in this exact field. Maybe even with these exact cows. And they didn't crowd us, so it must be true. Or we got lucky.

Next, I go to the woods where we played Brides of Artemis. I go to our tree, but I don't see the hamadryad, or anything else, not even a squirrel. The woods are cool and quiet, they smell green and damp and I breathe it in as deeply as I can, trying to commit to memory exactly how it smells, trying to remember the exact sound of a breeze through a canopy.

This is when I realize that I'm saying goodbye. That ever since I left my dad's house, without knowing it, I've been on a final tour of my old life, seeing the high street, and the school, and the cemetery, and the lake, and the field. I thought I wanted to come back so much, but now that I'm here I understand that I can't. The Island just isn't me now. I don't fully understand what

I am, but I know it's not a girl who lives on an island at the edge of the world. Not anymore.

The Underworld is the ugliest place I've ever seen. No stars, no clouds, no grass, no trees. But I could change that. I could cover the whole place in flowers. I could change it. *We* could change it.

Merry is going to be so angry with me for going again. Or at least she would be, if she remembered it.

Perennial

I THINK ABOUT GOING BACK TO MY DAD'S HOUSE, but there's nothing there I want or need. So I go to the lighthouse.

I haven't been here for a long time. We used to come, when we were kids, because lighthouses are exciting when you're a kid, but at some point, probably Ali-related, I'd stopped visiting. It's taller than I remember, and the white paint is flaking off. Yellow narcissi are dotted all around the base, and they look lovely against the blue sea beyond. It's a clear day, and I look out, but there's nothing there that shouldn't be there, or at least nothing that can be seen.

It's there, though. All this time, an entrance to the Underworld neighboring us like the other islands. I feel a bit stupid for not figuring out the Lethe thing. It always seemed off to me that Bree would be so casual about seeing a hamadryad when she was never casual about anything, but of course, she would have gone home and had milky tea, or squash made with the tap water, and that would have dulled it, until she forgot about it. Whereas I, who wouldn't touch the water, remembered.

I think about all the weird things that happen here, and how no one ever seems to dwell on them; it's always just *one of those Island things.* And I know I should be mad that we're basically being drugged by contaminated water, but if the alternative is everyone being sent away or—let's be realistic because the gods are involved—the Island being sunk into the ocean to keep people from it, then maybe being drugged is preferable. And everyone is happy enough. Why mess that up?

The lighthouse stairs are made of metal, so I know my father hears me coming long before I reach the door to the observatory, and sure enough, he's already boiled the kettle and is adding sugar to his coffee. He passes me a cup—black, unsweetened, which feels like a statement right now.

"I saw you coming down the track. Been a while since you've passed this way."

I shrug. "Thought I'd check up on the old place. Make sure everything's working." I pause. "Is it?"

My dad laughs. "You missed it last week. Ball vent got clogged and there was a horrible moment when I thought something had nested in it. I imagined Merry reading me the riot act when I told her, bringing all her bird squad here to set up guard over it."

"What was it?" It's safe to ask because I feel like this story, at least, ends well, and I'm proved right when my dad replies:

"Just muck. Cleaned it out and all's well."

Solid life advice.

I look out to sea. I see something flicker on the horizon, a wink, or a wave, and my heart leaps. I press my hand to the glass.

"You're going again, aren't you?"

He says it very softly, so I can pretend to ignore it if I want to. I nod.

"I won't see you again, will I?"

Still with my back to him, I shake my head. "Not for a while."

"But you'll be all right?"

I turn to him. "Yeah. I'll be all right. More than all right." I pause, and make a decision. "You won't remember this. You won't remember I came back. If you want to, stop drinking the tap water."

"You and that bloody water. You know that coffee's made with it." He nods at the cup in my hands.

"I know, which is why I'm not going to drink it. I mean it, Dad. If you want to remember things, stop drinking it."

He doesn't seem surprised and I wonder if perhaps he already knew, if maybe someone else told him a long time ago and at some point he decided to keep drinking it anyway, because there are some things you don't want to know and sometimes forgetting is easier. He all but confirms it when he says, "So, I take it you weren't really with your mom?"

"No." I smile. "And I'm not going to her now."

He sighs. "When she left, she told me to keep you here for as long as I could. To keep you safe."

"And you did. But I have a job to do, I think. I'll be all right. I promise that."

We put our cups down at the same time and meet in the middle of the observatory floor and hug. He's not a hugger, and I never used to be, but he is my dad and I am his daughter. He's the man who raised me, after my mom left us, before Mom left us, through every temperature and skinned knee and school play.

He holds me at arm's length and looks at me, really looks at me, drinking me in.

"Are you sure you have to go?" he asks, his voice tight.

"Just think of all the space you have for your barbecue now. You could have a whole firepit."

He pulls me back into his arms and I breathe him in.

"OK." He lets me go, and I step back.

I'm halfway out of the room when I spot an old succulent on his desk. I walk to it and lift it, pressing the tips of three fingers into the sandy soil and willing it back to health. I feel my dad's awed stare as the leaves fatten and turn from papery gray to green and tiny new leaves begin to grow and stretch. When I put it back down, it looks like something from a magazine spread.

I wink at my dad, then leave.

I'M NOT ONE HUNDRED PERCENT SURE HOW TO get back to the Underworld. I suppose I could pick one of the narcissi and see what happens. But in the end, I walk down to the infamous cove, scene of many crimes of my childhood and youth. It's empty midweek, middle of the day; no dog walkers, no school kids, no one at all. I don't really know what I'm doing, but I walk down to the shoreline and search for a piece of seaweed, or driftwood. I find some bladder wrack, dried in the sun, and grip it in my hand, imagining it into something new.

"Boatman," I say, closing my eyes and speaking to the water. "I want to come home."

Almost instantly I hear the sound of water slapping against the wooden hull of a small boat, and when I open my eyes he's waiting, standing in the sea, his hand outstretched for the golden bough my seaweed has become.

"Hello, Lady," he says, tucking the bough into his cloak.

I left his other one at the house. I hope he forgives me for it.

When he offers his hand to me, I take it, and he lifts me into the boat, my feet never touch the sea. I settle in the stern and keep my eyes on the horizon. I don't look back.

So this is what it's like to take the boat to the Underworld.

I'm not cold this time. I look down into the sea and see Nereids swimming alongside the boat, looking up at me with wide, wild eyes. It feels like an escort, like they're bridesmaids, and when I smile at them, they smile back, apparently delighted. It's very flattering. I lower my hand into the water and they reach out to touch me, gently caressing my fingers with their cool webbed ones. One dives, and returns with a handful of seaweed, offering it to me. I take it, and they look at me, expectant.

I push my power into it.

It doesn't flower but it does change color, moving from a deep maroon to a soft pink, the ends curling into fringed spirals. I hand it back to the Nereid, who weaves it into her hair, and then they all have seaweed, sea grass, all of them wanting me to use my hands to make them something new. I do, and every single one comes easier, until I barely need to think about it.

I think about what I could do in the Underworld. I could make a whole bunch of gardens. Connected ones, with different themes, different colors, different seasons. Some with big, tall trees, places for shades to wander and lose themselves. A maze, many mazes, to give them something to do. I wonder if Hades would put fountains or something in them, I wonder if we could ask one of the rivers to lend us some water. Groves, for people to wait for their loved ones so they can reunite in peace. Somewhere for the shades who've been punished to go to think about their crimes. The Underworld is so big, this is going to take forever.

It doesn't frighten me.

The Nereids leave us when ocean becomes the Styx, and Charon looks back at me.

I nod, to let him know I'm all right, and he smiles.

We row to the mouth of the Acheron, and then the boat picks up pace, moving fast, faster than I'd like, whipping us through the Asphodel Meadows, the gates to the Underworld rising from the gloom. They open before us, and this time the dog doesn't growl, like it knows I'm supposed to be here. Again, it's flattering.

I don't actually have a plan for what happens next. Part of me wants to go to the Furies, because they're what I know best, but I think they might be a bad influence on me. At least until I have a better grip on this thing inside me, I should keep a distance.

The first place I want to go to is my garden. That feels like the smart choice. I can build a house out of the flowers and wait to see what happens next.

I say goodbye to the Boatman on the dock and walk along it. My footsteps echoing. No one is waiting for me, and I get to the end and stare out into the blank space that is the Underworld. I suppose I could walk to my garden, I know it's near the Elysian Fields, but I don't know where *exactly* that is.

I haven't thought this through.

"Can I help you, Lady?" a silky, rich voice asks, and I turn to see a woman—a goddess—silently walking toward me. She is tall and slender, like a silver birch, one eye is jewel pink, the other black. Her hair is silver with streaks of black and she wears a black shift, like my old one, that shows her thin legs and long feet. There are gold bands on her arm.

"Eris, as it pleases you." She bows, and I do a funny little bob. I remember now she's a friend of the Furies, they lived with her when they lived here, before Hades; she's the one who waved to us the first time we flew past the towers. *Lady Strife,* Alecto called her. Discord.

I ignore the warning alarm ringing inside me. "I'm trying to get to my garden. It's near the Elysian Fields, except I don't know where they are. Could you point me toward them?"

"I can take you there, if you'll permit it?" she says.

I hesitate, then nod. "Thank you."

She holds out an arm for me, crooking it like Hades does, so I hook mine in hers. I wonder if I can learn to do this too, or will I always be dependent on other people to move me around the Underworld.

Eris leaves me outside the walls with a benign, practiced smile, then vanishes, and the alarm that started back near the dock is deafening now, every fiber of my being telling me not to open the door, to not go inside.

When I gently touch the handle, the door swings open.

The blow is instant, like a kick to the gut.

My garden; my beautiful, miraculous, impossible garden is in ruins.

Every single plant has been pulled from the ground and then shredded and crushed and torn so there is no hope of saving them. The ones that haven't been shredded have been ground underfoot, driven into the dust. Petals are scattered like confetti, pollen pools like blood. The bark of my glorious trees has been slashed by talons that can cut through rock, until they're barely standing, all the fruit smashed on the ground. The desecration is methodical and deliberate, no plant has been left undamaged, no hope has been left behind.

I can't fix this. There is no life here to coax. There is nothing to save. I came back for this, and it's all gone. All dead. My beautiful garden.

Bree stands at the center of the destruction. Her hands, her feet, her shroud, all are stained green.

Her eyes widen when she sees me. "I didn't—"

I hold up a hand and she falls silent, though her lips still move, flapping uselessly. All I can hear is a low buzzing in my ears, like I'm pressed against a hornet's nest. It's as if there's one inside my chest, and if I open my mouth the hornets will all come rushing out and I will never be able to call them back.

I reach out, trying to find something I can save, but all I can feel is red-hot rage eating through me, claws bursting from my fingers, eyes darkening like a predator's. I made it; it was mine, my secret and my solace and my miracle, and now it's dead. I don't want to be the bad guy; I don't want to be a monster, but what else am I supposed to do in the face of this? I'm standing in the wasteland that was my garden and the person I hate most in the world, never second most, no matter how much I pretended I blamed her and Ali equally, is covered in sap and smeared greenery like blood.

She was my best friend. I would have died for her.

I barely feel it as my wings force their way through my skin and expand.

They're not the dragon wings I imagined. From the corners of my eyes I can see them, dark and shadowy. Like Hades's shadow servants.

"Corey, please," Bree begs. "I didn't do this. Your friends— the Furies—they did it. They saw you coming back. They want you to hurt me. I know I deserve to be punished for Ali, but I didn't do this. I would never, ever do this."

I cover my ears because I don't want to hear her voice, don't want to hear her excuses. I want to blame her for this, even though I know she can't possibly have done it, doesn't have claws to shred trees and turn petals to ribbons. I know it but *I don't want to care.* My fury rises up inside me and it would be so easy just to let go, to let it out. To have vengeance. To have what Megaera would think is justice.

To become the Bringer of Death.

I see a vision of myself flying over the Underworld on my shadow wings, everything as barren and bleak as it's ever been, but now made worse by me, by the violence in my heart and what it's made me become. Worse than Tartarus, worse than the Phlegethon, with no mercy and no love at all, for anyone. A thing without hope, that only seeks to hurt everything in its path. To destroy. An eye for an eye for an eye forevermore.

Then I sense something, a weak, faint spark over in the corner where Hades had sown our seeds. Something alive.

I march toward it, the last good part of me clinging to it like a life raft. I fall to my knees and dig through the carnage, the sight of each broken stem piercing me like a dart, until I find that faint pulse of life. Somehow one tiny flower has survived. One in hundreds, and though it's trampled it's still alive. Barely, but maybe I can work with that. I saved the flowers on Bree's grave, I will save this. Because if I don't . . . If I can't . . .

I hold both my hands over it and will it to live. I put my whole heart into it, until my teeth are no longer pressing against my lips, until my talons are nails again, until my wings are folded away once more. I feel petals brush my palms and I open my eyes. A hyacinth, black as Hades's eyes.

I did this.

I stand and turn to Bree.

We look at each other across the ruins of my garden.

"Why did you do it?" I say. "Not this. Why Ali?"

Bree gives me a bleak look. "Here's the thing, Cor. I know I'm supposed to say because I loved him. And that I never meant for it to happen. And that I tried to stop it. But I didn't. I didn't love him, and I didn't try to stop it."

"Is that supposed to make it better?" I ask, incredulous.

"No. I just don't see the point in lying to you."

"Then what was it all for?"

She gives a single, humorless laugh. "Because it was the summer we were seventeen and nothing was happening for me. I always thought that summer would be the best summer of my life, and up until we jumped into the sea—remember?—it wasn't. It was the same old shitty summer on the same old shitty Island. And when we jumped, I realized if I wanted it to be the best summer ever, I had to make it happen. So when Ali kissed me—"

"*He* kissed *you*?" I interrupt.

She nods. "I would never have kissed him first."

I raise my eyebrows.

"I wouldn't. It was after the seal—"

I knew it.

"—We sort of grabbed each other because we were so excited, and he kissed me. I pushed him away. Then you came, and I tried to forget about it but I couldn't. I really did try. But in the end, I messaged him. I told myself it was to tell him it would never happen again but . . . It started."

I stare at her, unable to believe what I'm hearing. "So you threw away our friendship and trashed my relationship because you were *bored*?"

"No. Because I had nothing and you had everything, and, for once, I wanted something."

I am speechless, my mouth wide.

"You had your dad," Bree continues, "who just let you do what you wanted in the garden, dig it up, build whatever, and Merry, who was so cool and treated you like a person, and you had Ali. You liked being on the Island. Everything was so easy for you. You want to be vegan; sure, your dad just orders special food from the mainland, no problem. You won't drink the water; never mind, they'll get some bottled spring water in, just for you."

Her expression turns ugly, her voice bitter. "You want your friends to stay over; no worries, they'll go to the pub, let you have the house to yourself, leave some money for takeaway if you don't feel like cooking. You pierce your ears and you get grounded for a week because you sneaked off. I do the same and get grounded for the entire holiday for *violating my body* and my mom cuts them out of my ears with pliers because she can't figure out how to unscrew the balls."

"But you had earrings in," I say, horrified. "I saw them, at school."

She rolls her eyes. "I redid it myself with a safety pin the night before so you wouldn't know. I stole my mum's twenty-first birthday hoops. You were allowed to wear the clothes you wanted, to have a boyfriend, and I wasn't even allowed to cut my own fucking hair. My mom still dressed me, Corey. She still bought me smocked dresses, like I was a doll."

I shake my head, because this isn't true, none of it can be true. I would know if it was, because she was my best friend and best friends tell each other everything.

But then I think about all the places we used to go. Always at my house; we never stayed over at hers. Meeting at the cove. Breaking into the temple to hang out. All places we wouldn't be seen. Painting her nails red when she got to my house, then taking the polish off before she left.

I had no idea.

"I thought it would be better after the boys were born, but it wasn't," Bree finishes.

"And that's why you slept with my boyfriend?" I say.

"I just wanted something that was mine. And I know he wasn't mine," Bree says before I can. "I wanted to feel normal, and I did. For a few months, I did. I had a boyfriend and I cut my hair and I'm glad I did because then I died. I can't regret it, Cor. I'm sorry I hurt you, but I don't regret it. Because at least I lived a bit first."

Unexpectedly, shame and guilt flood me. I walk over to her, then lower myself to the ground. After a few seconds she sits too, facing me.

"I didn't want you to find out. I thought I could have you both, but then Ali started getting weird and talking about splitting up with you, and you knew something was going on and then it was too late."

"What did your mom say?" I ask. "When she found out."

"She *washed her hands of me*," Bree says. "We had a massive fight and she told me to break up with him, and I wouldn't because then everything would have been for nothing, and then she threatened to send me to the mainland, to the cousins, and I told her if she did I would never, ever come back. And then she said that was fine, because we were done. And that was the last time she spoke to me before I died."

I want to cry.

"She wouldn't even look at me. Dad wouldn't let her send me away, so she pretended I didn't exist. That's why I did this." She tugs on her hair. "To get a reaction. She's probably glad I'm here."

I think of how Bree's mother bent over her grave, chanting *sorry*, and the blanket in the coffin, and I know that isn't true.

What a total and utter mess.

"So what happens now?" Bree asks, resigned. "Are you going to change into a monster and tear me apart? Because I'd like to get it over with."

I don't feel much like turning into a monster. I suppose I could try making her into a plant. Maybe a cheese plant. The pun would really piss her off. But I take a deep breath and find I don't want to. Not even just for a second.

"Moment's passed."

She almost smiles. "Are you like, a goddess?" she asks.

I look at her from the side of my eye. "You know me, I get everything. It's all so easy for me."

Then she does smile.

"I'm the reason you're here, you know. In the Underworld," I clarify. It feels important to tell her. "I wished you dead at the Thesmophoria and Hades granted it."

"That isn't true."

"It is."

"No—I'm not denying you wished it. I know you did; I could feel it every time I saw you. But when you come here, as a human, you have to wait to see some judges so they can decide where you go and if you have to see the Furies. While you wait you read your fate, from start to finish. I was always going to die that night. It was written when I was born." For a moment she looks bitter. "So, you didn't actually kill me. I was always going to drown at age seventeen. You just got lucky with the timing. Sorry if that disappoints you."

On the contrary, I feel as though someone has taken a rucksack from my shoulders, one that was loaded with boulders, and laid it on the ground. *My dues are paid*, I realize. And I have all the answers I need.

We sit in silence for a while, but it's not the comfortable kind of silence you have with someone you've known almost all of your life. This is the silence of two people forced to share a table at a café. The silence of two people who don't have a single thing to say to each other anymore. I never imagined that would be us.

I stand up and walk to the door, opening it. Then I turn to her.

"I don't forgive you. I miss you like crazy; I think part of me always will. And I don't hate you as much as I want to. Even less now you've told me your tragic backstory." I soften it with a smile, and Bree smiles too. "That doesn't mean I forgive you. You did the one thing you're never, ever supposed to do, and you've said yourself you don't regret it, not really. So I can't forgive you. But I am sorry that you're dead. I wish more than anything that you weren't. I wish you could have another chance to find something good of your own."

She nods and swallows. "Me too."

She pushes herself to her feet and comes toward me.

"I know you don't trust me anymore, and that's fair, but I don't think you can trust those creatures either. The Furies. They knew what this place meant to you and they wrecked it anyway. They're trying to manipulate you. They left me in here because they knew you'd come back. They kept saying 'This is her home.'"

Home.

"They're right about that," I say. "So get out of my garden."

Bree raises one eyebrow, which almost makes me regret being nice to her. As she passes me, she stops.

"Can you fix it?" she asks.

I look at her until she walks away and closes the door behind her. It clicks shut with a gentle snap, like the breaking of a wishbone, or a heart.

I'm going to do better than fix it. I'm going to start again, and this time I'm going to do it right.

HARVEST

IT TAKES ME A LONG TIME TO GET THE WINGS TO come back. I can't get angry enough to force them out. I try gnashing my teeth and marching up and down, tossing handfuls of my poor dead flowers into the air. I really go for it, full-on funeral rites' tearing and moaning. I imagine Hades is there, invisible, watching me, to add some shame to the mix. Nothing works, until I do what I did with the plants and just will them to be.

I feel them unfolding, the same feeling I used to get when I stretched first thing in the morning, lengthening, tension and then release.

Flying is somehow even easier. I think *up* and they lift me, and then the direction I want to go in and I go there. I practice behind the walls until I feel like I've got it, that I can do it with almost as little thought as I walk or breathe.

I head to Erebus first.

The Underworld is silent and drab beneath me as I make the now-familiar journey back to the mountains. Not for much longer. As I fly, I start to sketch it out in my head; all the different areas, all the things I could do. Will do.

I land silently on the spit outside the cave, and pull myself together before walking in, realizing as I do that the height doesn't bother me anymore. It makes me a little bit sad; there's not very much of the old Corey left now. I leave my wings out as I enter the mountain home of the Furies.

"Corey!" Alecto drops down immediately and opens her arms, then hesitates. She looks at me, her lovely face watchful. "You're back."

"I'm back."

"Look at your wings. I never guessed they'd be like this."

"I never guessed I'd have wings. I should have listened to you."

Tisiphone and Megaera join us, but for once they don't crowd me.

"When did you return?" Megaera asks carefully, like she doesn't know.

"Just now."

"And you came here first?"

"No. I went to the garden." I smile.

If I wasn't looking for it, I wouldn't have seen the blink of surprise. "And how was it?" Megaera says.

I give her a long look. "It was how you left it."

"We left the girl—"

"Enough with the lies," I say, letting a little anger out, enough to make my fingertips tingle, though I manage to keep the talons in. "I know Bree didn't do it. I know it was you. For starters, she doesn't have the strength to rip up trees. And she didn't have the motivation, either. She doesn't want anything from me."

They're silent for a moment, looking at each other.

I know how badly they want me to join them, and I know they're not human. They're not made of flesh and blood, but out of the fabric of the universe, and I can't hold them to the same standards as humans. It's like expecting lions or sharks to show decorum, or have respect, or be merciful. It's a waste of time. But even so . . .

"I'm angry about how often you lied to me. I'm angry that you manipulated me. I'm angry you dragged me into your fight with Hades and tried to use me against him. I'm angry you kept secrets from me. I'm angry you dug up my seeds and tried to make me forget where I came from. I am angry with you," I say.

"We had to," Alecto says, her feathers flat, her eyes hopeless.

"Why? Why did you have to?"

"Because we wanted you to choose us," Megaera says. "Because we wanted you. Not just because of your power or what it might mean. We wanted *you*."

Oh. It knocks the wind out of my sails to hear her say it, but I can't let myself believe it. I speak very gently when I say, "Megaera, how many times do I have to tell you, I'm not a Fury."

"But you could be." Megaera smiles. "Look at you. You have the darkness for it. And the wings and the teeth and the claws. You're like us, just as we said. It would be so easy to join us. You're made of what we're made of."

"Maybe, but I'm made of other things too and you don't like those things."

"We could try to," Alecto says. "Couldn't we?" She looks at her sisters, who nod uncertainly.

I shake my head. "It wouldn't work."

"So you choose *him* over us," Megaera spits.

"I choose me."

Alecto and Tisiphone look down, but Megaera doesn't. I respect her for it. It reminds me of Bree.

"You shouldn't have destroyed the garden," I say. "And you should have told me the truth about why you wanted me to stay with you from the start. You should have given me all the facts and let me decide for myself."

"Would it have changed things?" Tisiphone asks. "Had we told you?"

I shake my head. "Probably not."

"Then it was our only chance." Megaera is unrepentant. Then she sighs, an oddly human sound. "But it wasn't enough."

"No," I agree. "And you can't ever do it again. I forgive you this time. But if you lie to me again, or try to trick me, I won't forgive you."

Megaera inclines her head. "So what will you do, now you've chosen yourself?" she asks.

"You can stay here," Alecto offers immediately. "With us. We don't mind you're not quite like us."

"That's kind, but I know where I'm supposed to be. And it isn't here."

"Then visit us soon." She leans forward and kisses my cheek, and I turn to kiss hers, making her chirp.

I open my wings to leave, when Megaera calls my name and I look back at her.

"We won't be on the same side, you know. If you align with the Olympian."

I'd expected as much.

"Will you be my enemy?" I ask.

All three shake their heads.

"No. But we shall do as we will, as you do as you will. And we will not go easy on you because we love you."

I smile. "Likewise."

SEEDING

THE AUSTERITY OF HADES'S PALACE IS WORSE to my eyes after the riches of my now-ruined garden and the bright violence of the Island, and I wonder what Hades will do when I fill his grounds with flowers. I should have brought him sunglasses from my world. The mortal world.

I almost fly over the walls but then spot a great wooden gate I hadn't noticed when I last flew by with the Furies. It looks like it's made of the same wood as the doors to the palace, and to my garden. I land in front of it and knock.

It swings silently open, not, as I think at first, by itself, but operated by shadows, and not the same as those who move in Hades's wake like an infernal train. These ones are soft-edged, like wisps of smoke.

"Hello," I say.

"Lady," the shadow replies, dipping into a deep bow.

"Is Hades home?" I ask, feeling like a child.

The shadow holds out its arm, gesturing to the door of the palace, which I take as a yes.

I am halfway to the door when it opens, another shadow waiting for me.

"Welcome, Lady," it says, stepping aside.

And I enter the house of Hades.

Windowless, it's lit by candles, spaced a few feet apart in mirror-bright silver sconces. A double staircase wraps the outside of the hall, the candles follow the curve of the stairs, a curlicue wrought iron balcony between them on the upper level. There are closed doors, the same dark wood as the front door, leading left and right at both the top and bottom of the steps. Dead ahead is another door, also closed.

The floor, stairs and walls are all made of black stone, jet flecked with white and gray quartz, polished to a shine that looks treacherous to me. The kind of floor children would fling themselves across on their knees, delighted at the velocity they could reach. The kind of floor that you'd break your neck on if you weren't careful.

"Where is he?" I ask.

"He's here somewhere, Lady," the shadow replies.

"So, should I wait for him to come?"

"As it pleases you." The shadow closes the door and then vanishes.

I manage to wait for all of a minute and then my curiosity gets the better of me.

I go through the left door first, but there is no sign of him in any of the rooms there. Most of them are barren, bare floored and bare walled, lit by candles and empty of anything else, but one is a study, stacked with paperwork, pens—*pens*. I'm amused by the idea he has, or needs, pens—parallel to each other, the same distance apart. It's very neat, which is exactly what I'd expect. It speaks of someone who hides behind order to reassure themselves. I must make him so angry.

I leave his study and return to the hall, taking the left-hand staircase, trailing my hand over the cool stone. I find more empty rooms; what was the point in building something so huge and vast if he isn't going to furnish it? The lack of windows is oppressive, and I make note that it has to change.

In the second wing, I find his bedroom and get a brief glimpse of something that looks more like a room in a budget hotel; a single bed, a cabinet beside it, a tiny wardrobe. But I don't pry further. I didn't like it when Hermes nosed around my things; I won't do it to Hades.

When I return to the hallway, planning to further explore the downstairs and see if my version of Hades's kitchen matches the real thing, I'm surprised to find Hermes standing in the center.

He looks up when he sees me, and smiles.

"Ah, there she is."

"Here I am," I say, leaning on the balcony.

"Welcome home." He bows. He looks like a god; fine, chiseled face, silver skin, the embodiment of beauty and power.

I walk down the stairs, stopping three steps from the bottom so we're eye level. "Do you think I'm a fool?"

He frowns, a rare moment when he's not smiling. It makes him look older. "Why would I think that?"

"Choosing here over the mortal world. There are at least a billion shades outside these walls that would give anything to go back to the place I just gave up."

"Why give it up then?"

"Because I don't belong there. Not anymore. And it's like you said, it's hard to live in between two places. To not belong to either. It would have been too hard, to try being part of both worlds."

Hermes sighs. "I shouldn't have said that to you. I was . . . jealous, if I'm honest."

I look at him, then sit on the stairs, patting the space next to me. He raises an eyebrow—seriously, can everyone do it except me?—and then sits.

"Jealous? Why?"

He pushes his hair back elegantly, not like when Hades does it, shoving his hand through as if his hair has gravely offended him.

"You *do* belong in both worlds. You have family in both worlds. You have a purpose in both worlds."

"So do you."

"No. I'm the Messenger. I exist *only* in the in-between. I have an uncle in this world who tolerates me because I escort some of his dead, and a father in the other who expects me to spy for him.

One of the things I am to spy on is Hades. He won't go *there*, and he won't allow *them* to come here, so it's down to me to tell them what he's up to, unless he decides to make himself accountable to them."

"Why should he?" I ask, surprising myself with how angry it makes me. "He drew the short straw in getting this place. If the others were bothered, they should have swapped with him or something. They don't get a say in what he does here."

Hermes smiles. "I absolutely agree. But it still falls to me to report back, which my uncle knows and subsequently keeps me at arm's length. And the others can't stand any mention of death or this place, so they avoid me when they can."

"You're lonely," I realize. All those little hints of bitterness and sadness hidden under megawatt smiles. He feels lonely.

"Whatever," he says, sounding like a mortal boy.

I slide along the step, nudging against him. "Well, I live here now, and I say you're welcome to visit me anytime. And you can stay for dinner."

Hermes doesn't say anything, but he nudges back against me, pausing for a moment so we are resting against each other. Then he stands, the movement fluid.

"Duty calls," he says, looking down at me with that trademark blade of a smile. "I'll be seeing you."

"I'm serious about dinner," I say as he saunters across the hall.

"You're going to regret joining this family," he says.

"I haven't joined any family."

"Yet," he calls over his shoulder as one of the shadows opens the door for him. "Bye, Auntie Corey."

My cheeks burn.

AFTER HE'S GONE, I CONTINUE MY EXPLORATION. I find a room with a white piano inside, the lid down, and when I lift it and press the keys the sound is discordant, long out of tune. I find what I guess is supposed to be a sitting room, with one small, hard chair, one table.

He must be so lonely too. He must think he doesn't deserve anything at all.

I find the kitchen, or at least what I think is the kitchen. It has a long table and an open fireplace, and there is food on the side; mortal food, bowls of fruit and piles of flatbread stacked in linen, bottles of olive oil, glass jugs of water. All for me. I unstopper one of the jugs, about to drink, when it slips from my hands.

Hades appears out of thin air and catches it.

"Hello," he says, holding the jug out to me.

I shake my head and press my hand to my chest. "Don't do that."

"I apologize." He puts the jug down.

"Hello," I remember to say as my heart starts to beat normally again. "How long have you been here?"

"Some time," he says evasively.

"Since I got here?" He hesitates, then nods. I'm not surprised. "Why didn't you say you were here?"

"I told you I wouldn't manipulate you, but the jug . . ." He trails off.

Something flutters in my chest. "Well, thank you for that. And seeing as I can see you now, you can give me the rest of the tour. I've already seen some of the empty rooms and windowless walls, but I'm sure you have plenty more."

He blinks, and suddenly I feel awkward and rude, insulting his home to his face.

"I'm kidding. Kind of. You don't have to. I shouldn't have—"

"I'd like that."

I crook my elbow, offering it to him. "Shall we, then?"

He gives me a strange look before taking my arm.

"This is the kitchen," he says.

"I see that."

"It's minimalist."

I look at him from the side of my eyes. Did he just make a joke?

"Tell me, what would you like it to have?" he asks.

I turn slowly, taking him with me. "Chairs, for the table."

"How many?"

"At least three. I'll be having Hermes to dinner sometimes."

Hades doesn't look at me as three chairs appear at the table. "So I heard."

"Is that OK?" I ask, suddenly unsure.

"It's OK," he says, and the word sounds strange in his mouth, too modern. "What else do you want?"

I look around again. We won't need a fridge, but an oven or stove might be nice. I don't think I need to eat mortal food, but

I want to. Shelves, for tableware. Also tableware. Candlesticks. A vase. I tell him all this and he nods seriously at each request, even though I'm just saying whatever comes into my head. I don't know how to play house. Live house, I suppose is more accurate now.

We move on, out of the kitchen, and I guide us back to the sitting room.

"You don't have to do this right now," I say. "But we're going to need sofas. Cozy ones. One each. Plus one for guests."

"Hermes?" he guesses.

"Yes. And maybe others."

He looks panicked, and I gently pull him around the room. "Windows, please. I'll deal with the garden so we have things to look at. Bookshelves."

"I don't have much time to read."

"No one does, but you still have to have them."

"I see."

"A fireplace. Maybe a mirror above it. A rug."

Hades stops. "Corey. Does all this mean you're staying?"

I nod.

"Here?"

Another nod.

"For . . . ?"

"Ever."

Then his hands are on the sides of my face. "Do you mean it?"

"Yes."

He shakes his head. "But all you wanted was to go home."

"I can't go back," I say, reaching up and taking his hands,

threading my fingers through them. "Firstly, I can't go back and live on the Island, and go to school, and do my homework, now that I've been here. Now that I know what I can really do. I have wings. Not right now, obviously," I say. "But they're in there."

His lips quirk. "That would be awkward at school."

"That was another joke." I stare at him.

"No," he says, eyes glittering, and it strikes me that I was wrong, in Erebus. He is handsome. Just not in an obvious way. He's the kind of good-looking that sneaks up on you and then hits you like a sledgehammer. "You said firstly. What's the second reason?"

I take a deep breath. "I can't go back because what I wanted to go back to doesn't exist. What I want—what I wanted," I correct myself, "was for everything to be the way it was. Me and Bree, best friends forever, growing old on the Island together. And I wanted that before I even came here. That's what I was waiting for. But it was already gone. I just hadn't accepted it."

"I see."

"I think this is where I'm supposed to be. If you'll let me. If you'll help me. You said this place was like this when you got it, but it's yours now. You can change it—you *should* change it."

"I didn't want it," he says quietly.

"Neither did I, at first."

He looks at me. "And now you do?"

"I'm getting there."

His eyes lower, looking at my mouth, and my stomach clenches. I don't know if I'm ready for that.

"I haven't picked out a bedroom," I say, releasing one of his hands but keeping hold of the other to lead him out of the room, back into the corridor. "But again, I'm going to want windows. And a double bed." I turn beetroot as I realize what that might sound like I'm implying. "I don't know where to get clothes."

"The Lampades will help with that. My servants," he clarifies, when I look puzzled. "Yours too now."

I don't *love* the idea of servants. Bree used to say she wanted them. I wonder how long it will take before she's not the first thing I think of.

"Your piano needs tuning too." I nod at it as we pass.

"Do you play?" he asks.

"No. Do you?"

"Sometimes."

"Will you play for me?"

"Yes."

"Are you just going to let me have everything I ask for?" I say.

"Yes." He nods. "I don't want to give you even the slightest reason to leave."

"I will want to go back sometimes," I say, and his face immediately falls. "Just to see my dad and Merry, to make sure they're all right. To see the stars, and the sun, and the sea. But you could come too, if you wanted. I could show you the mortal world." I have a flash of introducing Hades to Merry and my dad, and smile. "And in return, you can teach me how to be like you."

"I don't want you to be like me," he says quietly.

My heart aches and I squeeze his hand.

We walk on, until we're back in the hallway. There's no sign of the Lampades and I don't know what to ask to see next, what to do. I feel nervous, unsure for the first time since I came back.

"Corey? Ask the question," Hades says.

"What question?"

He pulls me gently around so I'm facing him. "The question everyone asks me when they come here. Ask it."

Oh.

I think of two little girls born exactly a month apart, four years old and holding hands in a supermarket. I think of them growing up together, running to the woods together, sharing beds and dreams and hopes and secrets. Sharing everything. I think of how there was so much I didn't see, and that I failed Bree in that.

I still don't forgive her for what she did. But I do wish she wasn't dead. I really, really wish it.

"Will you let Bree go back to the mortal world?"

He smiles, a big, broad smile that's as surprising as his laugh. "I've already asked the Fates."

I throw my arms around him, and a second later his wrap around me, his cold cheek pressed against mine.

"Thank you," I say.

"I gambled." He speaks into my ear. "If you were coming back, and I really hoped you were, I thought you might prefer it if she wasn't here. And you wish very, very loudly."

I laugh, and his arms tighten around me like he's trying to catch it, to keep it close. He releases me slowly.

"Do you need anything else?" he asks.

I think. "Not right now. Wait," I say. "Seeds. I'll need seeds."

He does that catching motion in the air and manifests a golden orb, tossing it to me.

It's one of the fruits that grew from the pomegranate trees, in the garden. He must have taken one before it was ruined.

I split it open and scoop out some of the seeds, pouring them into my mouth. He watches me, his eyes black and sharp. Hungry. "Have you tried it?"

He shakes his head.

I offer it to him and he lifts it, still in my hand, to his mouth.

When he lowers it, his lips are golden. Now I'm ready.

He tastes like ice, or salt, or diamonds—something clear and sharp and glittering, something that would quench or call a thirst, or buy an army, start a war. And he tastes sweet, like honey, like a new beginning.

Acknowledgments

Thanks and thanks and thanks again to Claire Wilson, my always-brilliant agent, for having the kind of faith in me that makes me want to believe in myself. And thanks to Safae El-Ouahabi at RCW, endlessly supportive and kind.

This book wouldn't exist without the team at David Fickling Books, in particular my editor, Anthony Hinton, who gave me permission to write whatever weird shit I wanted. This was the weird shit I wanted, and I love the book we made together.

Also at DFB, I owe a ton of thanks to Rosie Fickling, David Fickling, Meggie Dennis, Liz Cross, Linda Sargent and everyone who pitched in and helped me get this thing in shape. It was such a vast and nebulous and complex idea and there's no way I could have pulled it together without your help. Thanks to Kathy Webb and Julia Bruce, for the copyedits and proofreading that hide what a fool I often am. I feel terrible that it falls to you to fix my mistakes and make me look great while getting none of the public glory, so here I am, thanking you on the record. And thanks to Alison Gadsby, Phil Earle, Bronwen Bennie and

Jasmine Denholm for making sure this story finds its way to readers.

My editor and publishing team at Watkins, too, for being so flexible while I was trying to balance writing impractical fiction with practical nonfiction.

As ever, there is a ragtag bunch of ne'er-do-wells propping me up behind the scenes: Emilie Lyons, Franzi Schmidt, Papa and Mutti Schmidt, Katja Rammer and assorted Rammers, Antje Uhl, Catherine Johnson, Hannah Sheppard, Lizzy Evans, Hannah Dare, Neil Bird, Asma Zbidi, Sophie and Liam Reynolds, Laura Hughes, Steven Salisbury and Rainbow Rowell. Thank you forever and always.

Thanks also to my Bumfriends, for getting me through 2020 and 2021: Kate Hargreaves, Misha Anker, Gemma Varnom, and Laura Elliot. May our chat never be hacked.

About the Author

MELINDA SALISBURY is the four-time Carnegie Medal–nominated author of the Sin Eater's Daughter series, the State of Sorrow duology, and bestselling YA horror novel *Hold Back the Tide*, as well as *The Way Back Almanac*, a nonfiction title. Her books have been published in fourteen countries to date and have been short-listed for numerous national and international awards, including the Waterstones Children's Book Prize and the Edgar Award. Melinda lives by the sea in the south of England and is a keen wildlife photographer.

MELINDASALISBURY.COM